DANCE

OF

SOLDIERS

TANIA ROBERTS

First published in New Zealand in August 2024 by
Red Rose Publishing, New Plymouth

A catalogue record for the book is available from the National Library of New Zealand.

Format: Print ISBN 978-1-99-117469-7

Format: Print on Demand ISBN 978-1-0670288-0-0

Format: EPUB ISBN 978-1-0670288-1-7

Cover Design: Kura Carpenter Design, thebookcarpenter.co.nz

Cover Image: Arcangel Images Limited,

DANCE

Of

SOLDIERS

CHAPTER
1

"Hello love." Bill greeted Moira with a peck on the cheek. "Let me take your bag."

Moira still wasn't used to his gentlemanly ways. Very few of the men previously in her life had shown such consideration. Neither had they called her 'love'. She soaked up the term of endearment, holding tight to whatever promises it held.

She smiled as Bill put her bag on the tray of his truck and hurried around to open the passenger door. Although it was only a short drive from *Whipsnade Farm* to Bill's property, merely swapping one farm for another at the end of her training, Moira wanted to make an occasion of it and had discarded her land girl's uniform. Swapping, biscuit-brown, baggy overalls for a cinnamon-hued dress that hugged her curves and accentuated her hourglass figure. Her freshly washed hair, now more strawberry-blonde than red after three months in the outdoors, sat in soft curls on

1

her shoulders. Careful to avoid snagging her last pair of rationed silk stockings, Moira edged one leg up into the truck. Her dress's rear split parted, and she paused to glance back at Bill. Was that anticipation she saw in his smile as he watched the split rise revealing her shapely leg?

"I'm so glad you applied for me to be your land girl." Moira batted her eyelids. She planned to be much more than that.

Bill shifted awkwardly, cleared his throat, and rushed around to the driver's side of the vehicle. If Moira wasn't mistaken, his clean-shaven face, coloured as bright as the Besame Victory Red lipstick she wore.

The truck's cab filled with the aromas of tobacco and aftershave. Moira inhaled deeply, reassured that she'd made the right decision. There would be no more scowls from Duncan, the *Whipsnade Farm* manager every time she wanted a cigarette; Bill was a smoker too. Memories of the dance they'd attended at the Orari Hall were as vivid as Bill's Old Spice scent. He certainly had the moves and Moira always maintained that if a man had rhythm on the dance floor it would follow him into the bedroom.

Bill's farm was one over on the opposite side of the road. This would be the third time Moira had been in his house but only the second time Bill knew about. On her first visit she'd found no one at home except the ethereal presence of his late wife. Her photos, happy images of momentous occasions and loving poses with her husband, were neatly assembled on the sideboard. Moira had felt threatened by the portraits, imagined there would be no possibility of a relationship between her and Bill with this woman's

2

influence so real and potent, but when she had returned to the house at Bill's request, all but one of the photographs had been removed. She could live with a sole photograph. The six-by-four inch black and white image of a woman was just that, a record of someone passed. Moira was real, she was here in the present and she would make sure Bill knew that.

"Here we are then," Bill announced as he parked the truck by the back door. "Welcome to your new home. Come on in." He grabbed Moira's bag off the back of the truck and strode ahead to open the door for her.

Moira paused, hopeful that Bill might do something romantic and carry her over the threshold. She looked at him, but saw no sign in his tanned and weathered face of any romantic intent and laughed at her foolishness. She wasn't usually taken to whimsical fantasies; why was she doing now?

"The bathroom is in here." Bill opened the first of several doors off the living room. "We passed the toilet, out the back, off the porch. Sorry about that, not quite the luxury of the *Whipsnade* homestead."

"That's fine," Moira replied as she glanced around the living room. It was just as she remembered it; newspapers neatly stacked in the corner, firewood piled ready on the hearth and only the one photograph still on the sideboard.

"I'll put your bag in here." Bill had moved onto the next door and stood to the side so Moira could enter.

Sunlight filled the room. It was warm and welcoming but obviously not Bill's room. A single bed with a floral bedspread sat in the middle of the room, the mahogany bedhead matched the bedside tables and dresser. All very nice, but a single bed. Sleeping alone was not what Moira had planned. Her imagination had pictured a double bed, with Bill in it.

She coughed, choking back the reply that was threatening. At least she stopped before blurting out her frustration and disappointment. After all this was only the first day. Having to start in a single bed in a separate bedroom didn't mean she had to stay there. Moira had been able to tempt Bill before and she could easily do so again.

"It's lovely," she said. "Thank you." She turned to face Bill, stepped forward and kissed him. Her lips lingered longer than was necessary for a simple thank you and it had the desired effect. Bill dropped her bag to land with a thud on the wooden floorboards and wrapped his arms around her. She felt every inch of his body against hers, and every ounce of lust that surged in his loins.

When they finally broke apart, Bill cleared his throat.

"Sorry about that, totally ungentlemanly of me." He fidgeted, uncomfortable, his face flushed as he moved awkwardly on the spot as if he needed to escape. "I'll leave you to settle in, unpack your bags. I'll go make certain the truck is ready for you to drive the others."

Before Moira could say thank you again, Bill had gone. She smiled to herself, a satisfied grin, secure in the knowledge that no, she wouldn't be in the single bed for long.

⌘

Moira, along with Grace, Betsy and Alice were the first group of women to volunteer as land girls and be sent to

Whipsnade Farm for training. Christchurch city with its shops and dances was a train ride away, so Moira took the opportunity to learn to drive the farm truck and leapt at any chance to practise her skills. Today, that meant driving Grace and Alice to their next assignments. When she returned, Bill had a cup of tea waiting and they sat quietly at the table like an old married couple.

"Right, there's a fence at the back of the farm that needs fixing." Bill downed the last mouthful of his drink and stood ready to go. "You'd best get your overalls and boots on."

If Moira had been hoping for an easier assignment, she was wrong. Bill's farm was like a poor second cousin to the grandness of *Whipsnade* with a small flock of sheep, a dozen milking cows, several beef cattle for fattening and some pigs. Although the numbers were less, that didn't reduce the workload.

Moira placed her empty cup and saucer on the bench and looked down at her red toe peepers as she walked to the bedroom. Her shoulders slumped; she sat on the single bed to remove her shoes. So far, this wasn't going according to plan. She'd assumed Bill asking for her to be assigned as his land girl was just a ruse; a cover up so that they could be together without the judgement or condemnation of others but, putting her into a separate bedroom with a single bed and now, after a mere half hour, expecting her to change and go fencing; it appeared she had misjudged the situation. She put the toe peepers in the bottom of the wardrobe and silently promised them it wouldn't be for long.

⌘

"Can I drive?" Moira asked as they left the house. The use of Bill's truck was another advantage of being at his farm that she wanted to retain. There would be milk to take to the factory and Moira hadn't entirely forgotten that was where Jake worked. No harm in keeping him in the background in case things with Bill didn't progress the way she hoped.

"Sure. We'll just grab the posts, wire, and some tools first."

Moira stood to the side and lit a cigarette while Bill loaded the truck. Mid-morning, the temperature was steadily rising, and he stopped to roll his shirt sleeves up. Blowing her cigarette smoke skywards, Moira smiled. The mere sight of Bill's tanned and muscled forearms had her insides pirouetting.

The pigs, two sows and a boar, were in the paddock next to the cowshed. Even with rings in their snouts they'd managed to create mudholes. The sows' bellies sagged low to the ground; two rows of teats swollen as if they were feeding. Moira couldn't see any piglets and hoped there were none. She'd ended up in a mudhole at *Whipsnade* trying to catch the little blighters.

"Have you sold the piglets already?" she asked.

"The sows haven't farrowed yet," Bill replied. "I try to time it with calving so that I've got the whey to feed the weaners."

Moira stifled the swear word that formed by dragging on her cigarette. Milking and feeding pigs would start again soon. More physical work. There didn't seem to be any escaping it. She knew she was supposed to be grateful,

6

getting the opportunity to do her bit for the war effort but working in a shoe shop was certainly easier.

The track out to the back of the farm needed grading and Moira seemed to find every hump and hollow possible. The worn springs of the truck seat poked and prodded and made conversation difficult. They passed the cow paddock where all, but one of the herd sat lazily chewing their cud. The remaining animal appeared agitated, pacing backwards and forwards down the fence line as if it wanted to escape.

"They're close to calving," Bill said. "I'll come back and check on that girl later."

Moira felt for the beast, giving birth certainly wasn't on her agenda any time soon, if at all.

"Pull up here." Bill pointed to the broken strainer post they'd come to fix. "Sorry about that," he apologised when they finally stopped. "I haven't been able to back blade the track since they took the tractor. It's annoying to think of it smelted down as steel for guns."

"Can't be helped then," Moira conceded. She turned off the key and waited for Bill to be a gentleman and come around and open the door for her.

Another disappointment: he grabbed the shovel off the back of the truck and went to study the fence line without appearing to give her a second thought.

Reluctantly, she joined him by the sagging wires. At *Whipsnade Farm*, Duncan had insisted she dig a hole for a strainer post; the memory of the aches in her arms and shoulders from doing so, was still raw. She didn't fancy having to do it again.

7

"Too hard to get the broken post out. I'll just have to dig another hole to the side." Bill began scraping the grass and topsoil aside.

Moira's sigh of relief was carried away on a gentle breeze. "I'll undo the staples on the broken post."

"Thanks, that would be helpful."

The mound of fresh earth grew as the hole got deeper. Bill stopped often, to catch his breath and wipe away the sweat beading his brow with the back of his hand.

"How did the others like their postings?" he asked, removing his shirt, and tossing it toward the truck.

Moira gulped. She wished she could look as relaxed as Bill's shirt hanging casually from the side mirror, but answering his question would either involve lying or revealing Grace and Alice's secret. She returned the pliers and bent staples to the truck while she pondered her answer. Moira considered Grace and Alice her friends, but their swapping places was going to be discovered sooner or later, it was just a matter of time.

"Unlike me, they've both gone to places where they know no one," she replied, neither lying nor revealing.

"I hear Miss McPherson is like a mother to the women who work under her."

"Miss McPherson?" Moira feigned a lack of knowledge.

"At the linen flax mill. She's been there forever."

"I don't know her." That was the truth, Moira had heard the factory manager speak about Miss McPherson, but she hadn't met the woman. She momentarily considered offering to dig the hole to distract Bill from the conversation but the effort to keep a secret that wasn't hers, was too much.

"I'm certain she will look after Alice," Bill continued.

"Yes … umm … possibly," Moira stumbled over her words.

"What do you mean 'possibly'? Her reputation as a good boss is well known throughout the community."

"I've no doubt about Miss McPherson. It's just that … umm … Alice isn't at the flax mill."

"Pardon, I thought you said Alice was assigned to the flax mill. Did I hear wrong?"

"No, you heard right."

"Well, I'm sorry, Moira. I'm a simple man, not a simpleton but you are confusing me." Bill stood, his hands rested on the top of the shovel handle, a frown creased his forehead.

"Grace swapped places with Alice," Moira blurted. "Alice is at Orari Estate and Grace is at the flax mill."

"Why ever would they do that?"

"It was Grace's idea." Moira hoped Bill wouldn't let the secret go further. "Alice didn't have a clue until it happened, but she sure appeared grateful."

Bill shook his head in disbelief and resumed digging. "Well, I never," he murmured into the depths of the hole.

⌘

The following day dawned bright and sunny, but it didn't reflect on Moira's mood. She'd spent a restless night tossing and turning in her single bed. After the double bed

9

at *Whipsnade*, it was hard to get used to the narrow space where stretching out a limb left it exposed to the cool night air. The thought that Bill was asleep through the wall was even more frustrating. He'd excused himself shortly after dinner, claiming the fencing had done him in. The kiss he'd bestowed on Moira's forehead was the extent of his affections. She had lifted her face, paused in anticipation that Bill's next kiss would be on her lips but when she reopened her eyes it was to see him turning away from her towards his bedroom. She was still contemplating how to remedy the situation when she heard a steady rumble from behind the bedroom door. There was no point disturbing the snoring man.

"Good morning, my dear," Bill announced cheerfully when she emerged from the bedroom. "I've made porridge. Did you sleep alright? I hope so, we've got another big day ahead."

Moira turned away from Bill and sighed, the exhalation left her lungs as deflated as the rest of her felt but she didn't want him to see it.

"What are we going to do today?" she asked, deflecting his question while serving herself a big bowl of steaming porridge.

"There's an area down by the creek I want to get fenced off. When the spring floods come, as they always do around here, I need to be able to keep the animals safe. I've lost a few sheep over the years, been carried away in the rushing waters. I can't afford to lose any more."

The thought of more fencing, or more importantly, the outcome of more fencing leaving Bill too tired for anything else didn't sit well. Moira pondered various solutions as she stirred some milk through her porridge. There was no other choice. She was going to have to do as much fencing as Bill, to get in and get her hands dirty, not sit back and look pretty. The latter hadn't worked, hopefully the former would. Glancing down at her fingernails, Moira silently apologised to them as if they were a precious friend she would never see again.

⌘

"Park up over here," Bill suggested when they arrived at the creek. "Not too close, the weight of the truck might cause more subsidence."

Moira could see where the paddock dropped away, an existing fence suspended in mid-air between two posts sagged ineffectively, floodwaters having gouged out its footing. She parked the truck several feet away, pulling the handbrake on hard to ensure the vehicle didn't become one of the river's victims.

"Aargh!" Moira groaned as soon as she opened the truck door. "What's that stink?"

"Bugger," Bill muttered under his breath. "That's the odour of a decaying carcass, another one dead."

He grabbed a shovel off the back of the truck, although it was unlikely, judging by the stench, that there would be anything much left to bury.

Moira reached the embankment before Bill had time to warn her. The sight of the semi-decayed carcass, an eyeball staring blindly, and entails picked over by a scavenging magpie doubled Moira over. Regurgitated porridge spilled from her mouth. The vomit was indistinguishable from the dirty woollen sheep's flesh being slowly devoured by a wriggling mass of maggots.

"Come away, love." Bill dropped his shovel, put his arms around Moira's shoulder and led her away from the river edge, rubbing her back in calming circles.

Moira heard the term of endearment; she almost burst into laughter that it took a dead sheep to get Bill to comfort her. She wiped a dribble from her chin, feeling not the least bit beautiful. Now was not the time to take that comforting further. Moira grabbed her smokes from her overall pockets. She needed to draw on the nicotine, to calm her nerves and overpower the lingering smell of dead sheep and vomit.

"I'll get used to it," she said, hoping to convince both herself and Bill. "I'll have to if I'm going to be a farmer."

CHAPTER

2

"We'll get the fence in so hopefully there won't be any more dead animals for you to get used to." Bill shovelled some earth over the carcass to smother the stench.

"Right, where do we start then?" Moira took one last long draw before stubbing out the cigarette. With the odour dispersed she wanted to get busy, to distract herself from the image of the carcass.

"I think we'll build the fence back here. A straight line from there to there." Bill pointed left to right. "I'll lose a bit of paddock but at least the animals will be safe. We'll string a wire first and then if you lay the posts out, one every ten feet, I'll start digging."

Bill handed Moira the free end of the roll of wire he'd made a rough loop in. "You take that to the post over there and hook it over."

Moira did as she was asked, pulling on the wire so the spinning jenny would release another coil as she walked across the paddock. When the loop was hooked over the post, Bill cut sufficient wire off the coil to tie off both ends. He made another loop in his end, unravelled the spirals until the wire was straight and strung the loop over the opposite post, hammering in a staple to keep it secure.

Bill taught Moira how to use the wire strainers and then how to tie off the wires so none of the tension was lost.

"You can lay the posts out now, if you want."

Carrying posts wasn't something Moira wanted to do but she kept her end desire in mind as she slid the first one off the truck. It was heavier than she expected but if she hooked both arms under and balanced the weight on her chest, she was able to carry it the short distance required. Soon there a was a line-up of parallel posts laying on the ground next to the wire.

There was still half a dozen postholes to be dug when Moira had finished her task. Despite the ache in her arms, she grabbed a shovel and began digging. At least by the river the ground was soft. Digging was much easier than at *Whipsnade*. The sun was high in the sky by the time they had lifted each of the posts into its respective hole, shovelled the dirt back in and rammed the earth to pack it in tight.

"We'd better stop for lunch." Bill lifted his hat off his head to wipe the sweat from his brow. "You've been working really hard. I don't want to wear you out."

If she hadn't been so sore, Moira would have laughed. Every muscle in her body ached. She arched her spine, tried to stretch out the kinks, pressing her palms into her lower back for support. She wondered what Bill's wife had died of. Perhaps she had been worked into an early grave. Judging from the photos Moira had seen, she was a petite woman. Moira couldn't imagine her doing farm work.

"Did your wife help you with the fencing?" she blurted without thinking.

Bill's jaw dropped, his head jerked back, and his spine went rigid. Moira swallowed. She should have kept her mouth shut. All that hard work to get her in his good books and she'd probably ruined it all with one stupid comment.

Bill walked unsteadily to the truck and climbed in the passenger seat without speaking. Moira took this as a yes and climbed in the driver's side. The trip back to the house passed in silence. It was almost as if Bill's wife was seated between them keeping them apart. Bill lit his pipe and puffed away while he stared into the distance.

It wasn't until they were sitting at the table, halfway through a cup of tea, that Bill finally broke the awkward silence.

"Miriam was ill for some time before her death. She couldn't leave the house often and I needed to take care of her. The fence should have been fixed a long time ago, but I just never got around to it." Bill reached over the table and placed his hand on Moira's. "I am very grateful for all your help. You do know that, don't you?"

Moira nodded and smiled meekly. She saw the glassiness in Bill's eyes and a grown man crying was more than she wanted to deal with. "We'd better get back to it then."

They worked together over the afternoon and slowly and steadily the fence took shape. Wires were tightened and tied off. A barbed wire on the bottom to ensure the animals didn't go under the fence and another on the top to deter animals from trying to jump over. Moira braced the posts while Bill hammered in the staples. Each hit of the hammer reverberated through the post and into Moira. She tried hard not to flinch to prove to Bill she was up to the task.

"A job well done," Bill said as he hit in the last staple. He moved over to Moira, put an arm around her shoulder and stood back to admire their handiwork.

The weight of Bill's arm was almost more than Moira's shoulders could bare. She gritted her teeth determined not to reject the physical touch even though every muscle ached.

The sun had dipped down behind the Southern Alps radiating an orange glow to the underside of the hovering clouds.

"Red sky at night, shepherd's delight," Moira repeated the saying.

"You are my delight." Bill squeezed Moira into her side and kissed her forehead.

"Ouch!" Moira winced involuntarily.

"What's wrong? Are you alright? Did I hurt you? Do you need to sit down?"

"I've just found a few muscles I didn't think I had." Moira turned towards Bill and reached out wanting to return to his embrace.

16

"We'd better get you home," he said, holding her at arm's length.

"No, I'll be fine," she claimed, annoyed at herself for ruining the moment.

"No." Bill's tone was firm. "You go and sit in the truck. I'll just put the gear on the back, and we'll head home to pour you a nice hot bath."

The mere thought of a steaming bath made Moira feel better. She climbed into the truck, closed her eyes to the flare of the orange sky, slumped against the door and fell fast asleep.

⌘

Noises from the kitchen woke Moira. She edged one eye open and stretched, allowing wakefulness to seep in gradually. Daylight edged its way through the gap where the brown velvet drapes didn't quite meet. They weren't drapes she recognised, certainly not the floral drapes from her new bedroom at Bill's. Her body stirred, she spread her limbs and felt the softness of the sheets on her skin. Her heart skipped a beat; she was naked in a strange bedroom. Whose bedroom, was it? Why was she naked? What had happened? Why couldn't she remember?

She lifted the sheets and scanned her body. The cool air tingled her breasts. Although every muscle ached there was no evidence of anything sordid. There was a hint of maleness though, an indentation in the mattress beside her, a scent that held remnants of Old Spice. She sniffed. She knew the odour of fornication. A tiny smile crept across her face. Had she had sex or was it merely her wanton imagination?

"Blast." Moira cursed. Had she broken the vow she'd made to herself, never to have too much to drink that she couldn't remember?

She retraced her memories desperate for answers. She swallowed. Her throat wasn't parched, her head didn't throb with a hangover. She hadn't been drinking, not since the dance at the Orari Hall.

The Old Spice was Bill's. She was in his bed. She laughed. She'd got where she wanted to be, but she still couldn't remember what had happened.

"Morning, love." Bill opened the bedroom door. "It's good to hear you laugh. I thought I must have worn you out."

"I think you might have." Moira smiled suggestively, hiding her memory lapse. If they'd had sex, she wanted to encourage Bill. "But I'm not complaining."

"I've made the porridge, and the toast is cooked if you want to get up."

Moira folded the bedding back, exposing one breast and gifting Bill a tempting peak beneath the blankets. His Adam's apple bobbed as his eyes followed the curves of her body. He cleared his throat, looked skyward and hurried across to pull the curtains back.

"It's another lovely morning but those clouds are threatening. I reckon the weather will turn by lunch time. We're in for a bit of a storm. We'd better get all the jobs done before it arrives. And Mrs Terrill will be turning up soon. We'd better get this bed made before she gets here."

"Mrs Terrill?" Moira screeched. How had the conversation gone so quickly from sex to the neighbour?

"Yes, you remember her, don't you? She does the housekeeping at the *Whipsnade* homestead." Still stunned, Moira nodded, grateful no words escaped her gaping mouth.

"She's been helping me too ..." Bill's eyes glassed over. "Ever since Miriam died."

Moira threw the bedding back and climbed out of bed. Now the energies of two people too many were in the room, there was no point in her lingering. Bill stumbled back as Moira pushed past him.

"Where are my clothes?" she demanded.

"I folded them and put them on the chair in your bedroom."

Moira scanned the room, her frustration rising. There was no pile of clothes she recognised as hers.

"Next door," Bill mumbled.

Moira stomped from the room like a petulant toddler. *Her room.* He obviously didn't want a 'their' room. She was still just a land girl. Was Bill another man using her for what he could get? She thought he was different. Was she such a bad judge of character?

⌘

Breakfast was cold by the time Moira managed to temper her frustration and make it to the kitchen dressed in her overalls. Bill was nowhere to be seen. She swallowed loudly; a pang of guilt pulled at her heart. Had she overreacted? Was he going to replace her as his land girl?

19

Would she have to find somewhere else to live? Life had been simpler before the war. Wistfully, she wanted to go back to selling shoes Monday to Friday, dancing away her Saturday nights and sleeping away her Sunday mornings.

She slathered some crunchy toast with honey, so much that it was more toast on honey than honey on toast. It was easier to eat that way and had the desired effect of sweetening her mood so she could smile at Bill when he walked back in the door with a billy in his hand.

"Do you have a house cow?" She hoped her happy tone would start the day afresh.

"Yes, but this morning's milk is already in the safe." Bill pointed to the cupboard with its mesh doors that let the cool air flow through. "I've been feeding the scraps to the pigs. If you don't want those crusts, put them in this billy and we'll let the pigs enjoy them."

Bill's face lit up whenever he spoke about his pigs. Moira felt nothing to signal she would ever share his delight in the mud-wallowing animals. Would thoughts of her ever have that effect on him?

"The sow looks like she's started farrowing," Bill continued enthusiastically. "We'll have to go on piglet duty. We don't want her squashing any of her newborn."

"That's great." Sarcasm peppered Moira's response but it was lost on Bill.

"Mrs Terrill will be here soon." Bill glanced from the bedroom to the back door. "Did you make the bed, love?"

"Isn't Mrs Terrill coming to do that? Isn't she the housekeeper?"

"Well." Bill scratched his head as if he was wondering whether to continue. "She was but this will be the last day Mrs Terrill comes. I plan to tell her we'll be able to manage on our own. You can cook and wash, can't you?"

Moira's eyes went wide. The tea leaves in the bottom of the cup she'd been holding mirrored the storm clouds brewing both above the Southern Alps and in this very room as the cup clattered back onto the saucer. A land girl *and* a housekeeper. That wasn't what she signed up for. Sure, everyone had to make sacrifices in war time, but she could only go so far.

Bill shifted awkwardly. "I'll just go make the bed before she gets here."

Moira's frown drew a straight line above her narrowed eyes. "Why?"

"Don't get me wrong," Bill almost pleaded.

It seemed Moira had been misunderstanding Bill's intentions all the way. Irritated, she went silent, and he continued.

"Mrs Terrill is a lovely lady and I've really appreciated all that she has done for me."

The 'but' that was surely coming hung in the air, allowing silent seconds to pass.

"But she does like to gossip, and I don't want our business to be everyone else's business." Bill winked. "If you know what I mean."

Moira tilted her head to an inquisitive angle and spoke in an uncertain tone that resonated the doubts churning her stomach. "I'm not sure I do."

21

Bill glanced out the window before coming to Moira's side. He brushed an errant curl away from her face and gently placed his hands either side of her head, tilting it until their eyes met; his, the brown of earth, grounded and wise, hers the flecked hazel of leaves blowing about in the wind. Powerless, Moira surrendered to the moment. When Bill's lips brushed hers, it was as if the air was siphoned from the room. All doubt was removed as their lips meshed, speaking a language that needed no sound to be understood.

A knock at the door forced them apart. Bill straightened with a start and smoothed down his clothes as if it had been more than a kiss. He rushed to the bedroom and pulled the door closed on the still unmade bed.

"Mrs Terrill, how lovely to see you." Bill greeted the woman who strode into the room as if she owned it.

His face coloured a deep scarlet. Was it embarrassment or guilt that made him wring his hands behind his back? Mrs Terrill looked from Bill to Moira and back again, the corners of her mouth turned up in a knowing smile.

"I thought you'd be out on the farm already," she said.

"The house cow is milked, the pigs are fed. Just waiting for Moira to finish her cuppa and we'll be on our way to move the sheep and check on the cows."

"Mmm. Right." Mrs Terrill nodded but everything about her countenance said I don't believe a word you're saying. "I've made you a shepherd's pie for dinner. I'll get onto the housework and be out of your way."

"Thank you." Moira's gratitude was genuine. It was one meal she didn't have to cook.

"Yes, I am grateful for all you've done for me," Bill added. "I'm sure Moira and I can manage everything going forward though. You deserve a break and Mr Terrill will appreciate your company at home."

"Oh … oh … I didn't …" Mrs Terrill raised her eyebrows and gave Moira a dismissive glance. "I thought land girls were here to do farm work, not extras in the house. It's not like that at *Whipsnade*. Captain Boyle wouldn't hear of it if he wasn't away fighting."

Moira disguised her snigger behind her hand, pretending she had a cough. She doubted the extras she'd been wondering about, ever since she'd arrived at Bill's; were the same *extras,* Mrs Terrill was referring to.

"*Whipsnade* is a training farm," Bill explained. "It's not quite the same on a real farm. Everyone must pull their weight."

"Well then, I'll be off." Mrs Terrill huffed and turned on the spot, the shepherd's pie still in her hands. "Mr Terrill will be having shepherd's pie for dinner after all. Just as well it is his favourite."

The woman bustled her way from the house before Bill or Moira could protest. Moira had been going to offer to return the dish after they'd enjoyed the pie, but the food was the least of Bill's worries.

"That didn't go quite how I'd planned," he said. "I hate to think what story will do the rounds now. She probably saw us through the window."

"It'll be fine." Moira shrugged her shoulders. Her name had done the rounds on the grapevine so many times she

23

now paid no heed to the gossips. "There must be much more important things than us to talk about."

Bill shook his head. "I'd better go and make that blasted bed. A bit like shutting the gate after the horse has bolted but I hate climbing into an unmade bed."

CHAPTER

3

The storm clouds held their bounty until the clock's hands clicked past four in the afternoon but then they let go with a fury. Rain pelted against the windows and wind rattled the panes as the temperature dropped into single digits.

"I'd better go and check that sow." Bill put another log of wood on the fire. "You are alright to cook the mince and potatoes, aren't you?"

"It's unlikely to be as scrumptious as Mrs Terrill's pie but I think it will at least be edible." Moira had spent the last quarter hour peeling potatoes and carrots into a pot. She added half a teaspoon of salt from the salt pig and moved the pot to the top of the coal range to cook.

Bill came up behind her, wrapped his arms around her waist and peered over her shoulder.

"Are you going to make rissoles with the meat? They're my favourite. Especially with heaps of onion. There's one in the bottom drawer. And the mincer is in the cupboard under the sink."

He kissed her neck and was gone before she could protest.

Chopping the onion brought tears to her eyes. Moira always said, life was too short for silly tears. She wasn't one to cry but she didn't wipe them away. It was easier to think they weren't hers if she blamed the onion. It allowed her to deny the tightness in her chest, the uncertainty, her inability to see where the future might go when the present wasn't quite going according to plan.

"Aargh," she growled. "You're probably just hormonal, you silly woman."

The man kisses like he wants to devour you. He hugs like he never wants to let you go. So, what if he can't demonstrate his affections in front of others. It's not a crime. There are worse things that could happen.

Moira found the mincer in a box in the cupboard. She'd never used one before, fortunately the image on the lid of the box gave her some inkling how the various pieces went together. She tightened the clamp onto the end of the bench, attached the handle and selected the cutting blade with holes that looked like they would result in minced meat.

The first cut of meat she fed into the spout was too big and jammed the mincer. No matter how much pressure she put on the handle it wouldn't turn so she had to pull everything apart, cube the meat and start again. She turned the handle until globules of mince emerged from the cutting blade to fall on to the bench.

"Blast!" She glanced around the kitchen to check that there was no one to witness her mistake. Embarrassed she grabbed another bowl to catch the mince.

When that bowl was full, Moira tipped the diced onion in with the mince and mixed the two with her hands, cringing each time the raw meat squelched between her fingers. The things one must do to keep a man happy. She was still lost in her thoughts, moulding handfuls of mince into balls and flattening them between her palms, when the door burst open.

"Quick, I need your help." Rain dripped from Bill's raincoat, spattering on the floor. "The silly sow has farrowed out in the weather. I'll likely lose the lot if they're out overnight."

Moira left everything where it was, rinsed her hands and followed Bill out to the porch where her raincoat hung on a hook.

"I made a nice warm home too." Bill helped Moira into her coat.

It was obvious he was talking about the pig, but Moira acknowledged it was also true about the house she'd moved into.

"We'd better hurry, before it gets dark." Bill reached back inside to grab a torch and a tabby cat darted between his legs to the warmth of the house. "That's right, Buster, you keep warm by the fire."

Moira imagined the cat curled up in front of the fire, licking itself clean. She'd happily swap places, give her fingernails a much-needed manicure but she did the right thing and followed Bill.

Ominous clouds blackened the sky, hiding the view of the alps and dumping their fill in persistent heavy drops. With rain pelting her face, Moira could barely see twenty feet in front of her let alone the sow out in the paddock. The thought of chasing piglets around in this weather filled her with dread.

"The sow's over here." Bill led the way, beside the boxthorn hedge. "At least she sought a little shelter."

In the lee of the hedge, the sow lay on her side, stretched out, eyes closed, and a trail of afterbirth at her rear. Her four trotters created a makeshift pen between which lay a mass of wriggling pink piglets. Moira was scared the sow had died until the pig raised its head, squealed loudly, and pushed out another tiny piglet.

"How many is that?" Moira exclaimed. Merely witnessing the birth had drained her of energy. Thank goodness humans weren't so prolific in their offspring.

"I counted twelve before. She's only got a dozen teats. That last one, the runt of the litter, it'll likely die."

"Shouldn't you help it?" Moira emphasised the 'you'. Even though the newborn's baby-pink skin was bereft of hair from head to hoof, she had no intention of touching it.

"If it has the strength to get to a teat, it'll live. If it can't do that, it's better it dies now than later. We'll just stand here, provide them with a bit of shelter, wait a few minutes to see if its strong enough."

It sounded harsh. Moira thought of Alice. Petite Alice, the land girl who'd rescued every abandoned newborn at *Whipsnade* and was likely now doing the same at *Orari Estate*. Where was Alice when you needed her? She wouldn't begrudge standing out in this weather, rain pouring down her back soaking the legs of her overalls, dripping down into her gumboots to wet her socks. Moira never dreamt she'd say it, but perhaps she needed to be more like Alice.

The runt's natural instincts had it squirming, eyes still closed, away from the birthing canal. It followed the mucous trail of those who'd gone before, little grunts of effort signalling its journey. It burrowed between its mother's trotters, then stalled as if the effort had sucked the life from it, but it was only a momentary pause to gather strength for the biggest battle it faced. An older sibling needed to be pushed out of the way, off the teat that would provide the sustenance crucial to survival. The runt wormed its way between two slightly bigger piglets and rested again.

Moira knew life was all about the timing and for this thirteenth piglet time appeared to be on its side. Whether it was the tiny grunts it emitted or the swollen belly of the piglet beside it, that freed up a teat, it didn't matter. The outcome was the same. The runt wrapped its jaw around its mother's swollen teat and sucked.

"We'll give it another five minutes," Bill said. "Then we'll relocate them to the shed."

Moira glanced around the paddock. There were no buildings she would call a shed, just a few sheets of rusty corrugated iron nailed to an a-frame.

"Where?" she dared to ask, unsure if she wanted to know the answer. "And how?"

"Just over there." Bill pointed to the a-frame. "I've already filled it with hay and there are wooden bars at the sides to give the piglets somewhere safe to go."

"Won't they be safe with the sow?"

"Not when the sow decides to lay down or roll over," Bill replied, shaking his head. "I've had them squash the entire litter. Such a waste."

"And how are they going to get from here to there? Do you have a trolley or something?"

"We'll carry the piglets."

Moira gulped. She spread her hands in front of her, inspected her short nails, and the callouses on her upturned palms. Squelching in mince was nothing compared to what Bill was expecting of her now.

"Then hopefully we can just get out of the way and nature will take care of the rest," Bill continued. "You don't want to come between an angry sow and her offspring if she thinks you're trying to steal them away."

That's exactly what they would be doing. Was a pig intelligent enough to realise they were merely trying to help? Moira hadn't a clue, but she dearly hoped so. Being chased around a paddock by an enraged animal more than twice her size didn't enthuse her.

As the sated piglets gradually released the sow's teats, Bill picked them up two at a time. They flopped into his hands and thankfully remained that way when he placed them in Moira's. She expected them to be heavier but guessed each weighed only a couple of pounds.

"Quick, run them over to the shed." Bill murmured as if to keep their mission secret from the sow. "Put them in the hay at the side, behind the bar."

Moira hunched over to shelter the piglets from the rain and took off towards the shed. Unable to look where she was going and where she placed her feet at the same time, she lost her footing and rolled her ankle in a ditch.

"Ouch!"

She paused to catch her breath, but the jolt stirred the piglets and they started to wriggle and snuffle, tiny grunts that Moira prayed would be lost in the noise of the rain. Panicked, she turned back, glancing over her shoulder to check the sow remained by the hedge before casting aside her pain, and continuing to the shed.

The rain had wet the hay closest to the opening and Moira had to crouch to place the piglets in the dry behind the bar Bill had been adamant was necessary to keep them alive. The comforting smell of hay filled the tiny space and Moira wanted to sit down to rest her ankle.

"Here, crawl in and I'll pass you these ones." Bill came up behind her with another four piglets.

Moira hadn't heard him approach over the drumbeat of raindrops on the corrugated iron. Her head jerked up in fright.

"Ouch!" Her head hit the wooden frame supporting the roof reinforcing her dislike of pigs. "Can't the little blighters walk in themselves?"

"Too young," Bill replied matter-of-factly. "Not until they're about eight hours old. Quick, we need to get the last piglets. The sow's starting to realise something is amiss."

The last thing Moira wanted was to be trapped at the back of the shed with an angry sow between her and the only escape. She grabbed the piglets from Bill, hurriedly plonked them into the hay, and scrambled from the shed.

They rushed back to the sow. Moira followed Bill, mirroring his footsteps so she avoided further injury. The sow wrenched her head around, her snout sniffed out the intruders and she squealed a warning as Bill grabbed the last of the litter. He passed the runt to Moira and took off with the other four.

The thirteenth piglet may have been smaller than the rest, but it was feistier and thrashed about full of fight in Moira's hands. She wrapped her fingers around its girth, hugged it into her chest and rushed to keep up with Bill.

The sow's screech increased in pitch and volume until it was a battle cry announcing her charge across the paddock after them. Her short legs, swollen teats and recovery from birthing did nothing to dampen her maternal instinct to protect her offspring.

Terror and panic quickened Moira's heartrate. Blood pulsed at her temples. Her heartbeat thundered in her chest. She cursed the runt, clasped against her chest. It should have died, then she wouldn't be feeling she was about to be mauled.

Bill had already dropped the piglets into the hay and turned to grab the runt from Moira when she finally made it to the shed. With the sow fast approaching, there was no gentle placement of the last piglet but an unceremonious dumping between the others. It was almost as if Bill had decided that it didn't matter if the runt of the litter lived or died.

He grabbed Moira's hand and together they scurried out of harm's way, not stopping to catch their breath until the gate was shut and latched. The sow gave them a final grunt before disappearing into the shed, nudging, and sniffing each offspring to ensure they were present and alright, before lying down to offer herself as a milk bar again.

"Good job, well done." Bill was still holding Moira's hand and raised it to his lips.

She lapped up the affection, her hand felt safe in his, protected by its weathered strength although not safe enough to return the kiss to a hand dirtied by a sow and her litter. Instead, Moira tilted her face up towards Bill's, let the raindrops drip from her hood, and leaned in to kiss him.

In the pouring rain, Bill released her hand and enclosed her in his arms. There was no one or nothing to bear witness to the passion expressed in their kisses.

⌘

Hand-in-hand they made it back to the house with the promise of more surrounding them with a frisson of anticipation. In the shelter of the porch, Bill pulled Moira to him, and his lips found hers. Finally, Moira was going to get what she wanted. Nothing was going to stop it this time and she would remember every detail. If only, they could be rid of the constraints of raincoats, boots, and overalls.

"Shall we take this inside by the fire," she murmured between kisses.

"What? Yes, of course. Sorry, I got carried away." Bill pulled away to undo the buttons of his coat.

"I like it when you get carried away." Moira placed her hand on Bill's chest, widened her eyes and smiled suggestively. "I'll like it even more when we are inside in the warm."

Raindrops beat out a rhythm on the porch roof that echoed their ardour. They separated, long enough to clamber out of their wet weather gear, cast aside coats and boots to be left strewn about the porch. This was no time to be tidy, their ragged breathing paused only when Moira came into Bill's arms. Another kiss to fuel the desire sparked between them. This time. Nothing could be allowed to ruin the moment. Bill hugged Moira into his side and opened the door with his free hand.

"Aargh, what's that smell?" Moira turned her nose up at the stench.

"Quick, something's burning." Bill rushed to check the fire.

Panic took over from passion as they hurried to find the source.

In the sitting room, all was as Bill had left it, except Buster lay on the rag rug in front of the hearth, absorbing the fire's heat and licking his paws.

"Nothing wrong in here, is there, Buster?" Bill stroked the cat from head to tail and the feline purred.

"No, it's in here that there's a problem." Moira stood in the kitchen doorway, a dejected look on her face as she peered into the charred bottom of the pot.

34

Shrivelled carrots and blackened potatoes, her first effort at cooking tea for Bill, were inedible and the pot would take a lot of scrubbing to get clean.

"I think we should have been nicer to Mrs Terrill. These certainly aren't edible now."

"Oh no, did you leave the pot on the stove while we went out?" Bill stood with his hands on his hips. "You should never do that."

Moira felt like a chastised child. "Well, I know that now."

"At least we'll have the rissoles, we can still eat tonight."

They reached the kitchen bench together, eager to get the rissoles into the frying pan. The bowl was tipped on its side. A trail of discarded diced onions zigzagged across the bench to the plate that should have had more than enough rissoles for dinner tonight and tomorrow.

"Buster!" Bill growled. "You naughty cat."

"Oh, no, I'll put him outside."

"No point." Bill scooped what meat the cat hadn't eaten and moulded it back into a couple of patties. "That'd be like shutting the gate after the horse has bolted. Best you remember not to leave food out when Buster is around."

Moira huffed. She seemed to be getting the blame instead of the cat. She leaned back through the sitting room door and glared at Buster who continued to clean himself as if nothing was amiss. His tongue, the same pink tongue that licked the extremities of its body had also likely licked the meat. Bill seemed unperturbed but Moira's stomach was already squirming. She gulped loudly.

"Shouldn't we at least wash our hands first?" she asked.

"Oh, yes, rushed in, in such a state, I forgot." Bill rinsed his hands under the kitchen tap and dried them on a tea towel.

That *state* they'd been in seemed like a distant memory. Between piglets, cats and mince, Moira's hunger for everything had disappeared.

CHAPTER

4

Weeks whizzed by in a blur. Moira and Bill rose with the sun, worked all day except for brief stops for cups of tea and simple meals, and fell into bed exhausted not long after the sun disappeared behind the Southern Alps. As Moira had wanted, they shared Bill's double bed, but it was more to save the energy of making two beds than with romantic notions. Any passionate urges fizzled with aching bodies and the need for sleep.

"Sorry, love." Bill pecked Moira on the cheek. "I'm too tired. Maybe tomorrow."

Moira clung to the *maybe,* the hope it provided her current situation was only temporary. They just had to get through calving and lambing, and all would return to normal. She kept telling herself Bill was a good man, he had feelings for her, she wasn't just a land girl here for all she could do on the farm. Only two cows were yet to calve. There were now a dozen cows to milk morning and

37

night. Moira resigned herself to feeding the calves while Bill took the milk to the factory. It wasn't how she'd planned but flirting with Jake seemed pointless. He'd barely give her a second look and she no longer cared. Her nails were cracked, her hands dry and stained, her hair lank and lacklustre. Time and energy were precious, and manicures and hair treatments seemed a distant memory.

At least the sheep looked after themselves. When the lambs weren't bunting their mother's udders for milk they frolicked around the paddock, their tails wagging happily, stopping momentarily to nibble at fresh stalks of grass. Memories of docking and crutching at *Whipsnade* stopped Moira from describing the lambs as cute but they did bring a brief smile to her face.

The runt of the pig's litter remained smaller than the others but had just as much energy as they darted around the paddock, grunting and squealing. Moira wished for some of their gusto. The piglets had little need for her help, but the sows needed whey and meal to supplement their grazing in the paddock.

"Are you alright to finish up here?" Bill asked.

The rhetorical question caused Moira to sigh heavily. On a Wednesday night, Bill expected her to be responsible for hosing down the cowshed, shutting the cows away and feeding the pigs while he went off to Home Guard training. Bill's excitement for the Home Guard lit his face up more than she'd been able to. He might have been excused from fighting because he worked in an essential industry, but he still wanted to do his bit.

She understood that everyone was expected to make sacrifices for the war effort, and Bill volunteering for the

Home Guard was part of that, but the burden felt too weighty on her shoulders. Training took him away one night a week and all-day Saturday. She used to look forward to Saturdays before World War II turned everything upside down. Moira sighed. Her weekend sleep-ins were another distant memory.

When Bill wasn't at training, he was busy on the phone drumming up more volunteers or writing letters to those in charge lobbying for guns, training books and armbands or providing updates on the local situation.

"Nothing to report," Moira heard him say.

She wanted to scream there was everything to report, nothing was going according to plan, and changes needed to be made. Instead, she kept her thoughts to herself. It seemed no one would listen anyway.

Bill kissed her on the cheek and was gone from the cowshed before she'd let the last cow go. She filled two buckets of water, one for each set of cups to be submerged in, an easy way to clean any milk or excrement residue away. Next, she unravelled the hose from where it hung looped over the railings, turned the tap, and began hosing the yard where the cows had stood, chewing their cud, and emptying their bowels. Moira no longer cared that cow poop splattered her gumboots as she moved backwards and forwards trancelike across the yard. If only she could wash away her troubles as easy as the effluent.

When the concrete was back to a dark grey, Moira stowed the hose and set off up the race to shut the cows into their paddock. Her heavy feet trudged, one foot after the other, almost robotic. Fortunately, tonight's paddock was close to the shed. The metal hook clunked as she locked the gate, another task ticked off the list, one more to go before she headed home.

Beside the milking herd's paddock was another where the last of the cows yet to calve were grazing. There were only two of them. Moira glanced their way. For a moment it looked like one of them may be calving, but Moira had neither the energy nor the inclination to investigate further.

They're Bill's cows. He didn't ask me to check them.

She shrugged and kept walking.

The final task was the most strenuous, lugging buckets of whey to feed the pigs. Bill had made long wooden troughs for the whey to be tipped into. In their eagerness, the pigs always managed to upturn the empty troughs and bunt them about the paddock. By the time Moira trudged with a full bucket in each hand, to where the troughs lay strewn, the pigs and their offspring had gathered in anticipation.

"Get out, you mongrels." Moira yelled at the pigs sniffing and snorting her and the buckets, leaving a slobbery trail of saliva across her gumboots.

She put the buckets down and waved her arms to scare the animals. The piglets squealed, darted away, ran in circles and rushed back; their tails twirled in happy spirals as if it was all a game. The sows were too wise for that trick and eyed Moira up from under their floppy ears. She managed to right one of the troughs with her foot and quickly tipped a bucket of whey as pigs barrelled past her to get their fill. It took less than a minute for the trough to be slurped clean, just long enough for Moira to drag the second trough away, fill it and get herself back behind the closed gate.

"Phew!" Moira lent against the gate, her legs wobbly beneath her, relieved at having finally finished the day's chores.

⌘

"Bill's off doing what he enjoys. I should do something just for me." Moira paused in the porch and pondered. "I know! Never mind waiting until Sunday for a bath, I'm going to have one now."

Despite the chill of the night air, she undressed where she was. Nothing was allowed to ruin the moment. Moira dumped her smelly farm clothes in a heap in the porch. Naked she felt alive, her skin tingled, a shiver ran down her spine and her lips curved into a mischievous smile.

The cat meowed its arrival, smooched around her legs, his tail brushed across her thigh, and he purred.

"I know, Buster, it feels good, doesn't it." The cat likely wanted food more than her companionship, but it was nice to pretend otherwise.

Moira set the bath running, allowing the hot water to fill the small bathroom with steam before she added some cold. She closed her eyes, inhaled, and sighed, anticipating the instant when she could lower her body into the water, let the weight of the day wash away, the cleansing fresh water rinse her body and her thoughts.

"What else can I do to treat myself?"

Back in Christchurch, before the war, when she'd felt totally decadent, Moira would pour a glass of wine to sip while she soaked. She swallowed, imagining the taste, the smoothness of a Shiraz to relax with.

"Maybe," Moira whispered, a speck of hope sending her to the cupboards. "Where have you stowed your wine, Bill?"

She'd only ever seen Bill drink beer. Perhaps he had no wine. Maybe Miriam drank wine. Thoughts ran through her head as she rifled through the cupboards, first in the kitchen and then in the sideboard in the dining room.

"Nothing but a bottle of beer." Moira took the brown bottle from the sideboard cupboard and read the label. "Ballins Crystal Ale, seven percent proof. You'll do me."

She found a bottle opener in the kitchen, grabbed a glass, and returned with her treasure to the bathroom. She dipped her fingers, decided the bathwater was just right, not too hot to burn but hot enough to turn her skin a lovely, flushed pink.

Her first glass of gulped down beer was followed by a loud burp. Moira glanced around the room and giggled, realising there was no one to apologise to for her belch. She refilled the glass, set it down within arm's reach, and climbed into the bath.

As water rose over her body, air left her lungs in a sigh of relief. She almost purred like Buster. Moira closed her eyes and her mind to any thoughts that would steal the moment. As tension eased from her muscles, she let go of the list of chores that packed each day. She forgot the intentions she had when she agreed to be Bill's land girl, her expectations for their relationship which were no closer to being fulfilled than the day she arrived.

It was Buster who brought her back to the present. The cat meowed loudly as he jumped up onto the rim of the bath. The only hint at how long she'd dozed was the tepid temperature of the bath water and the goose bumps prickling her shoulders.

"What do you want?" Moira opened one eye and flicked some water at the cat. "You'll just have to wait. You're a cat and cats don't like getting wet."

Buster meowed in protest, flicked his tail and was gone as quick as he had arrived.

"I suppose," she mused aloud, inspecting her wrinkled fingerprints. "I'd better get out before I catch a chill."

Moira towelled herself off and wrapped the towel around her torso. Back in the sitting room she stoked the fire, pulled an armchair close enough for the fire's warmth to tickle her toes, and sat down with the beer bottle in hand.

"Bill wouldn't want me to waste you." Moira gazed at the two thirds full bottle. "And I don't want to have to cook. If only I never had to cook again."

⌘

It was a case of déjà vu when Moira woke the next morning, naked and alone in Bill's bed. Only this time her head hurt.

"You're awake." Bill yanked the curtains back.

"Oh, no." Moira scrunched her eyes shut and rubbed her throbbing temples.

"I have just the cure for your hangover. Well, two, but you can't choose hair of the dog because you've drunk the last bottle of beer in the house. So, it'll have to be warm milk and soot. It's an old English remedy. Apparently, my great grandfather swore by it. I've already milked the cows, so there's fresh milk that's still warm. I'll just get some soot out of the fire."

Bill was gone before Moira could protest. She rolled out of bed, clamped her hand over her mouth and hurried to the toilet. There was nothing delightful in her nakedness in the cold light of a new day, hanging her head over the toilet bowl. The only thing worse than losing the contents of her stomach was the thought of swallowing warm milk and soot.

⌘

"Where are you, Moira?" Bill opened the back door and called out.

Startled, she jumped up from the settee. She'd just laid down for a few minutes rest before beginning her long list of chores. Her head may have recovered from Thursday's hangover, but she still felt drained of energy on Saturday. It'd never taken this long before, perhaps she was getting old.

Bill was supposed to be at Home Guard training for the day. Their supply of rifles had finally arrived, and he was excited when he'd left earlier in the morning. *Whatever was he doing back now?*

"What did you forget?" she asked heading to the door.

"Oh, you're alright, that's good." His face showed genuine concern.

"Of course, I'm alright, what did you expect?" Moira saw William in the passenger seat of the truck and waved. "Won't you and William be late?"

Bill took Moira's hands in his. "There's been a shooting."

Moira was suddenly wide awake. "What? ... Who? ... Where? ... Has William been injured again?"

"No, no one you'd likely know," Bill replied. "Three policeman dead and another man seriously injured, over at Graham Stanley's."

"You're right, no one I know. So, why are you worried about me?"

"Stanley, the killer is on the run. Apparently, he's got a large cache of guns and is dangerous."

"Shouldn't you stay home then?"

Bill straightened. "The role of the Home Guard is to protect our local community in an emergency."

Moira slowly nodded, pulled her hands free and sagged against the door. *The community was more important than her.*

"You'd best be going then." She stared into a void above Bill's head and stepped back to close the door.

Bill's hand stopped her from closing it in his face.

"You'll keep yourself safe," he pleaded. "Be on the alert for any intruders. You can head over to *Whipsnade* if you're worried."

"I'll be fine." The words were uttered before Moira even considered whether they were true. It was easier to pretend than give into silly emotions. She straightened her spine, as if she'd donned an invisible coat of armour. "You'd better be careful too."

"I will. I'll see you tonight." Bill pulled the door closed.

Moira waited inside until she'd heard the truck rattle the cattle stop at the end of the driveway. She didn't need anyone to protect her. There was no point going to *Whipsnade*, Duncan would have enough on his plate with Nel, Betsy and the three new land girls. She'd just get her chores over and done with before dark. No fugitive was going to come around in broad daylight.

She left the house, slipped her feet into her gumboots, and headed off.

⌘

Moira's dinner consisted of poached eggs on toast with a serving of boiled silver beet so no one could argue she wasn't eating healthily. She ate at the kitchen bench, too hungry and too tired to wait for Bill to get home. He was late but she wouldn't let any thoughts of the armed fugitive send her into a worried frenzy. They probably just stopped at the pub for a beer, they'd be home any minute now, she was sure of it.

The house creaked as the outside temperature dropped. Every noise seemed amplified. The flames from the fire cast eerie shadows over the sitting room walls. Moira yanked the curtains shut; she couldn't see into the darkness of the night, so no one was going to be allowed to see her.

"Silly woman," she scolded herself. "There's no one out there. You're just letting your imagination get the better of you."

46

Seeking a happy song, Moira turned the radiogram on, but the serious tones of the war reporter did nothing to ease her nerves. She flicked the tuning knob from side to side. Static filled the room and filled her with frustration. She turned the radiogram off, stoked the fire and sat down to rest for a few minutes in the armchair.

The back door banging shut woke Moira from a deep sleep, her neck bent at an uncomfortable angle where she was still slouched in the armchair.

"What did you make me for supper?" Bill asked without so much as a greeting first. "Something good, I hope. I'm starving. It's been a big day."

Moira yawned and stretched her legs out in front of her. She stood, encouraging the blood flow to her limbs, waiting for Bill's customary peck on the cheek but he walked straight to the kitchen in search of food.

"I've only just got inside," she offered in explanation. It was only a little lie.

"Never mind then. I'll scramble myself some eggs." Bill bashed about the kitchen noisily.

"What about me?" Moira's whine sounded like a petulant toddler.

"I thought you would have eaten by now," Bill replied. "Did something go wrong to make you so late?"

She wasn't worried about food, just in need of acknowledgement for her efforts. Moira thought back over her day, nothing had gone wrong but there was more than enough work for two and she'd had to manage single handed.

"No, but …"

Bill glanced at his watch. "I'm back on duty in an hour. I need some sustenance. It's going to be a long night."

"What do you mean?"

"We've split into two," Bill replied. "I'll go out with one group tonight; William will take over with the other group first thing tomorrow and I'll come home for a sleep."

"Take over what?" Moira rubbed her temples; she was too tired for so many questions.

"The search for Stanley. The Home Guard are scouring the countryside inch by inch. We won't let him get away."

"Shouldn't the police be doing that?" *Leaving you home to help me on the farm,* Moira kept her thoughts to herself. "Not some vigilante group of locals."

"We're not some vigilante group." Bill stiffened as if the reference had offended him. "The police have requested the Home Guard's assistance, given their own numbers are substantially depleted."

Moira went quiet. The reminder that three men had already died, and another was injured drained the little energy she had.

Tomorrow was Sunday; it was meant to be a day of rest, even for those like her, who weren't religious. Before the war, Sunday started with a sleep-in, a long soak in the bath with scented bubbles. Did such luxuries even still exist?

Bill sleeping for the day meant a day of rest was the last thing Moira was going to get. Was she up to it? She was meant to be a land girl helping on a farm not running the entire operation herself. She glanced down at her dry cracked hands ingrained with dirt and sighed with exhaustion.

⌘

Later in bed, all was quiet except for the tick tock of the mantle clock. Bill's constant and regular breathing, like him, sturdy and reliable was missing. The ticking sounded like a time bomb, counting down to a catastrophe. What if something had happened to Bill? It wasn't just the workload that would fall on Moira's shoulders. Bill had made an imprint on her heart that wasn't expected. She wished he was lying next to her so she could feel his warmth emanate across the bed. She'd already forgiven his earlier lack of consideration of her. It was merely because he was tired, absorbed by his pursuit of the fugitive.

CHAPTER

5

Bill was overdue from his night-time shift in the search for Graham Stanley. Moira was pegging the washing on the line when the rattle of the cattle stop startled her. She'd kept herself busy trying not to think of what his lateness might mean. She hoisted the wicker washing basket to her hip and walked to the porch just as the truck rounded the end of the house.

Her heart thudded in her chest echoing the thud of the basket hitting the porch floor. William was driving the truck, not Bill. Since returning from fighting overseas, the eyepatch covering William's right eye and the jagged scar running the length of his cheek gave him a permanent seriousness so Moira couldn't tell from his expression whether his arrival brought good or bad news.

"Good, you're here." William rested the stump of his arm on the open window.

"What's happened? Where's Bill?"

Were the beads of perspiration on William's forehead, the result of his injuries or something worse?

"There's been an accident," he announced.

"Or another shooting?" Moira needed the truth.

William nodded slowly.

Moira swallowed. "How bad is it?"

"They've taken Bill to the hospital in Geraldine. I'll drive you in if you want."

Normally Moira would have refused such an offer, claimed that she was quite capable of driving and demanded the driver's seat, but an uncontrollable tremble started at her extremities. Her fingers and toes shivered, her legs felt like they were about to give way and her chin quivered. She managed to nod but couldn't utter anything coherent as she climbed into the passenger seat.

"Stanley snuck up on them," William explained. "In the pitch black, Bill didn't see what hit him."

"Is it bad?" Moira stared at the roof of the truck, cursing the tears that threatened.

"He took a stomach shot but the others made sure he got help as quick as possible."

The drive into Geraldine passed in a blur. Dazed, Moira was unable to comprehend the medley of emotions churning her insides. How had she allowed herself to become so attached to this man that life without him seemed unbearable? It wasn't like her at all. Life was meant to be fun; it was too short for dramas and catastrophes. She left those for other people.

51

"Here we are." William stopped outside a single storey weatherboard building and pulled on the handbrake.

"Geraldine Maternity Hospital." Moira read from the sign tucked in behind the property's front fence and laughed at the irony. She should be the one to be admitted here, not Bill but something would have to be happening between the sheets for that outcome to ever eventuate. "Whatever is he doing here?"

"There's nowhere else. They've dedicated some beds to general patients, in view of everything that's gone on."

"Right, of course, I keep forgetting we're not in Christchurch."

"Would you like me to come in with you?" William asked.

"No, I'll be fine," Moira replied as she climbed out of the truck.

"Take the key." William handed the truck key over to Moira. "I'll rejoin the search for Stanley and don't worry, we'll get the bastard who did this to Bill."

"Right, yes, thank you." Moira shook her head as if her thoughts needed shaking to become coherent again.

Her walk up the path to the hospital seemed surreal, like she was in a dream, or in this case a nightmare. She paused on the doorstep, took a deep breath unsure of what she would find inside the building. The hospital's white wooden door opened into an equally sterile corridor; the odour of disinfectant assaulted her nostrils.

"Hello. How can I help you?" A nurse, hair neatly tucked under a starched cap the same colour as her white uniform approached Moira.

"I'm here to see Bill ..." Moira couldn't remember his last name. She was used to just being on a first name basis. "He was brought in overnight, a shooting."

"You got here faster than we expected, Anne. I'll take you straight through."

"Anne?" Moira raised her hackles like a wary dog. "Who's Anne?"

"You're not Anne?" The nurse looked sideways at Moira.

. Did Bill have another woman all this time? Was the Home Guard just an excuse so she wouldn't get suspicious of him? Why did this always happen to her? Couldn't she find a man she could trust, just once?

"No, I'm Moira," she blurted. "Who on earth is Anne?"

"Anne is Bill's sister."

Moira sagged against the wall with relief. If the situation hadn't been so serious, she would have laughed at herself for jumping to unfounded conclusions.

"Are you alright, miss?" The nurse leaned in to check on Moira. "Do you need to sit down?"

"Nurse, you're needed in the ward." The matron approached, stamping her authority with every footstep. "What is all the kafuffle out here?"

"This young lady wishes to see Bill, but she isn't a relative of the patient."

"No, but ..." Moira wanted to scream that she was living with him, sharing his bed. She knew publicising their relationship would be the last thing Bill would want. "But I am running his farm for him, so I need to talk to him to get instructions."

"Well, he's not up to that, miss." The matron looked down her pointed nose at Moira.

"Can I at least see him?" Moira pleaded. "Reassure him that I have everything under control. Surely that will help in his recovery."

"Only next of kin are being granted visiting rights at this stage." The matron appeared adamant.

"Is it that bad? Is he going to die? Does he need to be moved to a better hospital?" Moira wrung her hands together as worst case scenarios filled her with dread.

"We are doing the best we can." The nurse ignored the matron and placed a comforting hand on Moira's shoulder. "The doctor will explain everything to Anne and John when they arrive. I understand they will be staying at Bill's so no doubt they will update you when they get back to the farm later."

Moira paced backwards and forwards across the corridor.

"I suggest you return home, miss, there is nothing more I can tell you." The matron ushered Moira towards the door.

"Is there someone who can pick you up?" the kind nurse asked.

"I can drive myself!" Moira snapped. It wasn't the nurse's fault, but she bore the brunt of Moira's frustration. She turned on her heel and stomped from the hospital, pushing the door to slam shut after her.

⌘

Moira continued to take her anger and frustration out on anything that came into her path. She slammed the truck door, the house door, and the kitchen cupboard door. She threw the bucket of food scraps at the pigs and tossed the empty billy on the ground. The sheep's hay was strewn about the paddock as Moira flung her arms around wildly.

She arrived at the cow paddock to find a recently calved cow flailing about on the ground.

"You look as angry as I feel." The thought of mimicking the cow, throwing a tantrum on the ground like a toddler brought Moira back to her senses. She stood, hands on her hips, looked around the rest of the herd who were sitting quietly chewing their cud. "Um … I don't think that's a good sign. That's all I need, a sick cow as well as a sick Bill."

Moira paused, rested her hands on the top of the strainer post at the gate and lowered her chin to sit on her entwined fingers while she contemplated her options. Hopefully the cow was just scratching in the dirt and would get up any minute now.

"That's wishful thinking, isn't it? Your eyes wouldn't be rolling about like that if you were just satisfying an itch."

If only Bill was still here, he'd know what to do. She'd have to prove she could cope. If his relatives turned up and she'd made a mess of things, already lost a good cow, she'd be down the road for sure.

Moira had no inkling as to what was wrong. She needed help. She remembered the small pile of books Bill kept on his bedside table. She had seen him flick through the pages, find what he needed and go off seemingly satisfied. Not being a reader herself, she'd left the pages unturned but noted the titles from their spines. One of the books was *The Science of Dairying.* Perhaps it held the solution to this dilemma. If only there were a manual for all of life's problems.

She hurried back to the house, kicked her gumboots off in the porch and rushed through to the bedroom. Her pulse raced as she scanned the table of contents: composition of milk, testing for fat content, herd testing, the list went on.

"Cheese making! What? I can't make cheese if I haven't got a cow to give me milk. What a useless book." Moira reached the bottom of the page almost ready to give up. She flicked the page over. "Some diseases affecting dairy cattle, Chapter XXI."

She recognised the letters as being roman numerals but couldn't remember from school what they stood for. Perhaps she should have paid more attention in the classroom. Fortunately, the page number was also listed, and she quickly turned to page 232.

"Contagious Mammitis!" Moira sucked in a breath. "Surely not contagious. I can't lose the whole herd."

The tiny words, full of scientific terminology and jargon she had no understanding of, blurred on the page. The bold type of the headings anchored her vision as she skipped ahead.

"Tuberculosis! Symptoms. Weak and emaciated. Well, you're not that or you wouldn't be thrashing about. Milk Fever or Part … Apo … I can't even pronounce that. Occurs in cows shortly after calving … a form of paralysis."

Moira jiggled on the spot. She'd found it. The cow likely had milk fever. She read on, under the heading of treatment was a diagram of the apparatus required and a description of what she needed to do. Re-invigorated, she rushed back to the porch, climbed into her gumboots with the book tucked under her arm and went in search of the syringe, nozzle and tubing shown in the diagram. Surely Bill would have them at the cow shed.

There was nothing in the small two bale shed that resembled the diagram. She checked the implement shed. She ran back to the house and checked the cupboards in the washhouse. Nothing. Dejected, she sat down on the porch step to ponder her next move.

The telephone's ring startled her, her spine went rigid. The hospital could be phoning with bad news.

"No, don't be silly, the hospital isn't going to phone you, you're not family, remember," she chastised herself as she stood, removed her gumboots, and headed to the telephone hanging on the kitchen wall.

It was a party line, so the call mightn't be for her. She couldn't remember which distinctive ring tone was theirs so didn't speak when she picked up the receiver.

"Hello … hello, is anybody there?"

The woman's voice sounded vaguely familiar. Was it the nurse deciding to help her out after all?

"Hello," she gingerly replied.

"Is that you, Moira?"

"Yes, who is this?"

"It's Betsy. Who did you think it would be? Never mind, I was just ringing to see if you were okay. I heard about the accident. I hope Bill is going to be alright. Are you managing on your own? Is there anything you'd like a hand with? Do you want to come over here until they find Stanley?"

Moira sucked in a breath while her mind ran through the questions Betsy fired at her.

"It's not good, Betsy. They won't tell me anything about Bill and now there's a cow that's looking pretty bad. I've got to do something."

"About Bill or the cow?"

"There's nothing I can do about Bill today. I've already tried. I couldn't get past the matron. I'll try again tomorrow."

"So, what's wrong with the cow? Shall I ask Duncan to come and have a look? He's out now but he could come by later maybe."

"Later might be too late." Moira's bleak mood sat heavy in her limbs. "I think it's milk fever, but I can't find the apparatus the book says to use to fix it."

"Oh, we had a cow down with that," Betsy replied. "She's alright now though."

"So, you have the equipment and know what to do?" A spark of hope twinkled in the distance.

"I know where the syringe is." Betsy hesitated as if unsure of herself. "And I've watched Duncan do it."

"Are you busy? Can you come over? Bring the syringe with you."

"I'd better. Duncan said the earlier you get to them the better their chances of survival. We'd best not wait for him to get home."

"Good, I'll see you soon." Moira ended the call and hurried back outside to check on the cow, hoping it wasn't already too late.

⌘

"You have to milk her out first," Betsy said as they approached the cow which was still cast in the corner of the paddock.

"How are we going to do that without getting kicked?" Moira already felt she'd been metaphorically kicked in the guts today; a physical injury would be the last straw.

"I'll talk to her, try to calm her down," Betsy offered. "The sick cow at Whipsnade stopped thrashing about. It must have sensed we were trying to help it."

"Or this cow doesn't have milk fever." Doubt stopped Moira mid-stride. "What if I've got it wrong and what we do kills the animal anyway?"

"Um." Betsy tipped her head to one side, before clearing her throat and continuing. "She's got the same symptoms as our one, so I'd say we've got nothing to lose. We're only going to milk her and put some air into her udders. It can't do any harm and if it doesn't work, we can get Duncan to come by later."

"I hope you're right." Moira rubbed the back of her neck.

She set down the bucket she'd been carrying, far enough to not be knocked over by the cow. It was half full of hot water, the syringe submerged to keep it sterile. Betsy knelt beside the animal's head, talking softly, stroking the cow's neck with one hand, and bracing its front legs with her other hand. Whether the cow ran out of fight or responded to Betsy's calm presence, Moira couldn't tell but she felt the same, as if a sense that everything would be alright washed over her. Her actions mirrored Betsy's. With one hand pushing down on the cow's hind legs, she slowly milked out each teat with her other hand.

"Do you think I've emptied her enough?" Moira asked, her voice laced with uncertainty.

"I think so. Give the udder a good wash with the warm water now," Betsy suggested. "We have to be careful to keep it as sterile as possible."

"It's just going to get dirty again on the ground."

"Here take my coat and put that under the udder when you've finished washing it."

"Thanks, Betsy, I don't know what I would have done without you."

With everything as clean as possible Moira gingerly threaded the syringe into the first teat and squeezed the rubber bulb to feed air into the udder until it swelled from a loose bag to tight.

"Another one now." Betsy continued to stroke the cow.

"How much is too much air?" Moira imagined the udder bursting like a popped balloon.

"I haven't a clue. Better to be less than more, I reckon. We can always have another go later."

When Moira had pumped air into each teat and massaged the udder like the *Science of Dairying* had suggested she moved out of the way and sat on the ground, wrapped her arms around her legs and rested her chin on her knees.

"Well, it's up to you now cow. Either you get up or you die."

"She'll live. You've done a good job, Moira."

"We'll see." Moira wasn't so sure.

"Right, I'd better get back." Betsy grabbed her coat from under the cow. "I've still got more jobs to do before milking."

"Me too. It's never ending, isn't it?"

"Sure is." Betsy's face mirrored the fatigue Moira felt. "And we've got calves for the A and P Show. Are you entering any animals?"

"No, Bill was too busy with the Home Guard."

"You will come along though?" Betsy asked. "It'll be a great day out."

"I'll see." Moira sighed. "I've got double the workload now with Bill out of action."

"I hope he gets better soon."

"So do I."

⌘

Pride put a spring in Moira's step as she headed home at the end of the day. The cow with milk fever was up and about, albeit a bit sluggish still but way better than before. When Moira made it back to the house, a shiny black car was parked in the driveway. Her breath hitched in her throat as she imagined a police officer had come to deliver bad news. She gingerly approached the porch where the back door was slightly ajar. Voices from inside stalled her entry.

"It's shameful, John. She's wormed her way into his bed."

Moira took an instant dislike to the woman the pious voice belonged to.

"Now, now, you don't know that for sure, Anne." The deep, even tone of the man's response was as calm as his words. Moira hoped the woman was listening.

"Well, I do. It's obvious no one has slept in the single bed for some time, and I'll be changing the sheets on the double bed before I sleep in it. It's atrocious," the woman huffed.

"We should keep an open mind."

"She's probably just a gold digger, not a land girl at all."

Heat boiled up Moira's face until her anger felt ready to explode.

"Bill's truck is here, and someone is out there feeding the animals," the man reasoned. "For all we know she is a very good farmer."

"Women don't do farmwork, John, and you know it. It's man's work for a reason. We cook and clean and you do the manual labour you're built for. It's the way the Lord intended. Just like he intended that conjugal rights are just that, the rights, and privileges of a married couple. It's sinful."

"Anne, you're getting yourself all het up. Bill is our first concern; the farm comes second. I'll have a look around tomorrow and see what needs doing. Bill managed by himself before, I'm sure I'll be able to too once I get up to speed."

"And then we can send her on her way. Miriam would be turning over in her grave."

There was no kind tone to the woman's words. Moira had been judged once again before she'd even been given a chance to prove herself.

"How about you put the kettle on, and we'll have a cuppa and wait until she gets home."

CHAPTER

6

Normally Moira would have barged straight in and given the woman what for, but she pulled herself up, aware that her anger would likely result in words that couldn't later be retracted. She knew the woman had misjudged her and she could prove it. She wouldn't allow them to send her away. She tiptoed back off the porch, waited a few minutes and then made her arrival known with a slam of the toilet door.

The last of the day's light seeped in through the toilet's small louvre window along with a cool breeze that helped further abate Moira's fury. Relieving herself physically allowed her to also let go of the lingering resentment. There was a sense of déjà vu. Judgement by people who didn't know her, in circumstances beyond her control, went way back to childhood. Her father divorced her mother when Moira was just seven years old. People looked down their noses at the single mother and her innocent child. Moira's mother ran out of fight, she chose to relocate rather than retaliate against their sneers and barbs. Moira was tired of running; it was time to stand and fight.

She was in this alone if the nurses wouldn't allow her to see Bill. He would back her up as far as her farming skills, but he would never reveal their relationship to his sister and her husband. The only way Moira was going to get to stay was if she could make herself indispensable on the farm.

Having finished her business, she stood, pulled up her overalls and hooked the straps back over her shoulders.

"You've got this, girl" she said to the determined looking image as she glanced in the mirror hung on the back of the door.

She straightened her spine, pulled her shoulders back and held her head high as she walked into the house.

"Hello. I'm Moira, Bill's land girl." Moira emphasised Bill's name as she smiled and held her hand out to shake theirs. It wasn't the done thing for a woman to shake hands, it was a challenge, to indicate she was equal. "You must be John and Anne. The hospital told me you'd be arriving today."

Anne looked down her nose at Moira's outreached hand as if it was contagious. She stood with pursed lips, clasping her own hands tightly into her body.

Seconds ticked by; Moira's hand remained outstretched, she didn't waiver. She watched John's eyes flick from her hand to his wife and back again. Eventually, he cleared his throat and returned the handshake.

"Hello, Moira," John said. "Sorry to be meeting you under such circumstances."

The look on Anne's face told Moira she was sorry to be meeting at all.

"How was Bill? Did the doctor give you an update. He wasn't around when I was there this morning and I wanted to get back to the farm to get everything done." The tiny white lie was justified, and Moira banished the pang of guilt that tightened her chest.

"John will be able to manage the farm work going forward." Anne ignored Moira's question.

"Oh, it's alright," Moira bustled on as if nothing was amiss. "I've got a good routine going. It's a big day but it's manageable."

Anne came to stand beside her husband as if his stature would add strength to her words. She barely came up to his shoulder and Moira was a good four inches taller which further boosted her confidence.

"Farm work isn't woman's work though." Anne stood with a hand on each hip.

"The government has decreed that it is in war times," Moira countered Anne's argument. "That's why they called for volunteers, that's what the Women's Land Service was formed for."

"I'll give you a hand tomorrow," John offered. "Do the hard and heavy bits that Bill would have done."

"And will do again soon." *Please, please, please*, Moira muttered under her breath.

"We hope so," John replied. "Would you like a cuppa? The water's hot."

"I'm famished. I need food more than a drink." Moira lifted the lid of the pot of mince and vegetables she'd prepared at lunch time." "I'll just fry some of this up, have a quick bite to eat and head to bed. It's been a big day."

"I can do that." Anne moved towards the pot.

"Because its women's work?" Moira's retort was laced with sarcasm.

She didn't wait for a response and busied herself stoking the coal range, adding a dollop of dripping to the frying pan, and tipping enough mince for a single serve on top. Anne had no choice but to retreat to the table with the teapot and cups on a tray.

John and Anne were still sipping their cups of tea when Moira sat down at the table with a full plate.

"What jobs need doing tomorrow?" John asked.

Moira finished her mouthful before answering. She tried to sound casual.

"Just the usual, milking, move the sheep, feed the pigs, get the milk to the factory."

"John can take the milk to the factory," Anne said.

"I'll do that." Moira was adamant but lightened her tone to continue. "It'll give me a chance to visit Bill again."

"You can't drive the truck." Anne nudged her husband with her elbow as if prompting him to support her. "Men drive trucks."

"Well, I can assure you, I'm not a man, I can drive the truck and I will be driving it tomorrow."

Anne huffed, stood, and carried her cup to the kitchen.

"She's worried about her brother," John offered an excuse for his wife.

"As we all are. How was he? Did the doctor give you an update?"

"It's a stomach wound. Quite serious. He lost a lot of blood." John paused and looked at Moira. "Sorry, you already know that."

William had told her it was a stomach wound but seeing John's worried look reinforced how bad things were.

"If it doesn't get infected," John continued. "He should be right but he's running a temperature, so they're quite concerned. We'll know more in the morning."

"Yes, we will." Moira wasn't going to let the matron prevent her from seeing Bill tomorrow. "Right, I'd better get to bed."

She bumped into Anne in the kitchen doorway and her fork clanged to the floor like a weapon cast down in a battle.

"Sorry," Anne apologised. "Let me clean that up for you."

Moira took the peace offering at face value. "Thank you."

⌘

Moira had to admit that John was very helpful. He was good around the animals and knew what to do.

"You're obviously a farmer," she said as they arrived back at the house, full milk cans from the morning's milking, secured on the back of the truck.

"I was," John replied. "Retired, sold up a few years ago and moved into town because Anne wanted to be closer to her ailing parents. We've got a big garden and there's plenty to do but I miss the land, there's nothing quite like fresh country air."

"Who is looking after her parents while you're down here?" Moira hoped John's answer would mean their stay was short-lived.

"They've both been dead several years now."

Moira swallowed so she didn't give voice to the disappointment she felt. John's move to Bill's farm could, and likely would, become permanent if Bill didn't make a full recovery and John would manage quite well without her.

"Right, I'd better get the milk to the factory." She needed to see Bill too, to get some indication that he was improving.

"You should have breakfast first," John suggested. "Anne will have cooked."

"I'll grab something when I get back."

Moira climbed into the truck, closing the door on any further conversation.

The drive to the factory was shorter than she remembered or perhaps it was just that her driving had improved. She backed the truck tray up to the loading platform and climbed out.

"Well, look here." Jake wolf whistled and his face spread into the widest grin. "Here's a beautiful vision to brighten our day. Moira! Long time no see, I thought you'd forgotten me."

The whistle brought a flush to Moira's cheeks. She tucked an errant strand of hair behind her ear, wishing she'd taken a little more effort to look her best.

"Hi, Jake. No one could forget you," she teased. "I've just been busy."

"Busy with Bill, I hear." Jake winked as he moved the full milk cans from the tray to the platform.

Unsure how to interpret the wink, Moira glanced around the factory to see if anyone else was within earshot. An older weatherbeaten farmer appeared to prick his ears up, alert for any gossip so Moira chose to neither confirm nor deny.

"He's been injured. He's in the hospital."

"I heard about the shooting. It's not good news. I hope they catch that bastard, Stanley."

"The Home Guard are working around the clock with the police," Moira said. "So, hopefully they'll get him soon."

"Then we'll all need something to cheer us up." Jake reloaded the truck with empty cans, tied them off and jumped down to stand beside Moira. "You'll be going to the A & P Show then? It's one day that's fun for everyone. You can't miss that. Not, that you need sweetening up, but I could buy you some candyfloss."

"Thanks, Jake, for the offer but I'll likely be too busy on the farm." *That is, if John hasn't taken over and rendered me redundant.*

"So, it'll have to be the next dance then. They're having one to raise money for the Home Guard. The weekend after the A & P Show. You'll have to come along to that."

"Umm, I don't know." Moira wasn't sure she'd have the energy for dancing, not with all the farm work.

"You won't be working at nighttime."

"No, but …" *It wouldn't feel right going to a dance without Bill, would it?*

"You promised me a dance last time, remember, and I'm still waiting for it."

Moira smiled. "You'd had too much beer. You would have stood on my toes."

"I promise to be on my best behaviour." Jake lay his hands across his chest and tilted his head looking all innocent.

Moira couldn't help the giggle that escaped. It was nice to have some fun, she'd almost forgotten what it felt like, the lightness that came when life wasn't all work and no play.

"Alright then. I'll see you at the dance." Moira made no promises other than to be there. If Bill was better, then she would go with him, if he wasn't then she would go alone and one dance with Jake couldn't hurt.

"Yes!" Jake looked like he'd just won first prize in the lottery. "You won't regret it."

⌘

Lightness filled Moira with a sense of anticipation, like a fluffy bumblebee buzzing about her insides, and came with her to the hospital. She bent to inhale the scent of an Iceberg rose, its fragrance another delight that made her believe all would be right in the world today as she casually sauntered up the path, her mouth curved into a smile.

"Hello." A friendly voice called out. "You're looking happier today."

Moira stopped, turned towards the voice, and saw the nurse she met in the corridor yesterday. The nurse's cap sat on the wooden bench seat beside her, allowing her dark curls to bounce about her friendly face.

"Hello," Moira replied, noticing the cigarette the nurse raised to her lips and drew on. "You smoke."

Whether the words were an observation or an accusation, the nurse didn't appear offended.

"Just getting a quick one in before I start work." She nodded towards the hospital building. "Matron doesn't approve."

"She doesn't seem to approve of much," Moira whispered, approaching the nurse. "I might join you, if you don't mind."

The nurse moved her cap to her lap and patted the seat beside her. "Be my guest. Have you come to see Bill?"

"Yes." Moira lit her own cigarette, inhaled, and blew a ring of smoke skyward before answering. "Are you going to let me in today?"

"It's not me stopping you. It's the rules, and the matron is a stickler for the rules, especially for the really sick patients."

The nurse went silent, as if she realised, she'd said too much. She looked everywhere except at Moira.

"Bill's not good, is he?" Moira dared to ask.

"I'm not meant to discuss patients outside the hospital." The nurse shook her head, the cigarette moving from side to side as she did.

"Has the infection got worse overnight?"

The nurse nodded. Her curls bobbed.

"Is he expected to make it?" Moira's cigarette trembled in her fingers.

The nurse turned on the seat, resting her free hand gently on Moira's shoulder. Her eyes reflected Moira's pained stare as she turned her head slowly, almost imperceptibly, from side to side.

Moira forced the lump in her throat down to block the hole that was forming in her heart. Just when she thought she had found a man who would respect her, a home where she could settle, a job where she could prove she was worthy, everything was turned upside down yet again. She wanted to scream, to howl like a child, to stomp her feet and protest that life wasn't fair. She lifted the smoke to her lips, inhaled deeply, waited for the calming effect of the nicotine to give her the strength to stand.

"Thank you." Moira looked back at the building, like it was a fortress she was determined to breach. "I will go and see him now."

"He's in the third room on your left," the nurse whispered a parting gift.

Moira dropped her cigarette butt to the ground and stomped its smoking embers with the sole of her shoe. She straightened her spine, pulled her shoulders back and strode up to the door of the hospital. It creaked on its hinges, like a warning bell announcing her arrival.

"Nurse Humphrey, you're late." The matron's voice bellowed from an office off to Moira's right. "There are babies in the nursery that need changing."

Fortunately, the matron continued head down with her paperwork and didn't notice Moira walk past. The sound of babies crying echoed down the corridor from the nursery, but Moira had no intention of changing dirty diapers, now or ever. She counted the doors on the left. One. Two. Three. A small silver name plate holder stopped her from turning the door handle. *William (Bill) De'Ath.*

Moira sighed despondently. Even is surname predicted his imminent fate. She sucked in a breath, wishing she had another cigarette to draw strength from, and opened the door. The only noise that filled the small room was Bill's raspy breath, raggedy inhales, and weary exhales symptoms of his struggle to live. His eyes were closed. If only he was merely enjoying a nap, resting up before another day on the farm. There was a greyness to his pallor as if the light within had already been dimmed. Moira itched to run her fingers over the stubble that prickled his unshaven chin, the only darkened pigment on his face.

Grey and white striped pyjamas were buttoned high under his chin, like the inescapable bars of a prison cell. Bill's left arm was hidden beneath the precise folds of a white hospital sheet, but his right lay atop the sheet to grant access to a drip. Moira glared at the upturned bottle, hung from a trolley beside the bed, giving Bill sustenance.

"You're not doing enough," she growled under her breath.

Moira's knuckles whitened as she gripped the steel frame at the foot of Bill's bed. She leaned on it for strength while she took everything in. The scene before her didn't paint a cheerful picture. Nothing gave her any hope that life would go back to how she wanted it to, but it had to, she had to believe that it could. If Bill knew she needed him, that she was here for him, then surely, he could get better.

She moved around to his right side, pulled a chair closer to the bed and sat down. His hand felt warm beneath hers. She entwined their fingers together, woven like a spider's web, wishing for the same resilience.

"Bill," she whispered. "It's Moira. I hope you can hear me."

Moira gasped. Did Bill's fingers twitch? Did he hear her? Or did she just imagine it?

"Please get better," she continued hoping for the slightest movement to signal his awareness of her presence. "Miriam might be wanting you to be with her, but I need you here. You still have so much life to live. Don't give up. Come back to me. Please."

Approaching footsteps and voices resounded in the corridor. Anne's screech was instantly recognisable.

"We haven't got long, Bill. Your sister doesn't want me around. I know you'd tell her I'm good at farming. If you'd

just get better, she can go home. We don't need her."
Moira released Bill's fingers and raised his hand to her
lips.

"I'm telling you, Matron, that is the farm truck outside,"
Anne growled.

"Madam. Keep your voice down. We have sick patients.
Only family are permitted in Mr De'Ath's room."

"That may be your policy but it's not one you're policing
very well. That woman is in with my brother when she has
no right to be." Anne barged into Bill's room. Her piercing
eyes bored into Moira's. "See! What did I tell you? She
can't even let a dying man be."

CHAPTER
7

Moira didn't wait for any more tongue lashings from Anne. She was so bitter and nasty it was hard to imagine she was Bill's sister; he was kind and caring. Moira walked from the hospital ward, shoulders back, head held high, past the matron whose face was red with rage.

"Nurse Humphrey, escort this woman out of the building," the woman ordered, her hands on her ample hips.

"Yes, Matron. This way, Miss." Nurse Humphrey came from the direction of the nursery and linked her arm around Moira's. "Did you get to say what you needed to?" she whispered.

"Yes, thank you, but I'm not sure if he heard me," Moira replied.

"Medical authorities will tell you patients can recognise voices even if they can't respond." The nurse gave Moira's hand a comforting pat.

"I hope you don't get into trouble."

"No more than usual." Nurse Humphrey smiled. "I'm just glad you got to see him. He had a rough night."

"He's not going to get better, is he?" Moira paused at the exit.

"I'll keep a good eye on him. You never know he might perk up after your visit."

"Thank you."

It was nice of the nurse to be positive, but Moira sensed she knew the truth, that Bill didn't have long to go.

⌘

Bill's truck must have known the way back to the farm. Moira had no recollection of the drive. Her mind seesawed between battling on to prove herself, clinging to the miniscule chance that Bill would come home, and John and Anne would leave, or just packing her things and moving on. So, what if she met everyone's expectations? Life was too short to stay where she wasn't wanted.

Rattling over the cattle stop brought her back to reality. She parked the truck outside the house, at least it was still her home for now, and got on with the chores on the farm. The sheep needed moving so she headed out to their paddock. Seeing all the lambs prancing around with their long tails wriggling reminded Moira that the lambs would soon have to be docked. Ringing lambs' tails and castrating ram lambs with rubber rings and elastrators made her insides squirm. It was not a job she wanted to do, and neither could she do it alone. Duncan would probably say she couldn't do it at all. And so would Anne, but Anne could be ignored as she obviously knew nothing about farming.

While she waited for the sheep to meander through the open gate to the fresh grass, unanswered questions raced through her mind. Would John insist he could handle the docking himself? Could she go ahead and do it without John to prove she was independent and capable? Could she ask Betsy to help? She splayed her fingers out, her nails were well beyond a manicure, cracked and ingrained with dirt, but the thought of having them touch the sheep's daggy behinds and testes made her cringe. Perhaps she could just leave the task to John.

She headed back to the house at lunch time, added an egg to a pot of boiling water and two slices of bread to the rack for toasting on the top of the freshly stoked coal range. It wasn't long before she was sitting down enjoying dipping the soldiers into the runny egg yolk.

"You've got to do what's right for you," she lectured herself between mouthfuls. "Stop beating yourself up for your choices. Why are you punishing yourself? You've done nothing wrong."

The food satisfied her hunger, and the personal pep talk lifted her spirits.

"It'll be my choice, if and when I choose to leave, nobody else's."

The need to prove herself still drove Moira to wash and dry her dishes. She took the piece of meat that was destined to be dinner from the safe, placed it in the largest pot she found in the cupboard and covered it with water. It was likely more water than necessary but proving she was just as capable in the house as on the farm, meant no more repeats of her first attempt at cooking.

Buster was in his usual spot on the mat in front of the fire, even though it wasn't lit. Moira eyed him up as she added salt to the pot and placed the lid firmly on top.

"You're not going to boil dry," she spoke to the pot as if it was human. "And Buster, you stay away, or I won't be as forgiving as Bill, I will kick your butt if you so much as sniff this meat."

Moira checked the coal range one last time, silently hoping there was just the right amount of heat to cook the meat neither under or overdone, before she left the house again and headed out to the pig paddock.

The piglets had grown so quickly and were close to weaning. That created another problem. She'd have to catch all thirteen of them and remove them from the paddock to separate them from the sow. It was bad enough having to carry them the night they were born. At least then it was four at a time, now when they must have quadrupled in weight, she'd struggle to carry more than one of them at a time. The sow had come after her and Bill then, what would she do if Moira tried to take her weaners? It didn't bear thinking about. Another job to add to the list of things she couldn't do.

Perhaps she should just give up and move on. Where would she go? With a new batch of land girls at *Whipsnade* there would be no room for her there. Alice and Fergus had left *Orari Estate*, they might have need for another land

80

girl, but that would mean living with a house full of men. Normally Moira would have leapt at the opportunity but all she could foresee from that relocation were more problems, more men doubting her ability to farm, more men she would have to prove herself to, more men to get into trouble with. Grace might be able to get her a job at the flax mill. No, Moira couldn't do that. The stench of rotting flax that followed Grace wherever she went was disgusting. Moira wasn't that desperate.

"Aha!" Moira stopped and smiled as the obvious solution came to mind. "Of course, why didn't I think of it before? The placement officer will know all the farms that want someone. I can telephone, find out what's available, just in case things don't work out here. It'll be good to have my options open."

Moira chuckled as she fed the pigs their rations of whey and meal. "And I'd better stop talking to myself before someone hears me and gets me committed to the loony bin."

⌘

Moira finally made it back to the house after the evening milking, emotionally drained and physically exhausted, to find John and Anne's black car parked outside. It looked like a gangster car she'd seen in the movies, poised ready for a shootout with the baddies. In this case though, she was considered the baddy, and she wasn't sure she had any energy for another confrontation.

Her stomach rumbled as the aroma of cooked meat beckoned her inside, but hearing John and Anne's voices, Moira tiptoed into the porch and pressed her ear against the closed door to glean whatever information she could arm herself with.

"Perhaps we should be nicer to her," John suggested.

He used the royal 'we', but Moira imagined that was just to placate Anne.

"Bill did say I love you, Moira." John's calm voice was the tonic Moira needed.

She felt giddy. She touched her fingers to her lips, remembered the times when Bill had kissed her. He was a good kisser. He mightn't have told her his feelings, but she felt them in his kisses.

"He was delirious," Anne huffed. "He meant Miriam."

It was a struggle for Moira to dampen the urge to barge in and give Anne a taste of her own medicine.

"He couldn't possibly love a woman who does farm work and drives a truck," Anne continued.

"Stranger things have happened," John replied.

Moira chose that moment to open the door, she faked a smile and pretended she'd only heard John's last comment.

"What strange things have happened?"

The pair turned and stared wide-eyed like possums caught in the car headlights. John coughed and Anne's cheeks coloured scarlet.

"I was just saying that the meat is cooked perfectly," Anne lied.

"Why is that so strange?" Moira wasn't going to let them off too easily. "I came in at lunchtime and put it on, planning for it to be ready by the time I finished milking."

It was more like a desperate hope that it wouldn't boil dry or still be raw, but Moira kept that to herself. "I'd best get some vegetables on too. I'm famished."

"Anne will do that." John nodded his head as if to nudge his wife towards the coal range. "You've had a busy day."

None too pleased to be ordered about, Anne huffed as she set about peeling potatoes.

"I'll be around to work on the farm from now on," John continued.

Moira's hunger pains vanished in an instant, replaced by a rolling stomach, like a tidal wave about to wash her and everything familiar away.

"Why?" she asked tentatively, holding her breath, afraid of the answer.

"We won't be visiting the hospital anymore."

"Ha … ha … has Bill died?" Moira clutched her arms to her chest.

"No, no." John patted her on the arm. "They're moving him to Christchurch. They're better equipped over there to deal with injuries as serious as his."

"I thought he should have gone there straight away."

"His injuries were too serious to risk the journey," John countered.

"So, he's got better already then?" Moira hated to think what he'd looked like before if the way he looked this morning was an improvement.

"I wouldn't say that, but he has stabilised enough to be moved which is good news."

It was good news, but it made contacting the placement officer even more urgent. She glanced at Bill's telephone. It hung on the wall in the kitchen meaning any call Moira made would have to wait until Anne and John were out of the house or she'd risk her conversation being overheard.

Half an hour later they were all sitting at the dining table. The room was silent except for the clang of knives and forks on plates. Moira was too tired for inane small talk so opted to keep quiet.

"I was thinking we'll need to start shutting up some paddocks for hay." John rested his knife and fork on his plate and steepled his fingers. "Do you know which paddocks Bill usually cuts, Moira?"

The question took Moira by surprise. It was nice to be consulted. She wished he'd asked a question she at least had some inkling about. She wanted her answer to sound intelligent but what she knew about haymaking could be written on the head of a matchstick. There was no point fibbing.

"No," she replied. "I haven't been here for haymaking before."

Anne rolled her eyes and settled her mouth into a satisfied smirk as if Moira had just ticked another item on the list that would send her on her way.

"There are several flat paddocks close to the hayshed though." Moira stared straight at Anne. "So those would be the logical ones to *shut up*."

Anne's jaw dropped as Moira's innuendo hit home. She huffed, looked down her nose and busied herself eating.

84

⌘

John and Anne didn't leave the farm until supplies were required at the end of the week. As soon as Moira heard the car wheels rattle over the cattle stop, she headed to the kitchen, where the Bakelite telephone was mounted on the wall. She held the earpiece to her ear and dialled through to the operator.

"Can you give me the number for the Women's Land Corps placement officer please?" Moira jotted down the reply. "Thank you."

She glanced out the kitchen window, to ensure John and Anne hadn't returned, before dialling the number. On the party line someone was bound to overhear her conversation, but hopefully they wouldn't gossip.

"Good morning, Mary McLean speaking."

For a split-second Moira thought she could pretend it was a wrong number and hang up but living under the same roof as Anne had become unbearable. There must be something better. If Bill ever came home, if the war ever ended, there would be options to return but for now she needed to leave.

"Good morning, um, yes, it's Moira Harvey here. I'm a land girl in need of a new placement. Do you have any farmers needing a volunteer?"

"Moira Harvey. That name rings a bell, you've only just gone to a new placement, haven't you? Why do you need another placement, Miss Harvey?"

Moira heard paper rustling in the background.

"Yes, I see, according to my records you were assigned to Bill De'Ath's farm, as a special request from him. Not usually how I like to run things, but I obliged in that instance. Has something untoward happened that you need to report, Miss Harvey?"

"No, no, it's just that my services are no longer required here."

"Mr De'Ath has sold the farm?"

Moira had no desire to relay the entire story, but the placement officer's questions kept coming.

"Bill's been injured. His family have come to run the farm. My services are no longer required. Do you have anything else, or shall I head back to Christchurch?"

As the words left Moira's mouth, she realised that Christchurch was a solution that meant she could visit Bill as and when she liked. Fatigue had seeped into her core, physical from the seven day a week dawn to dusk toil and emotional from having to deal with Anne's snide remarks while worrying about Bill. She imagined no more early mornings for milking, sleeping in a soft bed long after daybreak, visiting Bill at the hospital, helping with his rehabilitation.

"There are plenty of positions in the munitions factories," Mary replied, putting paid to Moira's wistful thoughts of an easier life. "But you've been through the land girl training, it would be a shame to waste the farming skills you've acquired. Just let me have a look."

Moira listened as Mary flicked through paper and murmured to herself.

"There is a placement that's just come in this morning," Mary eventually said. "I haven't had time to check what's involved yet or ensure the conditions are suitable."

"What type of farm is it?" Perhaps she could still avoid early morning milking.

"It's a high-country sheep station ..."

"I'll take it." Moira didn't wait for further details.

"Don't you want to know where it is and what's involved?" Mary asked.

"Lambing's finished, so it won't be that." Moira resisted the urge to squeal with delight that there would be no cows to milk. "Drenching, I've done that. Docking and shearing, I've done that. I can drive, so I can move the sheep."

"Can you ride a horse, Miss Harvey?"

Moira preferred the mechanics of a vehicle that she could control, not an animal taller than her with a mind of its own.

"Umm, no, but I'm sure I can learn."

"Do you know how to work farm dogs, Miss Harvey?"

Moira pictured herself, shepherd's whistle between her lips, rustling up Duncan's dogs at the *Whipsnade* woolshed. The dogs knew what to do themselves and only needed the odd whistle of encouragement.

"I sure do," she replied confidently, to not give any hint of exaggeration. "I'll take it."

"It is rather remote," Mary continued. "Will you cope with the isolation? Mr Masters only comes to town once a month."

There had been a day, before the war turned everything upside down, when Moira would have thought her throat had been cut if she wasn't within a mile of a shop but now that was a vague memory. What was most important now was no wife or female relative, dead, or alive, to despise her presence.

"Is there a Mrs Masters?" she asked.

"No, Mr Masters is a bachelor," Mary replied.

"Good. Let him know I'm on my way." In her head, Moira was already picturing the look on Anne's face when she relayed the news.

"Do you have your own transport?"

"No." Doubt started to creep into Moira's voice. "Can I catch the train or something? Or telephone him, Mr … what did you say his name was? He could make a special trip and pick me up."

"No trains go out that way. And Mr Masters doesn't have a telephone."

No telephone! That was remote. Did he live as far out as Alice and Fergus? Perhaps they'd be neighbours.

"I'll write to him," Mary continued. "Let him know you are keen and when he comes to town at the end of the month, he can pick you up."

End of the month! Two more weeks of putting up with Anne. Perhaps if John knew Moira was leaving, he would make Anne be nice to her, or at least civil.

"That'll be the Monday after the Home Guard dance. I'll contact you if there are any changes. Goodbye, Miss Harvey."

The telephone went dead before Moira could reply. She shrugged and moved on to picture herself at the Home Guard dance, a chance for a final fling before she went to the back of beyond. It couldn't possibly be worse than where she was.

CHAPTER

8

"The phone is for you, Moira." Anne held her hand over the receiver. "A woman."

Moira rushed to the telephone hoping it wasn't the placement officer and the news she hadn't yet revealed was about to be spilled.

"Hello, Moira speaking. Who's this?"

"Hi, Moira, it's Betsy."

Moira's sigh of relief was audible.

"Don't sound so happy to hear from me," Betsy joked.

Moira turned her back to John and Anne and curved her hand around the mouthpiece. "Sorry, I thought you might be someone else."

"Sorry to disappoint you. Have you got some beau chasing you? One of the American soldiers?"

"No! I haven't got anyone chasing me." Moira flicked from defensive to curious. "What American soldiers?"

"Haven't you heard?"

"No, I haven't heard anything, I've been busy working." Impatience brought a sharp tone to Moira's voice.

"There are American soldiers on leave being billeted in the area," Betsy replied. "They'll be coming to the Home Guard Dance."

"Mmm." Moira's mouth curved into a delighted smile as if was savouring the slow dissolve of chocolate on her tongue.

"Anyway," Betsy continued. "I was just checking to see if you've changed your mind about the A & P Show. It's going ahead despite Graham Stanley still being on the loose. It'll be a great day out. There'll be side shows and rides. Say you'll come. You don't have to have an animal to lead."

None of Betsy's reasons for going to the A & P Show appealed to Moira.

"You'll be too busy with William," she teased. "You don't need me for company."

"I have to help him with his calf, it's more difficult when you've only got one arm."

"It's really difficult when you've got two men." Moira chuckled.

"I haven't got two men, Moira." Betsy sounded defensive. "I'm engaged to Roland."

"I know, you keep telling me but I'm not sure who you're trying to remind."

"Oh, Moira Harvey, you're incorrigible," Betsy huffed. "I've hardly seen William anyway, he's busy with the manhunt. He's even more determined to catch Stanley after Bill got shot. It's like he's gone back to war. How is Bill?"

"They've moved him to Christchurch." Moira sighed.

"I'm sorry. Hopefully they'll be able to fix him up."

Moira glanced back over her shoulder. John and Anne were hovering within earshot, so Moira kept the news of her departure secret.

"I hope so," she replied.

"I'll see you at the dance then. I'm certain you wouldn't want to miss that."

Moira's mind wandered. She pictured the soldiers in their uniforms, imagined the drawl of their American accents, and mentally scanned the contents of her wardrobe. What could she wear? Her cinnamon dress and red toe peepers would enjoy another outing.

"I'll be at the dance with bells on."

⌘

John, Anne, and Moira were finishing up breakfast when the cattle stop rattled, announcing the arrival of a vehicle. They all strained to look out the window to see who would be visiting at this hour of the morning.

"It's William," Moira announced. "He's the neighbour's son. He was helping Bill train the Home Guard."

"I wonder what he wants with us." John stood and headed to the back door.

In the busyness following Bill's injury, Moira had forgotten the fugitive at the centre of the mayhem was still on the loose.

"He was leading the hunt for the fugitive that shot Bill," she recalled. "Perhaps he's got an update."

"They better have killed him." Anne scowled. "There has to be justice for my brother."

They all stood in the porch ready to greet William. He looked weary, not just the tiredness of war, but fatigue from hours without sleep. The sleeve of his shirt was stained with blood and hung loosely at his side.

"Oh, no," Anne gasped. "He's been injured too. He's hurt his arm. He's bleeding. Quick, John, help him."

John stepped forward but Moira interrupted.

"He lost his forearm in the war," she explained. "And an eye. That's why he wears an eyepatch."

"Hello, Moira." William stopped when he saw Moira wasn't alone. "And ... you must be Bill's relatives?"

"John Blackley." John stepped forward and held his hand out. He cleared his throat awkwardly when he realised William couldn't return the handshake. "This is my wife, Anne. Do you have some news about the fugitive?"

"Yes! We got the bastard. Oops, sorry ma'am, excuse my language. It's been a big week."

"That's alright, William," John said. "Understandable in the circumstances."

"Is he dead?" Anne asked.

"Yes, he is." William swallowed and lowered his head.

"The man who got him deserves a medal."

"It was a team effort," William replied. "I fired the fatal shot, but I couldn't have done it without the rest of the Home Guard."

"Well done, lad." John patted William on the shoulder. "Thank you."

"Right. Yes. Well, I'll be off, I'm in need of a hot bath and a long sleep. I just wanted to relay the news."

"Thanks, William." Moira raised her hands to her chest. Her gratitude was heartfelt.

⌘

There was no avoiding docking, drenching, and castrating the lambs. Moira was grateful Bill's flock of sheep was small compared to *Whipsnade's* but she and John had still risen with the first birdsong. The morning milking was over and done before the sunlight reached the sheep yards tucked in behind a barbary hedge, ensuring there was a full day to get all the jobs done.

A shepherd's whistle hanging on a string at the woolshed caught Moira's eye. It was covered in cobwebs and fly dirt, so she gave it a good scrub under the tap before wrapping her lips around it. Perhaps with a bit of practice she'd arrive at Mr Master's property as proficient as she'd implied. Moira set off with Bill's Huntaway dog to fetch the sheep. Whether the dog was excited to be released from its kennel, or understood and followed Moira's attempts at whistling, its deep bark echoed across the paddocks and garnered the attention of the sheep.

The flock was soon back at the yards and John and Moira worked well together to separate the lambs from the ewes, adjacent pens for each. Ignoring the racket created by lambs who could no longer feed off their mothers, the rams and ewes were then pushed through the drenching trough to emerge blue from head to tail from the bluestone mixed with the drench.

"It'll be good to have these big jobs out of the way." John let the rams and ewes back into the paddock.

Moira had kept the news of her departure quiet but seized the opportunity.

"I'll be able to leave you to it then," she said.

John paused and straightened his back. "Leave what to me?" His greying eyebrows drew together as he frowned at her.

"Farming," Moira replied matter-of-factly. "I've got another placement to go to."

"But … but you haven't been here long enough, have you?"

"There's no time requirement," Moira said. "We go where and when we are required, and you can manage fine without me, so I'm no longer needed here."

And your wife has never wanted me here at all! Moira kept her thoughts to herself. Although she had to admit Anne's acerbic words had been fewer and farther between since Bill had been moved to Christchurch. Perhaps Anne considered her brother out of Moira's reach.

95

"What about Bill?" John leaned in and lightly touched Moira's shoulder. "Won't you want to be here when he comes home?"

His soothing tone and caring gesture almost made Moira have misgivings about leaving. She paused, sorted through her thoughts, and pondered her reply.

"Bill's house isn't big enough for four." It was a fact that didn't give away her feelings.

"Yes," John agreed. "But Anne and I would head home and leave you two to manage."

"Well, it's a long way off." *If ever.* Deep in Moira's heart, there was a sense of peace and calm, she'd already said goodbye to Bill, this chapter in her life was over and another was about to begin.

They moved back to the lambs. Fortunately, the small pen meant the lambs were closely packed and Moira was easily able to catch the first. She wrapped her arms around its belly and grabbed hold of its front legs, braced its spine against her chest and rested its bottom on top of the fence post so John had easy access to the lamb's tail. It was over in a matter of minutes. A rubber ring stretched until it was high on the tail and then released to pinch in and cut off the blood supply, causing the tail to eventually drop off.

Moira let the first lamb go and picked up the next, developing a steady rhythm until all the pen, had been dealt to. She was grateful most of this year's lambs were ewes. Although they bleated, sat, stood, turned on the spot and generally looked uncomfortable, Moira had learned it was only temporary. Before they were ready to be released into the paddock, the tails had gone numb, and the lambs were back to their playful selves. There were only a few ram lambs whose testes received the same treatment.

"Would you like to enjoy a feast of mountain oysters?" John teased.

Luckily it was an expression Moira had already heard at *Whipsnade*.

"No, not for me." She laughed. "But you can snip some out for you if you like."

Moira squirmed at the thought of the ram lamb's small testes going anywhere near her mouth.

John laughed a deep belly laugh. "You're a smart lass, I can't catch you out. No wonder Bill asked for you to be his land girl."

Moira wasn't usually prone to blushing, but her cheeks coloured a deep scarlet. Was it because of the compliment she wasn't used to receiving or the real reason she'd agreed to be Bill's land girl, her intentions on that first day?

"We'd better let these back out to the paddock." She turned towards the gate to hide her feelings. "And head home for lunch."

"Yes," John said. "I hope Anne will have prepared something tastier than mountain oysters."

⌘

It was a fresh batch of scones that graced the table and filled the room with a tempting aroma when John and Moira arrived back at the house. Moira's stomach rumbled as she broke open a scone, releasing steam to waft past her face. She hesitated, counted the number of scones Anne had cooked, and divided it by three before deciding there would be plenty for her to enjoy. Butter on the first so it could melt with the heat; butter and honey on the second, jam on the third and then jam and whipped cream on the fourth like a dessert topping to finish the meal.

"Moira's leaving us," Bill announced. "She's got another placement to go to."

Anne's mouth gaped momentarily before she hid her surprise and responded politely. "Oh, that's a shame."

Moira wasunsure whether she'd detected a hint of sarcasm in Anne's words, or they could be taken at face value. She opted for the latter, looked directly at Anne, and replied.

"Yes, at the end of the month, after the Home Guard dance."

"They're having a dance." Anne's face lit up like a child who'd found a favourite lost toy. "We could go, John."

John nodded. The look that passed between husband and wife told Moira there was more to this story. It was another side to the couple that Moira hadn't seen.

"You know he was known as twinkle toes back in the day," Anne teased. "There isn't a dance he doesn't know. He whisks me around the dance floor, and I feel as light as a feather."

"That's how I met Bill," Moira added. "He's a wonderful dancer too."

"A shame he won't be there this time," Anne added.

They were all in agreement on that point and the room went silent as if to honour the injured man.

⌘

Anticipation for the dance brought an entirely different atmosphere to the house. Anne never stopped smiling.

"What are you going to wear tonight?" she asked Moira as if they were excited teenage girls. "Do land girls have a uniform they have to wear?"

"No! Some of them have a uniform but we've only been issued with overalls and gumboots and I'm certainly not wearing those."

Moira went to her wardrobe and pulled the cinnamon dress out on its hanger.

"I'll be wearing this." She held the dress out for Anne to see.

"Oh, that'll look lovely with your hair colouring." Anne's compliment came as a surprise to Moira.

"What will you be wearing?" she asked.

"I'm not sure," Anne replied. "I didn't come here expecting to get to go dancing but I'm not going to miss out for want of a pretty dress. I'll just have to make do."

Anne's eyes glazed over as if she'd got lost in distant memories.

"I used to have a figure like yours, you know." Anne giggled awkwardly and patted her hips. "But these child-bearing hips have served their purpose and now seem to want plenty of padding to keep them warm."

Moira felt for the woman. She'd judged her as nasty and bitter but there was a warmth hidden inside, it escaped when she smiled and took years off her appearance.

99

"Perhaps we could give ourselves a manicure and paint our fingernails," Moira suggested. "That'll add to the glamour, no matter what you're wearing."

"Oh, what a wonderful idea. A day of pampering is just what we need."

Moira blinked and raised her hands to her cheeks. Had she just heard what she thought? Had Anne's 'we' included her?

"John," Anne called out. "Moira and I need to get ready for the dance. You can manage the farm jobs today, can't you?"

It was voiced as a question, but Moira knew Anne only expected one answer.

"Yes, dear," John gave the obligatory reply and winked at Moira.

"Good, I'll run the bath." Anne strode towards the bathroom. "I'll have a quick wash first and then you can have a long soak to get all that farm muck out from under your fingernails, Moira."

⌘

Hours later, Moira and Anne were dressed and ready to go. It seemed fitting that Moira's last outing before she left the farm had her dressed in the same outfit, she'd arrived in. Her *Besame* Victory Red lipstick matched the red nail polish decorating her fingers and her toes peeking out from her red toe peepers

Anne's makeup was in more subtle shades of pink to match the flower petals in the floral design of her dress

100

"Well, would you take a look at you two." John chuckled and held his hand up as if to shield his eyes. "A man could be blinded by your dazzling beauty."

He angled his arms at either side of his torso and offered one to each of them. "May I be your escort for this evening's soiree?" he asked in a posh voice.

Anne blushed and giggled before looping her hands around her husband's arm. Moira followed suit. They had to turn sideways to fit through the door. John was a true gentleman and open and closed the house and car doors for them.

Sitting alone in the expanse of the back seat of John and Anne's car, a tinge of sadness made Moira sniff and retrieve a handkerchief from her purse to wipe her nose. If only Anne had been like this from the beginning, Moira wouldn't had found another job. She hoped it wasn't a decision she would regret.

"Never mind," she muttered to herself. "Have a good time tonight and worry about that tomorrow."

⌘

Cars and trucks hugged the sides of the road either side of the Orari Hall. Several horses were tethered to a fence rail and even a bicycle leaned against the wall. The district had turned out in numbers using whatever means of transport available to them.

Both the New Zealand and American flags had been hoisted up the flagpole at the front of the hall and fluttered in a light breeze. Goosebumps tingled Moira's bare arms; anticipation stole her breath away. She had both happy and sad memories from the last dance she'd attended here. Bill had been a wonderful dance partner, everything she'd dreamed of as they twirled and spun around the dance floor, shared smokes, beer, and kisses under the moonlight, but then he'd left her standing alone in the supper room. He'd disappeared into the night without a word, leaving her to face the gossip whispered behind hands, the looks of jealousy and judgement. She wouldn't let that happen again tonight, she'd dance with whomever asked her, enjoy the company of everyone and become attached to no one.

Moira lifted her chin and pulled her shoulders back to stride confidently into the hall. She rested her hand on John's arm as he escorted her and Anne through the foyer decorated with Ponga fronds. The hum of voices emanating from the hall was punctuated by an American drawl that flowed smoothly above the Kiwi accents, like treacle sweetening a toffee pudding. Moira's eyes were drawn to its source. She ran the tip of her tongue across her lips. She liked what she saw.

CHAPTER
9

"Moira. Moira. Over here." Grace called and waved to Moira from the opposite side of the room.

Moira wanted to ignore her friend and head straight towards the American soldiers. But the night was still young, and she'd just promised herself to become attached to no one, so with a drumbeat from the heel of her shoes she sashayed across the hall to sit with Grace and Betsy.

"Hi, Grace, hi, Betsy, it's nice to catch up. It seems like ages since we last saw one another."

"You're looking happy," Grace observed.

"It's dancing time, Grace. It's my final fling before I head off." Moira subtly raised the hem of her dress and crossed her legs, so her shapely calves were in full view of the soldiers. "And there are American soldiers here. What's not to be happy about?"

"What do you mean it's your final fling?" Grace's eyes went wide. "Where are you off to?"

"Why are you eyeing up the American soldiers?" Betsy looked more angry than surprised. "What about Bill?"

"What about Roland?" Moira retorted.

"Haven't you heard?" Grace asked.

"Roland's dead." Betsy looked up; her eyes were glassy.

Lost for words, Moira sucked in a breath. Her fun night wasn't starting off the way she'd wanted.

"Welcome, welcome to this evening's dance in honour of and to raise funds for the Home Guard." Announcements from the stage saved Moira from having to speak. "They have certainly been guarding the home front in the past fortnight and we thank them for their efforts in protecting our homes and ourselves from persons who shall remain nameless. If we could please observe a moment's silence to honour those who have given their lives in the call of duty and to send our good thoughts and prayers for a full recovery for those injured."

Chairs scuffed and feet shuffled as everyone stood and bowed their heads. Moira thought of Bill, silently wished he would recover. That was all she could do; the outcome was beyond her control. She wouldn't be made to feel guilty for her choices. She had to move on.

"Thank you everyone. We'll now welcome our musicians to the stage, and they can lead you into the first dance. You will have, no doubt noticed, that we have some special guests in our midst. We trust you will make our American visitors feel welcome."

Moira certainly planned to, but she had to make amends with Betsy first.

"Betsy." Moira rested her manicured hand on Betsy's leg. "I'm sorry to hear about Roland, but at least you can now move on, just as I'm going to do."

"What are you planning?" Grace asked.

"There is no need or room for me to stay at Bill's," Moira continued. "His sister and brother-in-law have everything under control. I've applied for another placement and I'm heading out to a sheep station on Monday."

"Where is it? What are you going to be doing?" Grace's incessant need to help kept her questions coming. "What conditions are you going to be living in? Who else will be there?"

"I don't know all of the details yet." In fact, Moira knew very little. She was trusting the placement officer but knowing there was no woman to be nasty to her was enough at the time.

"It sounds a bit sketchy." Grace looked worried.

"That's part of the adventure." Moira looked up to see another source of adventure she'd like to explore. A broad-shouldered, immaculately presented uniformed man was walking towards her. Her eyes traced the perfectly straight creases in his trousers, from where they brushed his polished boots to where they ended at his midriff.

"You'll have to telephone me when you get there," Betsy implored. "So, we know how to contact you and check that you're safe."

"There's no telephone," Moira replied but her focus had moved on.

"Evenin' ladies." The soldier bowed slightly. "Would y'all like to dance?"

Moira ignored Grace and Betsy's gaping mouths and stood to place her hand in the palm of the hand extended to her.

"Do you want to dance with all of us or just one?" she teased.

"Would y'all do me the honour?" The soldier ran his thumb lightly across Moira's hand. "A beautiful woman like you deserves to dance."

His words, his touch, both flowed over Moira like a silk cape. "With pleasure," she purred.

"I bought these here flowers." The soldier held up a corsage: a tiny white bud rose with some maidenhair fern. He gently placed it on Moira's chest. "May I?"

Moira's heart skipped a beat. She looked down at the neatly manicured fingers so close to her breast the warmth from his fingers radiated through the thin fabric of her dress. Feelings she hadn't felt for some months, hormones that had been stifled by the exhausting farm work of spring began bubbling deep inside. Where Bill had been reserved in showing his feelings in public, this man was almost brazen.

She swallowed and raised her head to subtly nod. She looked back at Grace while the soldier pinned the corsage to her dress. Grace shook her head and mouthed a warning Moira had no intention of following.

"You be careful."

"My fellow soldiers can take care of these other lovely ladies." The soldier rested his hand gently in the small of Moira's back and led her to an empty space in front of the stage.

Moira sensed the eyes of everyone in the hall following them. It happened at the last dance. If she was the source of gossip again then so be it. She wouldn't be around after Monday to worry.

"Frank. Frank Davis III. Private First Class." Frank took Moira's hand in his and raised it to his lips, brushing the softest of kisses across her knuckles.

Private First Class. Moira's breath quickened. She imagined Frank was first class in so many ways, from the tip of his neatly groomed hair, short and slicked back at the sides, to the soles of his highly polished boots. So much for her intention to keep her dance card open to any and everyone. She'd happily throw it out the door to remain in the sphere of Frank's aftershave, masculine with a hint of spice.

"Moira. Moira Harvey. Women's Land Army volunteer," she replied as the musicians began playing a slow waltz.

Frank drew her towards him, entwined their raised fingers and folded his arm around her back. The space between them disappeared. If not for Moira's quick shallow breaths her nipples would have touched his chest each time she inhaled.

He listened for the beat, stepped off in time to the music and glided them around the dance floor as if they were ice skating. Moira was mesmerised and not just by the intensity of his chocolate-brown eyes. She felt the power of his muscular thighs as they rubbed against hers. From his obvious strength she expected a roughness. Her only knowledge of Americans came from the cowboys she'd seen at the cinema, riding horses, lassoing animals, and killing Indians. Frank was a total contrast. His nails were neatly manicured, his hands smooth and callous free.

"Are y'all from around these parts, Moira?" Frank asked as he spun her around.

"I lived in Christchurch until earlier this year."

"A sophisticated woman from the city." Frank smiled. "I thought there was something special about y'all."

It would be easy to drown in his compliments. Moira reminded herself, just to have fun before she went away.

"What part of America are you from, Frank?"

"I'm a Southern lad. Louisiana is my hometown."

Moira was none the wiser. She'd have to see if Bill had an atlas in his bookcase.

"And are there three of you, Frank Davis III?" she teased.

"Only two now." Frank's eyes glazed over. "My Grandpa died just after I'd set sail with the troops."

Smooth and sensitive. Frank kept ticking boxes on Moira's unwritten list of the perfect man.

"I'm sorry to hear that. He would have been proud to see you in your uniform."

"Yes, he was an army man too."

They chatted away until the music stopped. Conversation came easy, like they'd been friends for decades.

"I'd like to keep y'all to myself all night," Frank whispered into Moira's ear, his warm breath tickling her neck, "but I'd better take y'all back to your friends."

Jake tapped Frank on the shoulder. "Moira's promised this next dance to me. I'll take her from here."

"What?" Frank stepped back in surprise. "Easy up. Let's ask the lady what she'd like to do."

Moira looked from Frank to Jake and back again. There wasn't much comparison and Jake wouldn't be her preferred choice, however she had promised him a dance. She'd also promised herself not to become attached to anyone. It wouldn't do any harm to let Frank think he had competition.

"I did promise Jake a dance." Moira placed her hand on Frank's chest. "But I'll save another one for you, Frank, if you like."

"I'd like that very much." Frank lifted her hand to his mouth and kissed the inside of her wrist before he turned and walked away without acknowledging Jake.

"Damn smooth-talking Americans," Jake groaned. "They think they can swan in here and steal our women."

"Jake!" Moira smelt the beer on his breath so waited until she had his full attention. "One, nobody is stealing anyone and two, I am not your woman."

"Do you know the American soldiers get paid twice what the Kiwi blokes do?" Jake sounded incredulous.

"You're not a soldier so why should that bother you?" Moira was getting impatient.

Jake flicked his finger at Moira's corsage. "They've got money to buy you things we can't afford. Sweet talk you with gifts."

"None of your talk is sweet," Moira murmured as the musicians began playing the next dance. "Do you want to dance or not, Jake?"

"Yes, yes, of course."

Fortunately, the dance was the Gay Gordon, so it wasn't long before Moira was free of Jake. John was the next in the circle to become her dance partner.

"I think your dance card will be overflowing tonight, Moira," he said as he swung her genteelly around. "The men around here seem to know a good thing when they're onto it."

Moira chuckled. "And you'll be danced off your feet by Anne. Just as well you're still nimble on them."

"Not bad for an old fellow, if I do say so myself."

Their light-hearted banter continued until John tipped his head in farewell and released Moira to her next partner. Moira soaked up the father-daughter-like interaction wishing she'd had more from her own father.

Grace and Betsy had joined the circle either side of Moira.

"Nice to see you dancing with William, Betsy," Moira said as the women stepped back to await their new partners. "He seems to manage fine with his injuries. There'll be no stopping him now."

Moira chuckled as Betsy's cheeks coloured scarlet. With her comment having hit the bullseye with Betsy, she turned her attention to Grace, waiting until the next time they moved to a new partner to tease her friend.

"And which handsome man are you trying to save now, Grace? Is it Ben you're still rescuing?" Moira eyed the next soldier looking eager to sweep Grace into his arms. "Oh look, this soldier looks like he wants to save you."

"Very funny, Moira," Grace replied. "It might just be you who needs rescuing."

"I can look after myself," Moira declared before marching forward, one, two, three, with her new dance partner, another of the American soldiers.

He was just as smartly dressed as Frank, but he didn't have the same effect on Moira. There was something about Frank Davis III that had instantly appealed. Love at first sight was a silly notion that romantics believed in, not Moira, she was too wise to know that would never happen.

When they changed partners again, it was Frank who arrived at her side. He held her hands ready to step forward.

"That's better," he sighed. "Back in my arms again, right where y'all belong."

Moira giggled. "Oh, Frank, you're such a charmer, you could sell ice to the Eskimos."

"Can't y'all feel it too, Moira?"

She could. The smouldering that began deep inside when he'd first touched her, was kindled by his breath on her skin, like blowing the embers of a fire, anticipation of the flame pulsing through her veins.

"You're only here for a few days on leave, aren't you?" Moira said to deflect her desire to feel the heat, weary of getting burnt.

"Yes, true." Frank spun them around before he had to release Moira to her next partner.

By the time the Gay Gordon wound down, Moira was dancing with William. There was an awkward moment when she instinctively went to rest her fingers on his missing right hand. She quickly lowered her hand to rest on his shoulder and tried to pretend William's injuries were negligible.

"Nothing to stop you and Betsy now," she said.

William's head jerked back. "You've never been one to mince your words, have you, Moira."

"No point beating about the bush, William," she replied. "Life's too short not to enjoy."

"Are you planning on enjoying it with an American soldier?" William smiled, so Moira took his question as teasing instead of an accusation.

"I'm leaving on Monday to work on a sheep station so I'm not planning anything." It was the truth.

"I heard they were being billeted on a sheep station. Is that the one you're going to?"

Moira closed her eyes and pictured Frank's face. Imagine if it was the very same sheep station. Anticipation made her glow.

William spun her around for the final time and she had to bring herself back to reality as the dance finished.

"I'm being picked up by Barry Masters. I don't know where his farm is or where the soldiers are billeted." *But I intend to find out.*

"Barry Masters," William repeated in a tone that indicated nothing good as he walked Moira back to the table. "Good luck going out there."

"What?" Moira gasped. "What do you mean?"

"He's a bit of a hermit. Doesn't like spending his money."

"Shouldn't I go?"

"He'll probably want his pound of flesh ..." William cleared his throat. "Sorry, I mean, he'll likely expect you to work from dawn to dusk and I doubt it will be the luxury living conditions you had at *Whipsnade*."

Moira had been working all day every day at Bill's, that seemed to be the expectation of all farmers and Bill's house wasn't luxurious. Comfortable, and warm was all she needed.

"I'll cope," she declared.

"You'll cope with what?" Grace asked.

"Farming in the back of beyond with a hermit," William replied on Moira's behalf. "At least it's nearly summer, the snow will have melted on the high country."

"Thanks for your positivity, William." Moira flopped down into a seat. "I think Betsy would like this next dance with you."

113

"You could change your mind, Moira," Grace suggested. "Tell the placement officer you don't think it will be suitable."

"It'll be fine." Moira was unsure if she was trying to convince Grace or herself.

"Y'all look worried, Moira." Frank's voice was soft and caring as he approached. "Is everythin' alright?"

Moira stood, shook her head, and smiled. "It will be when you dance with me again."

She took Frank's hand and pulled him onto the dance floor.

"How about some swing music to liven things up?" the pianist called from the stage as his fingers splayed over the keys to create a lively beat.

"Perfect," Moira purred.

The rest of the musicians joined in, the music was loud, the tempo fast and Moira's and Frank's feet and hips twirled and whirled with the rhythm. Frank had perfect timing. He was strong but gentle as he held Moira's hand and flung her out in a spin and then pulled her back into his body. *Rhythm on the dance floor equalled rhythm in the bedroom.* Moira smiled at the realisation Frank ticked off another of her unwritten criteria for the perfect man.

She glimpsed John and Anne on the dance floor, their faces were lit up, they danced like excited teenagers experiencing love for the first time. Was that even possible? Could a couple be married as long as they had, and still have a spark between them? It certainly wasn't the case with her parents, divorced when she was just a child,

114

divorced when it was still a dirty word, and considered a sin by the very people who should have offered support.

The exuberant music didn't allow her to dwell on these thoughts for long. Moira jiggled her hips, slid her shoes from side to side on the powdered floor, held Frank's hand and trusted his lead. She felt the heat rise up her body, her blood pulsed, her breathing quickened. This is what it felt to be alive, and Moira revelled in it.

⌘

"Are you ready to leave now, Moira?" John asked as he and Anne approached her.

The last dance had finished, the musicians were packing up their instruments. Frank held Moira's hand as they sat alone at the side of the hall. He hadn't released it since they'd started the last waltz and Moira hadn't wanted him to, as if doing so would be the end of their brief encounter, an ending neither of them desired.

"Promise me y'all see me tomorrow." Frank's look implored Moira to say yes. "I could take y'all on a picnic, down by the river."

Moira glanced up at John as if he was her father and she needed approval. There were probably farm jobs to be done but he would cope without her after she'd left, another day wouldn't make any difference. She looked across at Anne to see if she was judging her. Anne was flushed, exhausted but glowing from a night of doing what she loved. Moira needed to do the same.

"I'd really like that." She smiled at Frank.

He lifted her hand to his lips. He kissed her skin, let his mouth linger until his warmth permeated her body. "Until tomorrow."

CHAPTER
10

Girlish giggling brought Moira from her sleep. She had no memory of any laughter in her dream, and it continued as she stared into the darkness of her bedroom.

"John, stop it." Anne's feigned protest was just audible through the wall before she giggled again.

"You know you like it. You don't really want me to stop."

"No, but ..." The giggle became a stifled groan of satisfaction. "Moira might hear."

It was Moira's turn to chuckle. She clamped the blankets over her mouth to ensure she kept her amusement to herself, imagining Anne's horror if Moira revealed she'd heard their interlude. It would be sweet revenge for all the times Anne was nasty, but Moira had seen a different side of Bill's sister and couldn't be so cruel. She would likely miss the couple when she left.

Being around them had showed her a bond she didn't know was possible between two people. Her parents had bickered and fought until they'd finally parted ways when Moira was only seven. Marriages didn't last long, why would anyone bother, better just to party and have a good time or so she thought.

It wasn't just reassuring that they were still having sex at their age, it was the laughter and fun they enjoyed, the knowing looks with unspoken words and the special touches and gestures that came from memories they'd created together.

Moira replaced the disconcerting image of older people having sex by visualising her and Frank on a picnic blanket by the river. Would he be able to make her giggle like a teenager? Warmth flooded through her. She hoped so.

Would he still be a part of her life when they were John and Anne's age? What memories could they create? Would there be a Frank Davis IV? *Now you're getting carried away. Go back to sleep and stop being so silly.*

Moira turned onto her side, muffled one ear into the pillow and pulled the blankets up over the other, leaving John and Anne to do whatever they wanted, without an audience.

⌘

John and Moira got in early from the morning milking. It was like he had an extra spring in his step, a burst of energy that seemed to get the jobs done in half of the time. Moira smiled knowingly but that was all she could do.

They opened the back door to Anne's happy singing.

"Here I go again.

I hear those trumpets blow again.

All aglow again.

Taking a chance on love.

Here I slide again. Anne slid from the bench to the coal range to flip the eggs frying in the pan.

About to take that ride again.

Starry eyed again.

Taking a chance on love."

Moira waited until Anne paused at the end of a verse before applauding.

Anne jumped with fright. "Oh, I didn't hear you."

"You were too busy singing." Moira chuckled. "What's got you in such a good mood?"

Moira turned away and rolled her eyes at her own foolish teasing. She already knew the answer, it was the last question she should have asked. When she turned back around Anne had gone scarlet.

"Are you that happy that I'm leaving tomorrow?" Moira tried to deflect.

"No, no, nothing like that. Sit down. You must be hungry. I've cooked bacon and eggs and fried up the potatoes left over from last night's dinner. Here." Anne jabbered as she carried the frying pan to the table. "Help yourself. You must be hungry."

I would be hungry if I'd been making love all night like you. Moira smiled widely but managed to keep these thoughts to herself.

"I could eat a horse." John gave Anne a sheepish grin as he filled his plate with a generous helping.

"What was the song you were singing?" Moira asked.

"Benny Goodman's just done a remake of it that's gone to number one in the charts." Anne's face lit up. "It's *Take a Chance on Love* from the musical *Cabin in the Sky*. John took me to see the movie just before we came down here."

"Dancing and the movies." Moira's eyes held a twinkle of mischief. "What else do you two sweethearts get up to?"

John stuffed his mouth full, and Anne turned back to the bench. An awkward silence filled the room, making Moira feel she may have gone a step too far even though her insides were somersaulting with delight.

"Would you like a cuppa?" Anne filled the kettle from the tap. "I could make you a thermos to take on your picnic with Frank. He's a bit of a sweetheart, isn't he? Are you going to take a chance on love, Moira?"

It was Moira's turn to blush, not something she was usually prone to do.

"He's American."

"Yes," Anne agreed with the obvious. "He's got a charming accent. What part of America is he from?"

"Louisiana. It's in the south."

"That would explain it," John joined the conversation.

"Explain what?" Moira frowned.

120

"They have slaves in the south. The whites don't like the blacks. They buy and sell them and whip them when they disobey. Have done for centuries." John continued eating his breakfast as if this information was nothing horrific.

"And what does that explain?" Confusion still crinkled Moira's forehead.

"All the trouble they're having in Wellington," John continued. "You read about it in the newspaper. Brawls between the American soldiers and the Maori. All because of the colour of their skin."

"Oh, I don't think Frank would be like that." Moira defended him but then considered she really knew very little about Frank at all. There were no Maori at last night's dance, so no opportunity to witness his reaction. He was at least the third generation of his family to live in the southern states and it appeared he came from money with his genteel manners. Perhaps his family had slaves too, she couldn't imagine him doing anything brutal but then he was a soldier, he'd be expected to kill the enemy. Moira shook her head, there was no point speculating, she'd just have to ask him later.

⌘

By the time the cattle stop announced Frank's arrival, Moira had already been hovering around the back door for a good half hour, doing up and undoing the buttons on her cardigan as if that would make the time go faster.

"Don't look too keen there, lass,' John teased. "You've got to make him think he has to win you over."

121

"Like you have to win Anne over." Moira winked as she sat at the table trying to look calm and collected. "With movies and dancing."

"Happy wife, happy life." John put his hand to his chest and smiled.

Moira leapt out of the chair when Frank knocked at the door.

"Hello there, Frank." John opened the door and extended his hand.

Frank swapped the box of chocolates he was carrying to his left hand so he could return the handshake.

"Morning, sir, I'm here to collect Moira. Is she about?"

"She was around here somewhere," John chuckled, his exaggerated voice filled with mischief. "I'll just go see if I can find her."

"I'm right behind you," Moira swallowed the bait and nudged John aside. "Hi, Frank, it's lovely to see you again."

"The pleasure is all mine." Frank extended his hand with the chocolate box. "I bought y'all some chocolates. I hope y'all like them."

"Mmm, chocolates, delicious," John continued his teasing.

"Thank you," Moira replied. "We'd better take them with us, or John will likely eat them all."

John patted his stomach.

"Have you told that boy to look after our Moira?" Anne called from the sitting room where she was clearing the ashes from the fire.

It was nice to be thought of as their daughter, but Moira wanted to assure Anne she could look after herself.

"He's not a boy, Anne," John called back. "He's a soldier and a perfect gentleman, aren't you Frank?"

"Yes, sir." Frank clicked his heals together as if he was standing to attention to receive an order. "Understood, sir."

"Good then," John said. "You two had best be off and have some fun."

"Is he y'all father?" Frank asked as soon as the door was closed.

"No … no definitely not." Memories of Moira's father had faded over time. Like newspaper left in the sunlight, they'd yellowed and curled at the edges, the story they contained had blurred, with the facts distorted by her mother's hatred of the man who'd abandoned them.

"I didn't see any likeness." Frank hurried ahead to open the passenger door of the car. "But I thought perhaps y'all got y'all beauty from y'all mother."

Frank was smooth in every aspect. His compliments felt like the silk undergarments Moira had on, especially selected and softly caressing her skin. She innocently brushed her hand against his as she climbed into the vehicle.

"Mmm, something smells yummy." The aroma of fresh baking emanated from a picnic basket that sat on the seat between them.

"Edith knew I'd want to impress y'all, so she got up extra early and baked some scones for us."

Edith! Who was Edith? Moira caught her jealous thoughts. It was way too early for her to be having these. She'd only just met Frank. She was merely having some fun before she went away, and he went back to soldiering. She lightened the tone of her voice.

"Edith, who's Edith?"

"She's one of the land girls at the station we've been billeted to on our leave," Frank replied casually. "I think she's the farm owner's niece. She was at the dance last night. She saw how besotted I was with y'all and thought I'd need a helpin' hand to win y'all over."

You don't need any help, you're doing fine all by yourself, Frank Davis III. Moira smiled, slowly nodded but stayed silent, following John's advice to not look too keen.

They hadn't driven far when Frank turned off onto a gravel track that led down to a grassy area beside the river.

"This looks like a nice spot," he said as he pulled on the hand brake and turned the engine off.

"How did you know it was here?" Moira had been in the area eight months now and she never knew the reserve existed, tucked down below the road level, sheltered by willow trees whose leaves rustled in the light breeze.

"Edith suggested it." Frank's eyes sparkled as he looked across at Moira and smiled with a perfect row of white teeth. "She said it was a nice private spot."

"Thank you, Edith." Moira wondered if she was destined to have relationships with men where the presence of another woman was so strong it felt like they were a threesome.

They found a spot under the shade of a willow and Frank spread a tartan picnic blanket over the grass.

"Would y'all like to eat first?" Frank asked, opening the lid of the picnic basket.

Moira's insides fluttered like the leaves in the trees. *First?* What was Frank planning for seconds? She smiled in anticipation.

"It would be a shame not to eat the scones while they're still warm."

Steam rose from a triangle-shaped scone as Frank sliced it in half. The dollop of butter he dropped between the two halves quickly melted and soaked into the doughy baking.

"Y'all better eat it before the butter drips." Frank passed a scone to Moira. "I don't want to be responsible for ruinin' y'all pretty dress."

"Mmm, delicious," Moira purred.

"Y'all land girls are amazin'. Y'all can turn y'all hands to anythin'. Cookin'. Farmin'."

Moira laughed as she recalled her first attempt at cooking, between the cat and the coal range, it had been a disaster.

"Well, we have to step up while you men are busy protecting us from the enemy."

"Yes." Frank's look became serious. "I'll be headin' back the day after tomorrow."

"Back to where?" Moira asked.

"Wellington. We're stationed at Par-cack-car-rye-kie."

"You mean Paekākāriki?" Moira corrected his pronunciation.

"Yeah, there. Bloody native words, why don't they just stick to English?"

Moira straightened. It was the first time she'd heard Frank swear. It wasn't so much the swearing, she could do that herself when the moment called for it, but it was the linking to Maori that made her eyebrows draw together. Perhaps Frank was used to having slaves.

"Do you have something against Maori?" Moira needed to know.

"Nah. Apart from the fact that they beat up our troops." Sarcasm peppered Frank's reply. "They're like savages. They come at y'all lookin' all fierce, tongues pokin' out, like warriors goin' into battle."

"And your troops wouldn't have done anything to provoke them?"

"Only have too much beer." Frank laughed. "Anyway, we don't need any help hurtin' ourselves, we seem to be able to do that unaided. We've already drowned ten soldiers without even seein' the enemy."

Moira gasped. "How did that happen?"

"A vessel had engine troubles. Those aboard were supposed to establish landin' positions and communications but had to be towed back out." Frank's face glazed over as if he was reliving the moment. "It was late at night, the water was freezin', a rogue wave capsized the boat. One officer and nine good men drowned." Frank's eyes went wide, and he sat up suddenly. "But I didn't tell y'all that and y'all not to let it go any further."

"Your secret is safe with me, Frank." Moira patted his thigh. "I won't tell a soul."

"Anyway, I'm not here to waste my leave talkin' about the war, especially not when I've got a pretty girl to talk to. Tell me all about y'llself, Moira. What made y'all become a land girl? Besides the war, I mean."

Moira could hardly tell Frank she came to the country because that's the only place there were still young men, those who worked in essential industries and excused from fighting.

"I used to work in a shoe shop," she said. "But they stopped making the fancy shoes I used to sell so I was out of a job. What did you used to do, before you enlisted?"

"I was studying for a law degree at Louisiana State University."

"Brains and good looks, you are blessed Frank Davis III." Moira was beginning to think this man was too good to be true, a figment of her imagination that would all too soon disappear.

"I am blessed to have come halfway around the world to find y'all." Frank moved the picnic basket out of the way and slid closer to Moira. "I'd like to take y'all home with me when I leave."

Moira giggled. "You don't have to promise me the earth, Frank, just for a kiss."

She leaned closer, tilted her head back and grinned playfully, hesitating only momentarily to check she wasn't being too bold. Seeing her own desire mirrored in Frank's eyes, Moira kissed him, deep and full mouthed, seizing the moment.

"Mmm," Frank groaned. "A woman who knows what she wants. Would she like more than a kiss?"

Frank moved closer, gently brushed a strand of hair from Moira's face, ran his fingers around her hairline, trailed his forefinger across her bottom lip, and down over her chin until it settled in the hollow at the base of her neck.

Moira's breath hitched in that hollow, her eyes urged Frank to continue his exploration, to trace a line to the valley between her breasts, to notice that her nipples were taut with desire beneath the cotton barrier of her dress.

She lay back on the blanket, and pulled Frank to her, wrapping her arm around his torso, feeling his muscles beneath the heavy fabric of his shirt. She'd seen his erection bulging against his trousers and now felt it pressing into her thigh. Life was too short to consider the rights and wrongs of the situation. It felt right, her body was telling Moira this American could give her what she desired in the now and if it was wrong in the morning then so be it. She was moving on and would do so with no regrets.

"Are you sure this is what you want, my lovely Moira?" Frank's fingers freed the button at the front of Moira's dress from its buttonhole.

"Yes," Moira's voice was husky, blood pulsed to every nerve-ending in her body. "All of me wants all of you, Frank."

Their lovemaking flowed like the river they lay beside; it lapped at the edges, rippled over the curves of their bodies, and bubbled in the hollows. With depth came intensity, until they rode the current, cresting the cascade to tumble through the rapids. With a sense of floating, they lay in each other's arms, luxuriating in the aftermath.

"Move over will y'all," a deep voice with an American accent interrupted. "Come on, Frank, share y'all treats."

Frank leapt up; one hand went automatically to his hip where a weapon would have been holstered, the other to his groin.

"What the …?" Hitching up his pants, Frank stood in front of Moira so she could recompose herself. "What are y'all doing sneaking up on us like that, Chad? Come to think of it, what the hell are y'all doing here at all?"

"Calm down." Chad splayed his hands and waved them as if trying to cool the situation. "We didn't sneak up. Y'all and y'all lovely lady were just a little pre-occupied, to notice our arrival."

"How did y'all know I'd be here?"

Moira was unsure whether Frank was red-faced with anger or embarrassment. She stood, smoothed down her dress and moved to stand beside him.

"Morning, Moira." Chad was bright and cheery. "Nice spot for a picnic."

She remembered Chad, she'd danced with him in the Gay Gordon. Although he wore the same uniform as Frank, he wasn't anywhere as nice. Chad moved to the side and Edith stepped forward. She wasn't at all what Moira had expected for someone who seemed to have so much influence. The determined look on her face belied her tiny stature. Perhaps she was like Alice, her petiteness requiring more grit than normal.

"Edith said there was more than enough food for four and we should come and share it with y'all. Have y'all met Edith, Moira?"

"No, I haven't." Their intimate moment was lost. Unsure what the visitors had witnessed, Moira tried to act innocent. "Hi Edith, nice to meet you."

"Nice to meet you too, Moira. I saw you at the dance last night and Frank wouldn't stop rabbiting on about you, so I thought I'd better come and meet you in person."

Edith smiled but Moira wasn't convinced it was genuine. Edith seemed to be mothering Frank, needing to assess whether Moira was good enough for her boy.

"Thank you for the scones." Moira diverted the conversation away from her and Frank. The passion ignited between them felt like it had now been dunked in a cold river. "They're delicious."

The four sat down on the picnic blanket. Chad and Edith enjoyed the contents of the picnic basket and Frank and Moira lit cigarettes and blew smoke rings into the air. It was the only way to communicate their frustration at the untimely interruption.

CHAPTER
11

Edith insisted Frank drive Chad back to the farm as she had to visit a sick friend in town so that was the end of Frank and Moira's picnic.

"I'll drop Moira off first and then come back and get y'all," Frank suggested.

"No need for that," Edith was adamant. "I'm going that direction; I'll drop her off on my way."

"But ..." Frank's normally cheery face had a stony expression.

"No buts, remember we've got petrol rationing." Edith busied herself packing up the picnic basket and folding the blanket. "You were lucky to get use of the truck in the first place for a joy ride."

Joy ride. Moira hid her amusement. They'd rudely interrupted their joy ride.

"I'll walk y'all to the car." Frank took Moira's hand in his. "I'm so sorry," he whispered as they walked away. "This hasn't turned out the way I'd hoped. Can I see y'all again?"

"I'm leaving tomorrow to go to my next placement." Moira glanced back at Edith. "And I don't imagine Miss Bossy Pants will allow you the use of the truck again."

Frank's fingers tightened their hold of her hand. A desire to pick up where they'd left off, a need for more time to explore whatever was between them, or just a casual wartime fling? Moira wasn't sure. She knew Frank had ignited something inside her, but she wasn't naïve enough to think it was love.

"What's y'all address going to be?" Frank's face lit up. "I could write to y'all."

Moira had no intention of being like Betsy and sitting around waiting for letters to arrive.

"I don't know yet. I won't find out until tomorrow." She couldn't mirror Frank's eagerness. She imagined he'd just find another woman. There would be plenty of them in Wellington. She was a fling and nothing more.

"Don't worry, I'll find a way." Frank pulled Moira into his arms. He tilted her chin until their eyes met. "There is something special about y'all, Moira. I know it."

Cocooned against his body Moira felt protected. He was a man who was both gentle and strong. She didn't know much else about him and maybe never would, but he'd made her last day in Orari a memorable one. Their farewell kiss lingered with unspoken promises of what might have been.

⌘

Moira's last night in the single bed in Bill's house left her lethargic, a heaviness in her chest. She couldn't decide if she was coming down with something or mourning a loss. She walked heavy footed to the kitchen, her belongings packed away in her suitcase.

"Are you all ready to go there, lass?" John asked.

Moira clamped her mouth shut to stop her chin trembling. *Silly emotions*, she refused to give into them.

"Are you sad to be leaving us?" John was aware enough to detect Moira's sadness but not wise enough to leave her be. "You can always come back and visit you know."

"There. There." Anne patted Moira's back like a mother winding a baby. "It'll be that soldier, not us, she's missing. Seems she's fallen for his American charm, hook, line, and sinker."

Moira allowed the couple to talk about her as if she wasn't present. Was it Frank, or was it Bill, or was it simply the need to have somewhere more permanent that left her melancholy? Whatever it was there was no point stewing.

"I might have a cup of tea before I go." Moira dropped her suitcase in the porch. "I think it's going to be a long drive."

The tea had the desired effect, soothing her nerves. She paid no heed to the telephone's ring until she heard Anne mention Bill's name.

"That's great to hear. Thank you for letting me know. Goodbye for now."

"Is Bill coming home?" Moira's head shot up and she bounced on the edge of her seat.

"Not before you leave."

The words themselves were innocent, merely a statement of fact, Bill wouldn't be home before Moira left this morning but Anne's tone carried the same malice it had the day they'd met. It silently added 'so you won't be able to get your gold-digging fingers into him.' Was Moira imagining it? *No.* Anne's mouth curled into a smug sneer.

Anne's stance surprised Moira. She'd never known someone to change so quickly, from nice to horrid in a split second. It was just as well Moira was leaving.

"It's wonderful news that he's recovering." She refused to let Anne spoil the good news.

"Yes, great to hear," John stepped back into his role as mediator. Standing behind Anne, he scrunched his shoulders up to his ears and mouthed an apology.

Moira returned her empty cup to the bench just as the cattle stop rattled once again. A glance at the clock, confirmed it was too early for her expected ride. It wouldn't be Bill, but it might be Frank, come to rescue her from Anne. She bounced from foot to foot and peered out the window, filled with hope that he'd been able to bribe Edith for the use of the truck. Her pulse quickened as she raised a finger to her lips. She could still feel Frank's kiss. Her skin flushed with the thought of his body on hers.

It was a rusty old truck that chugged into view followed by a cloud of black smoke from the exhaust.

The back was piled high with supplies, a rope net slung over top and tied down to secure the precariously stacked load.

"Barry."

Moira looked down at her cinnamon dress and back at the man driving the truck. He was as hairy as the border collie dog seated beside him. It was hard to tell where his unkempt hair stopped, and his long straggly beard began.

"Perhaps you'd better change, Moira," Anne suggested. "You might ruin your dress."

Moira had intended to go out in the style in which she'd arrived. Unsure whether Anne's advice was well-meant or spiteful, she ignored it, hoping she wouldn't regret her decision.

"Nope, I'll be fine," she said to herself as much as Anne and headed through the porch with her bag.

"Moira."

She heard the deep grunt of her name and surmised it was Barry who spoke from a mouth hidden beneath a nicotine-stained moustache.

"Gotta hit the road." Barry flicked his grime-ingrained fingers to indicate Moira should get in.

"Would you like to stop in for a cup of tea?" Anne offered. "The kettle is hot."

"Long drive."

Barry's response was either a good reason to have a drink or an excuse not to, his voice and expression remained unchanged, so it was difficult to tell which. But he left the engine running, pulled a pipe from his pocket and put a match to it until puffs of smoke rose from him as well as the truck.

"Looks like Barry is a man of few words." John stood beside Anne. "You'd better go, lass. All the best."

There was no room on the back for Moira's suitcase. She'd have to have it in the front with her. The passenger door creaked on its rusty hinges, coming slowly open to reveal an interior as dishevelled as its owner. The seat covering was split in several places, dog hair clung to what stuffing remained. The border collie looked inquisitively at Moira, its tongue hanging to one side as it moved to sit between the two seats.

"Climb in. Molly won't hurt ya." Barry wrapped his arm around the dog and pulled it towards him.

Moira hesitated. Perhaps she could change her mind, move to Wellington, look up Frank.

"Long drive," Barry repeated. "Better go."

Moira edged her red toe peepers in between the assortment of tools that littered the floor of the truck. She squeezed in beside her suitcase, using it as a barrier between her and the dog. It wasn't that she didn't like dogs, but she was unsure if the unpleasant odour filling the cabin was human or canine. It stunk like the sheep's carcass she'd found when she'd arrived at Bill's. She almost smiled at the irony, *leaving as she'd begun*, she'd have to be careful what she manifested.

She waved goodbye as Barry backed through the shroud of black smoke that engulfed the truck. Choking on the fumes, Moira reached for the window winder only to find a knob where it should have been.

"Does the window go up?"

"Nup."

Moira held her breath until Barry shoved the vehicle from reverse to first and headed down the driveway with the fumes behind them.

"How long will it take to get to your farm?" Moira asked.

"A few hours."

"Is Molly your only dog, or do you have more?

"A few."

"Did you manage to get all the supplies you needed?"

"Missed a few." Barry puffed away on his pipe. "Always next time."

Trying to make conversation with this man of *few* words was futile. Moira lit a cigarette, rested her head back on the seat and let the wind that whistled through the open window blow away any remaining resentment she held for life not turning out the way she thought it would. She was starting another chapter, and she would do her darndest to ensure it was a better one.

⌘

Moira must have nodded off at some point. She woke with a jolt when Barry turned the truck from a tar-sealed road onto a gravel track. A full bladder told her they must have travelled some distance. Barry took no care to dodge the potholes on the rutted track and Moira hoped they'd arrive at their destination soon.

She stretched to ease a kink in her neck and came face to face with Molly. The dog rested its head on Moira's suitcase. Mismatched eyes, one blue, one hazel looked beseechingly at Moira.

"Hello, Molly." Moira patted the dog's head, thinking perhaps she'd get better responses from the dog than its owner.

Molly's barked reply made her laugh. If only she understood canine, they could form an alliance. A nudge from Barry silenced the dog.

"How much further?" Moira was curious whether they were passing through the steep brown hills that rose on either side of the truck or she was expected to farm in this treacherous terrain. It was nothing like she'd seen before.

"Not far."

Not far turned out to be quite some distance. A pass between the hills opened to a wide expansive valley. The track wove its way from one end of the valley to the other, zig zagging to follow the river that ran its length. They reached a ford and had to cross the crystal blue waters, ambling slowly over the rocks that formed a platform of sorts.

The river's source appeared to be a waterfall tumbling from the brow of the hill. The cascade exasperated Moira's need to urinate. She wangled one knee across the other, hitting the dash in the process.

"I need a toilet," she groaned.

Barry looked sideways at her, grumbled under his breath, and brought the truck to a stop in the middle of the track.

Moira scanned the area. There were no buildings, not even a long drop. Barry flicked his filthy fingers in the opposite direction, indicating Moira should get out. She stared at him, too stunned to move while he nonchalantly took the opportunity to relight his pipe.

"You going or not?"

Gingerly, Moira climbed out of the truck. Tussock grew haphazardly amongst moss covered rocks that looked as if they'd been there since dinosaurs roamed. Over to the left she spied a boulder. With no other option, she headed towards it, glancing back over her shoulder to check Barry wasn't abandoning her in the middle of nowhere.

She cursed herself for wearing the cinnamon dress. It wasn't easy to hitch the fitted skirt up over her thighs and pull her underwear down, all the while remaining alert to every strange sound and movement. Overhead a hawk circled, high enough to utilise the updraft to hover effortlessly, low enough to site its prey. Moira hoped it wasn't her the hawk was keeping an eye on.

The boulder provided the privacy she needed, but the thistles growing in the lee of the rock, pricked her bare skin as she squatted.

"Ouch!" She muffled her squeal. Heaven forbid Barry would come running to her aid. She doubted he hurried anywhere but it wasn't a risk she wanted to take.

She heard the rev of the engine and hurried to finish. If only she'd remembered which leaves were safe to use as toilet paper or what stinging nettle looked like. She hitched her underwear up, smoothed her now wrinkled dress down and walked briskly back to the truck avoiding the thorns that threatened to stab her legs.

The track pitched skyward at the end of the valley. Barry changed down a gear and they began the climb. Brown turned to grey, as earth became rock, a narrow track chiselled from the hillside. On the driver's side the rock rose steeply, disappearing into a lingering fog. On the passenger's side it fell rapidly, plummeting to the river below. Moira's knuckles lost all colour as she clung to the frayed edge of her seat. It was a futile protective measure; the scree slope would become an avalanche tumbling anyone unfortunate enough to slip.

Moira looked straight ahead and kept silent. She wanted nothing or no one to distract Barry. He'd likely driven this track a thousand times, but she needed him to do it safely this time. She tried to picture what would be at the end: another valley, lush with grass, a beautiful homestead, fat healthy animals. It had to be something special, otherwise who would go to all the trouble to build a track to nowhere.

"Bugger." Barry changed into first gear and the vehicle slowed to a snail's pace.

Moira gasped when she noticed the reason why. Just ahead a channel of water came across the track. Like a sharp knife it carved a segment of the track from the outside, the edge where Moira was sitting. She glanced across at Barry, itched to suggest they could stop, walk the rest of the way, and carry the supplies. She looked back at the precarious load, the likely culprit of their demise but gripped by fear she remained silent, unable to speak.

Barry drove on, hugging the hillside until it was close enough to touch. Moira held her breath, as if that would make her lighter, less likely to fall. The front wheels went over, one scrunching on the wet gravel, one rotating in midair. It was only a matter of seconds, but it seemed like a lifetime. The front wheels were safe but the rear wheels, under the weight of the supplies, still had to traverse the chasm.

Molly whimpered. Even the dog sensed the danger.

"All right there, girl." Barry took his hand off the wheel to give Molly a reassuring pat.

Moira's arms flew up, ready to wrest the steering wheel from Barry, wrench the wheels to the right. She opened her mouth to scream.

"No worry," Barry muttered as the rear of the truck safely reached beyond the slip.

Craving the calming effect of nicotine, Moira grabbed her cigarette packet from her handbag. Her trembling fingers struggled to remove a smoke and light it, but the shaking abated with the first long inhale. Two cigarettes since leaving Bill's, Moira hoped her wartime ration would last until she next made it to town. As she was discovering, it was a huge journey in more ways than one.

They were nearing the summit when a gust of wind howled down the hillside, chasing a cloud across the windscreen, blanketing the truck in a mantle of whiteness that dropped the temperature several degrees. A shiver ran the length of Moira's spine. She'd need a hot bath when they finally reached their destination, both to warm the chill and ease the fear that had seeped into her bones.

Thankfully, Barry stopped, pulled on the handbrake, and waited for the fog to drift away. It settled in the valley like a bed of cotton wool, but Moira had already surmised there was nothing soft about this terrain.

Crossing the crest of the hill brought a hint of civilisation into view, not another human, but yards with lichen covered rails, a small woolshed with silvered weatherboards, fences strung with animal hides, several ramshackle buildings, a corrugated iron water tank towering on rickety stilts, and a long-abandoned tractor sitting lop-sided with a flat tyre. Moira scanned the area, wondering, if this was their destination and if it was, where was the homestead?

Her first question was answered when Barry turned off the track and parked the truck beside a building whose only window was covered by a faded sack. She rubbed her eyes and shook her head. This couldn't be real. Nobody lived in conditions like these. Perhaps they were just stopping off to visit a neighbour or drop supplies at an outpost.

Barry climbed out of the truck and Molly followed. "Help unload, would ya."

"Who lives here?" Moira was afraid of the answer.

"We do." Barry looked down at Molly and rubbed her ears.

A rabbit darted out from the strangled roots of a gnarly fruit tree and Molly took off after it.

"Where's the house?"

The grimy fingers Moira was beginning to despise pointed to an oblong area of charred ground.

"Burnt down," was Barry's matter-of-fact reply. "Not enough water to put the fire out."

He'd finally strung more than three words together, but they weren't ones Moira wanted to hear.

"Where do I sleep?" Moira stepped back, creating much needed space between her and Barry and his response. If walking back to town hadn't been an impossibility, she might have hightailed it out of there.

"Shearers' quarters."

Moira's eyes widened in disbelief. If Barry expected her to sleep in the same decrepit hut as him, she'd steal his truck and risk driving the road herself to escape.

CHAPTER
12

"I sleep here." Barry pushed the door open on the hut with the sacking window. "You have that one."

The building Barry indicated was Moira's looked identical except its tiny window still held a pane of glass. She carried her suitcase to the doorsill and dropped it at her feet with a thud that echoed the dread hitting the pit of her stomach. With no need for security in this isolated spot, the unlocked door swung open with a tentative push. Moira held her breath as she peered into the semi-darkness, while her new abode revealed itself. It was as if the brown of the earth had imbued itself within, there was no hint of a woman's presence, no colour to lift her mood.

Moira's only choice was forward, there was no going back. She stepped over the threshold, onto wooden floorboards, bereft of any floor covering, other than a generous coating of dust. In one corner, a set of single wooden bunks provided options for sleeping. Neither of the mattresses looked comfortable. Moira walloped the lower one with her hand and nearly choked on the dust particles she disturbed, immediately deciding the top bunk was the better of the two.

A simple table and two chairs occupied the opposite corner, an unlit gas lamp signalling the hut was without power. Moira thought back over the journey, there hadn't been a power line for miles. She'd been so concerned with the dangers of the drive; she hadn't registered the disadvantages of the destination.

At the foot of the bunks was a plain set of drawers with a wash basin and water ewer on top. Moira swallowed hard; tears welled in the corners of her eyes. She wouldn't let them fall. She wouldn't let them be the only running water in her new room. Surely there must be another building that housed the bathroom, the bath she'd been hankering for. There was the tank on stilts, there was at least gravity fed water for something.

"You coming to help, or what?" Barry had already undone the ropes and removed the cargo net.

His gruff voice pulled Moira from her self-pity. There would be plenty of time for her to reflect on the stupidity of accepting this placement without further information. She'd volunteered as a land girl because the only young men left in New Zealand seemed to be farming in the country. Now she was stuck in the back of beyond with a male that looked more like a woolly ram than human.

"I'll just change," she called back. Her dress was covered in dog hair and didn't need to be ruined further lifting boxes of supplies.

She pushed the door shut and lay her suitcase on the bottom bunk. The tightly packed case sprung open when she flicked its catches. Without a wardrobe to hang her dresses, or an opportunity to wear anything other than her farm clothes, Moira might as well left half of her belongings behind. She grabbed her overalls, a blouse to wear underneath, some farm socks and her gumboots and began to undress.

She lifted her dress over her head and sat down to remove her toe peepers, disturbing a mouse with the scuff of the chair. The vermin scampered from its hiding place beneath the table and ran across Moira's bare toes. She clapped her hand across her mouth to muffle her scream, more terrified that Barry would barge in, than the tiny fieldmouse which huddled by the door.

"I'll let you out in a minute," she whispered. "Just let me get dressed first."

Overalls and gumboots provided Moira the much-needed bravado to confront the mouse, Barry and the work that lay outside the hut. When the door opened, she'd have liked to run away as fast as the mouse did, but Moira helped Barry carry the stores into a third building that acted as the kitchen.

The building sat low to the ground and its thick walls anchored it into the landscape.

"Cobb cottage." Barry must have noticed Moira's curiosity. "Local mud and straw."

"Looks like it's been here forever," Moira said. "How old is it?"

Barry tilted his head and looked skyward as if he was searching for the information.

"Least fifty years," he eventually answered.

More than twice as old as Moira. She hoped she'd feel this stable by that age.

An open fire spanned one end of the building. Barry added some wood to the fire and stirred the ashes with a poker until the hot embers sparked. He lifted the lid on the cast iron pot suspended from a steel bar above the fire.

"Rabbit stew," he announced, sniffing the pot.

There was a gleam to Barry's eyes as if he was proud of his cooking. He may have been smiling but Moira couldn't tell, his mouth hidden beneath wiry facial hair, the furrow in his weatherbeaten forehead a permanent frown. She wondered how old he was, how long he'd lived this isolated life.

A sack of flour was stowed away in a metal-lined bin; another of potatoes was tipped into a wooden box that doubled as a seat. A bag of onions hung on one of many wire hooks curved over the open rafters supporting a thatched roof. Moira imagined the rain dripping through the thatch but there was no evidence of water damage, and the mustiness of her hut was missing, replaced with a dryness that felt comforting.

The trestle table doubled as a chopping board. Knife marks ingrained with a myriad of food stains assured Moira at least she would be fed. Barry grabbed several potatoes from the bin, a parsnip, and an onion. The unpeeled and unwashed vegetables were roughly chopped and tossed into the stew.

147

"Did you want some of the carrots, as well?" Moira offered, recalling the sack of carrots on the truck.

"Nah, they're for the rabbits."

Moira shook her head in disbelief. *Feeding rabbits? Wasn't Barry a sheep farmer?*

They returned to the truck and unloaded wool sacks, twine, and shearing blades.

"Shearers turning up soon," Barry informed her as they stacked everything under a platform by the sheep yards.

Any concerns Moira would normally have had about the effort required for shearing were far outweighed by the pending arrival of more people. Where on earth were they going to sleep? She hoped that *soon* was like *not far* and it would be a long time before she had to deal with the issue.

The sun was painting the clouds a pastel orange by the time they finished unloading the truck. Molly reappeared with a rabbit hanging from her jaw.

"Good girl." Barry patted Molly's head, took the rabbit from her mouth, and threw it to Moira. "Skin that, would ya."

Instinctively, Moira reached out to grab what was being thrown at her. She wished she hadn't when her fingers disappeared into the neck wound that caused the rabbit's demise. The carcass was still warm.

Barry pointed to the fence strung with rabbit skins. "Knife in the post. Hang the skin to dry. We'll save the meat for tea tomorrow."

Moira cringed. Every time Barry strung sentences together, they delivered bad news.

148

She'd watched *Whipsnade's* farm manager, Duncan skin a sheep but she'd never seen a rabbit being skinned, let alone done it herself. She imagined Barry wouldn't take kindly to a request for help on the first task she'd been assigned. Surely it couldn't be that different. She'd have to give it a go.

It took all her strength to wrench the knife from the top of the fencepost. She looked down the line of skins stretched between the fence wires. They were all missing their heads, feet, and tails.

"Sorry," she whispered an apology to the glazed eyes of the dead rabbit before hooking the tip of the blade into the neck wound and cutting the pelt around the neck.

The eyes were a distraction, a reminder of what she was having to do so she sliced through the neck until the head fell to the ground. Moira's stomach squirmed. She felt like an executioner, beheading a wrongly convicted criminal, even though it was Molly that had done the deed and now rushed in to grab the reward.

It soon became apparent removing the head was the wrong thing to do; there was little left to hang onto while she tackled the rest. She dangled the rabbit by its front legs and ran the knife down the centre of the breast. The blade pierced the animal's gut. The stench made Moira retch and drop the carcass.

"What the hell are ya doin?" Barry stomped over and grabbed the knife from Moira's hand.

He picked up the rabbit and lay it spine down on a piece of wood. A run of the blade from the breast to the groin, allowed him to peal the pelt aside. He reached into the breast, took hold of the heart, and wrenched it, the gut, and the intestine out and tossed them over the fence as pickings for a hovering hawk. Barry crunched the knife through each of the legs, removed the feet and cast them aside. With deft hands he then ripped the pelt to leave a naked, sinewy carcass.

"Do ya think ya can string this over the fence?"

Moira hurried to redeem herself, took the skin and stretched it between two wires as the others appeared to be. Barry didn't hang around to inspect. He headed back to the cob cottage. Dinner was likely ready. Moira's hands were covered in blood and rabbit fur, she felt tarred and feathered, a punishment for what, she didn't know. She headed towards the water tank in search of the bathroom.

A tap at the bottom of the tank was connected to a hose that branched off at a T-connection. One side of the hose was strung across to a fruit tree where a shower head hung from a branch. There was a lovely view out over the landscape but without any privacy screen there would also be a lovely view of the bather. Moira didn't know enough about Barry to risk it. Cast off to the side she found a rusty tin bath. Rainwater and rotting leaves had collected in the bottom of the bath creating a brown slime. The bath would be usable; it just needed a clean first.

The other side of the hose led to another tree. Between its gnarly roots a porcelain basin, still blackened from the fire, was rigged up on wooden posts. Excited by the prospect of running water, Moira turned the taps. The hot gave nothing but a pained screech; the cold coughed and spurted before gifting Moira sufficient water to wash her hands. She grabbed a grimy bar of soap and lathered up her hands, wringing them together. Water drained from the basin to splash at her feet.

Twenty feet or so out to the side stood a tin shed, its corrugated iron walls a mixture of second-hand sheets in an assortment of colours. The door was a collection of wooden slats roughly nailed onto a plank. It could have been designed to provide air flow for the long drop or a view down over the valley, but Moira chose to hitch the wire hook that kept it shut. Shafts of lights squeezed through the cracks between the slats and the nail holes in the iron, resembling the shimmer of the Milky Way on a cloudless night. Moira had to appreciate the small moments of beauty amidst the harshness of her new environment.

Barry was already tucking into a plate of rabbit stew by the time Moira made it back inside. He was so used to being alone, table etiquette would be like a foreign language to him and even simple consideration of another's presence seemed long forgotten.

"Help yaself," he said between chews, his cheeks bulging.

There was nothing appetising about the congealing sludge on Barry's plate, nor the rabbit carcass hanging from the rafters next to the onions. Moira's stomach rumbled, more from emotional strain than physical exertion. What had she got herself into? Whatever tomorrow would bring, she needed sustenance, so she spooned a generous helping onto a chipped plate, its gold edging long since worn away, and sat down on the bench seat opposite Barry. Molly lay under the table, head resting on the floor, doleful eyes on the watch for any morsel that would come her way.

Moira closed her eyes to erase the image of a pristine white tail flicking as a rabbit hopped past and fed herself the first chunk of meat. The gaminess of the meat was familiar, and she remembered Nel had cooked rabbit stew at *Whipsnade*. Barry's version wasn't nearly as tasty and much drier, needing copious amounts of gravy.

"Tasty, eh?" A dribble of gravy edged its way down Barry's beard.

Wishing to avoid insulting the cook, Moira just nodded, exaggerating her chewing motion to imply enjoyment while she struggled to swallow the sinewy meat.

Wind whistled under the door and flickered the gas lamp.

"Wind's getting up." The creases that fanned out from Barry's eyes wrinkled with humour. "Ya have to turn the sheep in the morning."

Turn the sheep. It wasn't a task Moira had done before or even heard what was entailed. Was Barry trying to catch her out, that glint in his eyes, how should she interpret it?

"Where are the sheep?" she asked.

"Over in the north paddock. Sounds like a westerly out there." Barry cackled, an evil laugh that gave Moira no confidence to believe him. "Need to turn the flock or there'll be no point shearing them."

Moira turned her ear to the door, straining to hear anything that would indicate there was a modicum of truth to Barry's words. She imagined if a person stayed in one place for as long as he had, then you'd be able to tell the wind was from the west, even when you were inside a building with walls a foot thick. But a wind from any direction didn't mean sheep needed turning. They had four legs; they could turn themselves. They had their own insulation, a woolly fleece to keep the warmth in, it was going to take more than a brisk westerly to remove. Moira decided to call Barry's bluff.

"Surely," she tried to sound like a seasoned farmer, "they can turn themselves."

Barry's cackle filled the cottage, echoing off the walls. He laughed so much he nearly fell off the seat.

"So, ya not just a pretty girl from the city." He calmed as quick as he'd started. "Just as well, we'll head out soon an' lay the carrots out."

"Shall I clean up here first?" Moira asked, eager to give the plates and utensils a decent wash.

"Nah, we'd best get them out before it's too dark."

Barry grabbed several sacks from outside: the new one full of carrots and two empty sacks. He tipped half the carrots onto the table and passed Moira a knife.

"Chop these up," he ordered as he began doing the same.

The chunks of carrot were loaded into the empty sacks. Barry swung one over his shoulder and indicated for Moira to do the same, before they headed out the door. Fortunately, the moon was a large orb illuminating the night sky and their way down a dirt track carved out of the hillside. Where the track flattened out, they entered a paddock, a rickety gate lay on its side incapable of keeping livestock in or out. Running around the perimeter of the paddock was a trench of recently dug earth.

"I'll go this way. Ya' go that." Barry pointed to the fence line that went off at a right angle. "Drop a piece of carrot in the trench every so often."

Oblivious as to the why of this instruction, Moira did as she was told, relieved as the heavy sack digging into her shoulder gradually lightened.

"What's it for?" she asked when they met at the opposite corner.

"The rabbits." Barry frowned at Moira.

"I realise that but what is feeding carrots to the rabbits supposed to do?"

"They like scratching around in the fresh earth and they like carrots even more." Barry's evil cackle echoed across the valley. "Tomorrow night, I'll let them go hungry then we'll lace the carrots with poison."

It sounded like an easier way to kill them than trapping or shooting but Moira hoped they weren't eating the poisoned meat.

"Then what do you do with them?" she asked seeking assurance.

"Skin them. Bury them."

Moira's relief quickly turned to dread. They'd laid out a hundred chunks of carrot. If there were going to be that many dead rabbits, she'd better hone her skinning skills.

Halfway back up the track, they stopped and turned to see rabbits scampering from all directions, out of burrows, through from other paddocks. The field had become a seething mass, a cacophony of honking noises.

"What's that noise?" Moira had never heard anything like it.

"That's their happy honk." Barry lit his pipe and puffed his way home. "If only they knew."

CHAPTER

13

Birdsong woke Moira at first light. With no electricity and Barry's limited conversation, they had retired early on her first day at the high-country station. Her lumpy mattress hadn't made for a comfortable sleep and despite ten hours in bed Moira felt irritable. She crossed and uncrossed her legs beneath the rough grey blanket, the only bedding provided, and couldn't stop scratching her arms. Was it simply a bad sleep? Could she roll over and snatch another hour of slumber? Her stomach gurgled loudly, but she felt more nauseous than hungry. She closed her eyes and inhaled long and slow. Images of carrots, rabbits and rabbit stew filled her thoughts. Panic that she'd eaten poisoned rabbit had her down off the bunk and racing to the toilet.

The ground was chilly beneath her bare feet, the long drop seat cold and unwelcoming. The toilet door swung open as she sat unable to move, her hand over her mouth hoping she could stifle the urge to vomit. Worried Barry would discover her in this vulnerable position, Moira listened intently for any noise to indicate he was close.

Relief, both physical and emotional came gradually as Moira inhaled the fresh morning air, focusing on the day unfolding before her. Sunlight coloured the sky a golden hue. Rays of light painted swathes down the hillsides, reaching further into the valley as the sun edged higher. Other than the cheery chirping of birds, and the distant bleat of sheep, the landscape sat in a serene quietness. Last night's wind had yet to pick up its morning momentum. There was beauty amongst the chaos.

Moira's stomach settled but in the light another problem became apparent. Red spots dotted her arms, her legs and she imagined her torso beneath her nightie. She clenched her fists to resist the urge to scratch but she could only sustain that for so long, one by one her fingers unfolded, they touched her skin, lightly at first, then desperately to ease the irritation, scratching until her limbs glowed red and hot.

She noticed a speck of black on her leg. A flea. The source of her suffering.

"I'll get you, you little sod," she threatened as she finished her toileting.

She stood, lifted the hem of her nightie with one hand and readied her other thumb and forefinger as pincers, all the while keeping an eye on the insect feasting on her leg. Without delay, she grabbed and squeezed, pressing the flea until the tips of her make-shift pincers went white.

"Gotcha!" Moira smiled triumphantly.

She turned and lifted her finger, ready to flick her squished quarry to the bottom of the long drop. The black speck seized the moment and leapt for freedom.

"Bloody hell!" Moira jumped back and cursed. Unable to see where the flea had gone, she felt certain it was back on her and madly brushed her skin, shook her nightie, and leapt about.

A cold shower suddenly seemed like a wonderful idea. Moira glanced back at Barry's hut and the cob cottage. There was no sign of life, the chimney was without smoke, and Molly must have still been tucked up beside her owner.

The first splashes of cold water felt icy on Moira's face and sent a shiver down her spine. As she overcame the initial shock, relief flowed like rivulets over her skin to puddle at her feet. Feeling soothed but wanting to be certain the fleas weren't clinging to her nightie, she peeked over her shoulder to check she was still alone, before tugging the wet garment over her head.

Looking down over her body she felt like a pin cushion, dotted with red spots where the pins had been pushed in. Conscious that she shouldn't waste the precious supply of water, Moira made certain there were no black dots amongst the red or on her nightie before she turned the tap off.

Her body may have been flea free but her bed and hut likely weren't. Moira wrung the excess water from the nightie and unravelled it to hold against her torso while she scurried back to her hut. She had no choice but to dress in the farm clothes from yesterday. She'd hung them over the back of the chair overnight so hopefully the fleas had been too preoccupied with her to infect the clothes.

The clothing chafed her skin. Were there more fleas or was it merely an irritation of the existing bites? Her imagination played havoc and she had to grit her teeth to resist the urge to scratch so she busied herself dragging the mattresses out of the hut, standing them on end against a tree trunk. A discarded broken handle from a garden tool became her weapon as she beat the mattresses with as much force as she could muster. Apart from the clouds of dust that rose and threatened to choke her, it was therapeutic. Each beat of the stick was a release of her frustration: with fleas, the mattress, the limited water supply that allowed the homestead to burn down, the dusty hut that was now her bedroom, her placement in the back of beyond with a man that was more at ease with himself than others, with Anne for her nastiness forcing Moira to leave Orari, with Graham Stanley for injuring Bill in the first place, for Chad's interruption of her interlude with Frank, and for Edith not allowing Frank to return for a final visit. Even Hitler took a whack for inciting a World War. The last and final thump, the one that broke the stick in half, was for her parents' divorce, Moira's first and harshest lesson, the one that kept coming back to haunt her, the one that taught her the world was not always kind.

Catching her breath, Moira realised the only person who hadn't been a source of frustration was Frank. She pictured his cheeky smile, heard his southern drawl pouring compliments like treacle, smooth and full of sugar and spice and all things nice. What was it he'd said: that there was something special about her? What did he promise? That he'd find her?

"Yeah, right." Moira shook her head to bring herself back to reality. "You're in the back of beyond covered in flea bites, no one is going to go out of their way to find that."

"I see ya' had a shower."

Moira jumped. Lost in her musings, she hadn't heard Barry approach but was now aghast at his comment. The best interpretation was he'd noticed her wet hair and assumed she'd showered; the worst interpretation was he had seen her naked under the shower. She eyed him, looked for the glint in his eyes, a flicker showing his amusement. Fortunately, she saw none. She decided to adopt his approach, one-word responses.

"Fleas," was all she offered in explanation.

"Need thick skin." Barry pinched at the leathery skin on his forearm. "Can't get through."

Moira needed thick skin for more reasons than fleas. To survive in this harsh environment, to prosper in a man's world, every woman needed to toughen her resolve.

"Ya' hungry?" Barry patted his stomach. "Fry up's ready."

Clutching her own stomach Moira wondered if the fry-up was of leftovers from last night's dinner she'd rather avoid. There was only one way to find out, she abandoned the mattresses, a dose of sunlight would do them good and followed Barry to the cottage. He had the same grubby clothes on as yesterday. The creases hinted that he'd likely slept in them, and Moira judged from the sweaty odour that followed him, he'd probably worn the same shirt and trousers for the last week, possibly month. The smell did nothing to ease her stomach, but after all her whacking, she assumed the rumbles from her belly were now hunger pains.

On an iron plate suspended over the fire, a frying pan sizzled with rashers of bacon, chunks of leftover potatoes and slices of meat which Moira couldn't identify as rabbit. Approaching the frying pan, her first whiff was of the bacon's tasty aroma. She licked her lips in anticipation but there was a hint of rotten egg, not enough to make gag but enough to have her questioning the menu.

"So, what is it we're eating this morning?" she asked.

"Lamb's fry, bacon and spuds." Barry moved to the table with a generous serving.

"Lamb's fry?" Moira eyed Barry dubiously. Hadn't she heard somewhere lamb's testes referred to as lamb's fry?

Barry cackled, piled his fork high and sighed as he shovelled his mouth full. Trying to avoid the lamb's fry, Moira dished herself up a smaller helping and sat opposite Barry. She fished around with her knife and fork, pushing the lamb's fry aside, to eat the bacon and potatoes first. When all that remained on her plate, the same plate she'd eaten dinner off the previous night, were slivers of dark brown meat, Moira eyed Barry suspiciously.

"What do you call lamb's fry?" She watched for any hint of lie in his response.

"It's okay," he conceded with a wink. "It's liver, not testes. Eat up. Iron's good for ya'. Big day ahead."

Moira had just finished chewing the last of her breakfast when a bell jingled outside.

"That'll be Joe the hawker," Barry answered her unspoken question.

"Hawker?" Moira had never heard the term.

"He travels around the back country farms with his wares," Barry explained. "He'll take the rabbit pelts, swap them for more poison."

"Well, good morning, good morning." Ducking his head to pass through the doorway, Joe entered the cottage with a friendly greeting but stopped suddenly and stared wide-eyed at Moira. "Well, I never! Who would have thought Barry would have a lovely looking thing like you sitting at his breakfast table. Where did you spring from? Are there any more of you? A sister, a cousin, perhaps?"

Joe's large frame blocked the only doorway, leaving Moira feeling vulnerable. She wanted to believe the big man was harmless. The muscles bulging beneath his shirtsleeves hinted he'd easily have the strength to pull his wagon by hand.

"Sorry, I'm one of a kind." Moira hid her uneasiness with a chuckle.

"Moira's a land girl," Barry explained. "Giving me a hand."

"She could give me more than a hand." Joe laughed raucously.

"Did ya' get that poison?" Barry ignored Joe's remark and changed the subject.

Joe shook his head and finally turned from Moira to Barry. "Sure did. Looks like you've got a fair, few pelts. Are you getting on top of the rabbit problem?"

"Doesn't feel like it," Barry groaned. "Need to be able to do the whole farm at the same time. The damn things just breed and re-infest. I'll have no decent pasture left come winter at this rate."

Barry must have seen the leer Joe sent Moira's way and came to her rescue.

"Moira, ya' go bundle up the dry pelts on the fence," he suggested.

"Surely, the lady would like to see my wares first," Joe countered. "I've got some fancy laces and bolts of fabric to sew a pretty dress."

"No use for that out here." Moira stood, slipped her hands into her overall pockets, and turned for the door. She already had several dresses that were unlikely to leave her suitcase.

"How about a fine hat to keep the sun off that peachy skin of yours?"

"Already got one, thanks." She didn't, but she wasn't going to let Joe know that.

"What about some luxury cotton sheets? My last offer," Joe pleaded. "Women tell me there's nothing quite like slipping between clean sheets at night. Can't see what difference it makes myself. Don't need sheets when you're sleeping under the stars."

Moira was half out the door when she heard Joe mention sheets. The thought of cotton against her skin, soothing the flea bites, instead of the rough grey blanket, stopped her instantly. She looked from Joe out to his open wagon and back again, imagining the sheets were likely ingrained with dust from the trip.

"How do you keep them clean on your wagon?"

"Mrs Humphrey, bought single instead of double by mistake, still wrapped in cellophane, they are. She was going to take them back, but I traded them for ..." Joe scratched his head. "Can't remember now, but doesn't matter, I've got them, and I can see you'd really like them."

It was true. She'd love the sheets, but she was wary of what he'd want in return. What did she have to trade, other than herself, which wasn't on offer.

"I'd better get the pelts bundled up." Moira left the men to their business and headed outside.

Leaving the pelt that had been added to the fence line last night, Moira collected two piles of hard, dried skins, two dozen in each stack. She hunted around for something to bundle them up with and found some lengths of baling twine saved from when the hay had been fed out. She secured the twine and carried the piles back to Joe's wagon.

"Four dozen," Moira declared as she placed the bundles beside the wagon.

"That'll be plenty then." Joe handed Barry a small glass bottle, its label had a skull and cross bones and POISON written in big letters.

"Strychnine!" Barry's eyes lit up. "The little buggers won't stand a chance."

Moira stepped back; it was a warning she too would need to heed.

"And for you too, my lady." Barry bowed in a gentlemanly fashion and presented the sheets to Moira.

"But … but." Unsure Moira hesitated, resisting the urge to grab the pristine linen. "I don't have anything to trade for them."

"Four dozen pelts is more than enough," Joe replied. "Barry should be supplying you with bedding anyway."

That was true. Her living conditions were deteriorating. She'd gone from a double bed at *Whipsnade,* to a single bed at Bill's, both with clean cotton sheets, and now an uncomfortable bunk infested with fleas and only an itchy blanket.

"Thank you." Moira grabbed the sheets and hugged them to her chest.

"Right then," Joe turned to Barry. "Can you spare a cuppa before I head on my way?"

The men went back into the cob cottage leaving Moira alone with her thoughts. She took the sheets back to her hut and found a cigarette. She needed one. So much had happened in a short space of time. She savoured the nicotine fix, felt its immediate calming effect while she pondered her predicament. How had she gone from dancing in Frank's arms to covered in flea bites and bargaining for clean sheets? More importantly, how long was she going to have to stay here with Barry? She had no means of escape on her own and Barry only went to town once a month. Was Joe another option she'd be prepared to risk? Where was he even heading next? Perhaps he could take a message, deliver it to the placement officer and demand they come and collect her. Even if she made it out of here, what were her options after that. The placement officer had made it clear they weren't impressed with land girls who couldn't stick it out. Maybe she just wasn't cut out for farming. There was always the option of moving to Wellington, closer to Frank. Surely, she'd be able to find a job in a shop in the capital city.

Moira stubbed the cigarette butt into the dirt, satisfied she had options. She would give it her best shot in the meantime but if it didn't work out, she could move on, find something better; life was too short not to.

She carried her mattress back inside and made the bed up. Smoothing down the crisp white sheets, she imagined climbing between them, the soothing effect on her skin, the cool relief, perhaps she'd could catch forty winks while the men were having their cup of tea.

"Right, I'll be off then," Joe said as he shook Barry's hand and climbed back up on his wagon. "See you next month."

Moira sighed wearily. No time for a sleep and no opportunity to leave or get word out for a whole month. She was stuck here. She'd just have to make the most of it. Molly wandered over to sit at Moira's feet.

"You don't mind living here, do you Molly?" Moira patted the dog's head. "I guess it can't be all bad."

Molly scratched her belly then bent herself around and nipped at her thigh.

"Oh, no, don't tell me you've got fleas too?" Scared that more fleas would jump her way, Moira stepped away from the dog. She'd solved her bedding problem only to be presented with another dilemma to solve.

The bell on Joe's wagon signalled his departure as he drove off down the track.

"Better get a move on. Gotta shift the sheep. Get them heading this way so they'll be close when the shearing gang arrive." Barry grabbed two rope halters from a hook on the side of the woolshed and passed them to Moira. "Horses are over yonder. Bring them in, will ya."

Moira gulped. Her farming skills, or lack thereof, were about to be tested again. Where was Alice when you needed her? If that petite woman could ride a horse, then surely there was nothing to it. Moira headed off in the direction Barry had pointed. Down over the brow of the hill, two horses stood expectantly beside the fence. Any confidence she'd had at the top of the hill dissipated by the time she reached their paddock. The horses towered over her and had hooves the size of Barry's frying pan. One was clearly a stallion, everything about them was huge.

Moira looked from the horses to the halters and back to the yards where Barry was waiting for her.

"Can you help me out here, horse? I'll be nice to you if could be kind to me."

CHAPTER
14

Moira held a halter out in front of her trying to figure out which way the loops and long length of rope were meant to fit over the horse's head. Fortunately, the horses co-operated, lowering their heads, and even flicking their ears forward to hint that one of the loops needed to go behind their ears.

"Now stay there while I open the gate." Moira hitched the horses to the fence while she ducked along the fence line to unhook a rickety wooden gate.

With a fear of being trampled mixed with the dread of revealing her complete lack of equine skills, Moira hung onto the very end of the halter ropes as she led the horses back to the yards. The rhythmic clip clop of their hooves behind her was somewhat soothing. Barry had bridles and saddles ready on the yard rails. She waited, watched what he did with the stallion and attempted to mirror his actions with the horse that seemed to be assigned to her.

"Does the horse have a name?" she asked attempting to feign nonchalance while she struggled to heave the saddle over the horse's back.

"Storm," Barry replied. "Stallion's Leo."

Storm! Moira gulped; her trembling fingers fumbled with the buckles on the saddle. Did the name reflect the horse's temperament or its smoky black colouring? She hoped the latter. Leo sounded much gentler.

"Better check that." Barry moved over to inspect the saddle straps. "In case ya saddle like ya skin."

She did. He had to undo the buckles and tighten the girth strap and adjust the stirrups.

Barry released half a dozen farm dogs from their run, collected a shotgun and stowed ammunition in his saddle bag. He mounted the stallion with ease, one foot in the stirrup, and up into the saddle in a fluid movement. Moira tried to emulate. It was an effort to lift her foot high enough to hook it into the stirrup and she didn't have enough strength in her arms or bounce in her other leg to lift herself the height of the horse. After several failed attempts Storm began to fidget. Moira noticed Barry's stony expression and the slow shake of his head, so she opted to climb on the yard railings and swing her leg across. She winced as her pubic bone walloped into the pommel and she imagined splitting in two as her legs spread over the horse's broadness.

Barry moved off and instinctively Storm followed, at a slow amble, down the track they'd arrived by. Each plod of the horse's hooves rocked Moira from side to side. She gripped the reigns tightly, and grabbed a handful of Storm's mane, as an extra precaution. One glance down at the ground left her frightened to do so again, least it tempted a fall, from what seemed like a great height.

When they reached the valley floor, they branched off on another track Moira hadn't noticed on the journey in. It was a single file, beaten path that wound its way between the tussock, rock, and a spattering of bushes with sharp thorns that were best avoided. The farm dogs sniffed and followed scents with their noses to the ground, tails wagging excitedly. They took off at a sprint barking loudly at the hares that bounded across the paddock. Molly was content to run alongside the horses, perhaps aware of the long tiring day ahead. Moira hoped the dog was sensible enough to stay away from the horses' hooves.

Moira's confidence lifted; if they were riding at this pace all day, she could manage. She relaxed her hold on the reins a fraction and began to take in her surroundings. At first glance, the landscape would be described as brown, but Moira noticed the tussock took on a golden hue where the sun caught its spindles, the willows growing beside the river were an apple green, the lichen that lived on the shaded side of the rocks wasn't a solid mass but a multitude of tiny peppermint hued leaves with tips dipped in white. They passed shrubs whose delicate branches resembled a copper filigree. Other plants that crept across the countryside were in shades of mustard and rust. She was reminded again there was beauty amongst the chaos.

Lost in her thoughts, Moira only noticed the track veered into a gulley when a sudden drop in temperature sent a

170

shiver down her spine. The sun hadn't breached the brow of this west facing hill and it sat in a cold shadow. Ahead the dogs had gathered in a pack and barked to announce the quarry they'd surrounded. Moira tried to get a glimpse but all she got was a whiff of unpleasantness, a stench she remembered from her first day at Bill's; there was a dead animal ahead. She tilted her head up and gulped in some fresh air, planning to hold her breath until they'd passed the carcass, but Barry pulled up right beside the fetid smell and dismounted.

"Pluck it." He pointed at the sheep indicating Moira should dismount and pluck the wool from its pelt, while he grabbed a small spade hitched to his saddle and began to dig a hole.

Moira looked aghast at the sheep that had clearly been dead for some time. There was no avoiding Barry's instruction so reluctantly she dismounted. She pinched her nostrils between her thumb and forefinger and knelt to pluck at the wool with her other hand. It came away easily but only because a wriggling mass of maggots was busy devouring the sheep's hide, burrowing into its internal organs. She wanted to close her eyes against the image but that would risk her fingers touching the fly larvae. She clamped her mouth shut as her breakfast threatened to leave her stomach; grabbed a handful of wool, stood, and moved away to get some fresh air.

"What do you want me to do with it?" she asked Barry.

"Saddle bag," he replied between his grunts of effort in digging into the hard ground. "Can't waste it."

The thought of maggots in her saddle bag prompted Moira to inspect the wool before she stuffed it away, took

171

another long breath of fresh air and returned to the carcass to pluck some more. By the time Barry had finished digging the hole, she'd gathered all the wool she thought usable, leaving the underside where the belly must have been pecked at by a hawk as well as the maggots. Barry dragged the carcass by its feet across to the hole and shovelled the dirt back on top, gradually smothering the stench.

He gave Moira a leg up onto Storm. Remounted, they continued along the track. Moira was grateful Barry was a man of few words, she didn't want to discuss what they'd just done, and she hoped she'd never have to do it again.

Over to their left a stand of native bush grew, like a green oasis in the middle of a desert. The dogs took off again, their barks echoing off the hillside. Moira hoped they were merely drawn to the shady copse of trees as an opportunity to cool down but when the horses started to get jittery, she knew it would never be that simple. The ground in front of the trees had been gouged out as if someone had overturned the dirt to weed but abandoned the task without finishing.

"Pig rooting." Barry reached back, withdrew his shotgun from its pouch, grabbed some ammunition and loaded the gun. "Wild boar," he explained, raising the gun, and whistling the dogs to chase the pig out.

Moira wanted to calm Storm, to tell the horse it was okay, but she needed to be convinced first. She let the horse back off, happy to have thirty feet or more between them and the bush which was alive with dogs barking. A squeal pierced the air, followed by a dog's yelp before a boar ran between the spindly trunks of the manuka and kanuka trees with dogs nipping at its trotters. It was hard to imagine the high-pitched screech coming from such a fierce-looking animal. A squat black pig with vicious tusks jutting out either side of its long jaw, one covered in blood where it had ripped a dog, looked straight at Barry just long enough for him to pull the trigger. The bullet hit dead centre on the boar's forehead, and it dropped instantly to the ground.

"Get back," Barry yelled.

Moira pulled on her reins to get Storm to step back further only to realise the command was for the dogs which had rushed towards the dying beast. Barry jumped down from the horse, grabbed a knife from his belt and sliced through the pig's neck. Blood gushed from the wound, puddling beneath the boar.

Can't waste it. Moira didn't bother to ask what they needed the boar for. She was fast learning that everything in this remote land had a use, and nothing would be wasted.

"Dig a hole will ya." Barry rolled the boar onto its back, sliced down from the breast to the groin, pulled back the skin and yanked out the innards. "Bury these deep."

The gut and intestines sat like a wobbly jelly while Moira took Barry's spade and dug a hole. A blowfly buzzed passed her head, already drawn to the offal as if the gun shot was a signal to come prowling. The thought of more maggots added an urgency to her task. She chipped away at the hard ground, only managing a small spade full each time. By the time the hole was deep enough, perspiration dripped from her brow.

Barry kicked the offal into the hole. "Cover it up."

He disappeared into the bush with a tomahawk and reappeared a few moments later with two long branches hacked from a tree and delimbed. The boar was tied between the stakes which Barry then attached to the back of his saddle so when they remounted and continued to the sheep paddock the boar was dragged along behind Leo.

The sun was high in the sky by the time they reached the paddock where the sheep were grazing. Barry whistled and the dogs, including Molly, took off to the left, skirting around the mob of sheep, following their master's commands. Deep barks from a black and tan Huntaway got the sheep moving. Molly crouched and eyed up any sheep tempted to be stubborn, creeping forwards to nip at their hocks until they were moving with the flock.

Perhaps the day was going to run smoothly now, Moira hoped so; her hips ached each step of the horse and as the temperature rose so did the itchiness of her flea bites. Keeping her hands on the reins prevented her from scratching. If the sheep obeyed the dogs as they seemed to be, they could all be on their way home soon with little effort from her or Barry.

"Head around the fence line." Barry interrupted Moira's thoughts, indicating for her to follow the path the dogs had taken. "Round up the stragglers."

Reluctantly Moira followed the instruction, wincing with every step as she rocked from side to side. If her bottom wasn't bruised, then it must surely have blisters. She soon came across her first obstinate sheep. It stood, looked straight at her, and stomped its hoof. Moira urged Storm closer until he towered over the sheep but still the woolly animal held its ground, unafraid of the Clydesdale. Molly came to the rescue, circling around behind the sheep and darting in to bite its rear.

"Good girl, Molly." Moira encouraged the dog, wanting to ensure she'd stick close by.

It was a huge paddock, and it took a good half hour to ride the perimeter. By the time Moira made it back to Barry the flock of sheep was headed in the right direction, a chorus of bleats meandering across the paddock. The combination of Barry's whistles, the dogs' barks and the sheep baaing blended like a foreign language Moira had no hope of understanding.

Unable to contribute other than allowing Storm to amble along behind, Moira's thoughts wandered. If this was the effort required each day, she wasn't sure she was cut out for high country farming. There were far too many sheep to count, at least ten times as many as Bill's. They would all have to be drenched, dagged, and shorn. She felt exhausted just thinking about the workload.

When they finally made it back to the yards late in the afternoon, Moira sighed with relief. Weary to the bone, she was afraid her legs would give out beneath her as she dismounted. She stood, leaning against the horse for support, grateful for the small respite while Storm drank from a trough by the yards. If there hadn't been a green slime coating the walls of the concrete trough, Moira would have drunk from it as well.

"You take as long as you like, Storm," she murmured into the horse's side.

"Unsaddle the horses will ya." Barry had untied the boar from its makeshift trailer and hauled it onto his back, a front trotter in each hand over his shoulders. "Feed em in the paddock."

Moira groaned. Her rest was over. At least she was excused from processing the boar.

The saddle felt double the weight it had this morning. Moira stumbled backwards before she was able to hook it over the fence rail, grunting with the effort. The horses wandered back to the paddock on their own accord, and she followed them with a slab of hay wishing she too could retire for the day. *Forever.*

"Give us a hand." She heard Barry yell from a building she hadn't noticed before.

It was tucked away in the shade of some trees, as tall as a Ponga but smaller than Moira's hut and with an earth floor. Barry had a rope looped over a rafter and attached to either end of a steel hook through the pig's trotters. He couldn't manage to hold the carcass and pull the end of the rope at the same time.

"Hoist it up."

How did he ever manage on his own? Moira hoped to be eating the pork for tea, not having the beast hanging upside down, its lifeless eyes staring at her. Her arms ached from holding the reins all day, she had little strength to pull on the rope so leaned back and let her body weight raise the boar towards the rafters.

"Don't want bone taint. Should process this now." Barry scratched his head and glanced out the door. "Too late. Tomorrow'll do."

Moira would have clapped her hands if they weren't so sore. Delight brought a smile to her face, her working day was done. Moira's stomach rumbled as they headed back to the cob cottage, she was ready for dinner.

"Stoke that fire," Barry ordered. "Get a rabbit cooking while we finish the other jobs."

Moira's shoulders slumped. *Other jobs! More rabbit for tea! Surely, he couldn't expect more from her!*

More work was exactly what Barry expected. When the fire was generating a steady heat for the pot suspended above it, Barry and Moira headed back outside.

"Need to get the woolshed ready," he said.

The wooden building attached to the sheepyards had seen better days, its horizontal plank walls looked as weatherbeaten as Barry, buckling where the nails had popped and in need of a paint. They climbed the stairs and went inside where cobweb-covered windows filtered the last of the day's sunlight. Their presence stirred the sheep in the holding paddock and pens and a cacophony of bleats echoed off the woolshed's corrugated iron roof. The slatted floor had been worn smooth, season after season, the trampling of hooves rounded the corners of the slats and the lanoline from the sheep's wool coated the timber. Instead of the gaps Moira expected to see between the slats, discarded wool, excrement and dirt had been left to build up, as if awaiting her arrival.

"Ya can clear out underneath." Barry pointed to the area beneath the slats.

Moira eyed the rusty blade of a knife stabbed into one of the timber dwangs. It took all her determination to resist the urge to slice Barry's finger off so he couldn't point to any more horrid jobs.

"Make a pile," came Barry's next instruction.

"No waste, right." Moira's voice reeked with sarcasm.

Barry nodded, oblivious to her tone. "Good fertiliser."

The same spade that had earlier buried dead sheep and pig offal, was now being used to clear out years of accumulated muck. Unable to get between the ground and the floor, Moira was down on her hands and knees, chipping away at the side of the pile where a gate should have led to a covered pen.

The only good thing was that she didn't have to sit on her bottom, it was too sore already. She tucked an errant strand of hair behind her ears and shook her head. How on earth was she going to move the pile before the shearers arrived, or even enough to allow a gap so the debris from this year's shear could fall between the slats?

Slowly, inch by inch, the pile beside the woolshed grew as Moira edged her way under the floor. Dust caked her face, clinging to the sweat that dripped from every pore. She wheezed and sneezed, breathing and swallowing dust particles that danced in the fading light. Whenever she dislodged a chunk, she squeezed her eyes shut until the dust motes settled but still, she felt a layer of grit each time she blinked.

Hidden beneath the floor, Moira didn't notice when the sun finally dipped down behind the hills.

"That'll do for now," Barry called out as the last rays of sunlight were extinguished. "Tea's cooked."

Moira crawled out from under the woolshed, wincing each time the blisters on her hands touched the ground. She was ravenous, even rabbit stew now sounded tasty, such was her appetite after the physical exertion of the day but first she needed a wash. Thoughts of soaking her aching muscles in a hot bubble bath were soon quashed by the reality of where she was and the knowledge that she had no energy left to lug buckets of hot water to fill the tub.

She settled for a cold shower, watching as the water running down her body gradually cleared from brown to translucent, lost in thoughts of how long she could sustain the effort required to be a high- country farmer.

CHAPTER
15

A loud clang dragged Moira from a slumber that had been plagued with nightmares filled with dead animal heads staring with vacant eyes, innards circled by buzzing blowflies, and squirming with maggots.

The noise reminded her of a church bell summoning its congregation to the weekly service, but she remembered where she was and knew it wasn't possible. The sound of water hitting steel followed and her mind's eye tried to discern its source. *A bath!* Moira jumped down from the top bunk energised by the thought of a long hot soak.

Still in her nightgown, she ventured into the cool morning air and poked her head around the corner of her hut. Barry had pulled the bathtub out and was using water from the shower to give it a clean. Moira averted her eyes in case he'd undressed already. She might have joined the land girls to meet men and have some fun but seeing Barry naked in the bath was an image she'd rather not endure.

"Give us a hand, will ya," Barry yelled out.

Moira's head jerked back. He must have heard her hut's squeaky door. Surely, he didn't expect her to help him bathe. He certainly needed a bath. His body odour said it had been a while since the last one, but he was a grown man, he could wash himself.

The idea of a soak lost its attractiveness.

"I'll just get dressed," she replied, ducking back into the hut to change into her farm clothes.

"Gotta scald the pig," Barry explained when she arrived clad in her overalls.

What was worse? A dead pig in the bath or a naked Barry. Moira considered them on a par. She tentatively approached, unsure exactly what scalding a pig involved.

"Ya haven't done that before, have ya?"

Moira shook her head. It wasn't one of the questions the placement officer asked so at least she hadn't lied about her skill set.

"Light the fire." Barry tossed a box of matches to Moira and pointed to a heap of leaves and twigs piled on a clear patch of dirt beneath a tree.

She glanced at the overhanging branches, wondering if the instruction was a wise move. Assuming Barry knew what he was doing, she struck a match to the tinder. They lifted a metal frame over the burgeoning flames and then added larger pieces of wood until the fire was well alight.

The frame had been made so the bath was suspended over the fire and the water they bucketed into the tub heated up.

"We'll eat breakfast while the water heats up."

"Do we need it boiling?" Moira hoped to sound intelligent.

Barry shook his head. "Scalding, not boiling."

Moira was none the wiser but guessed she'd find out soon enough, more important now was food. Working dawn to dusk, she was starving. She rubbed her belly, silently promising to fill it and followed Barry to the cottage.

The acrid aroma of fried liver wafting from the open door stopped in her tracks. She doubled over, dry retching.

"Ya sick?" There was no caring tone to Barry's inquiry as if he worried about her wellbeing, rather the inconvenience of her being unfit for work.

"Just my stomach adjusting to a high-country diet." There was no sympathy to be gained by being a helpless female. She breathed through her mouth and rubbed her stomach again, this time to soothe the queasiness.

Barry frowned at the plate of lambs-fry, bacon, and potatoes he dished up for Moira.

"Good tucker."

"Don't worry, I won't waste it." Moira picked up her fork and began eating. She needed all the sustenance she could get.

The food was eaten, plates scraped clean, and they downed a tepid cup of tea. Moira held her breath as they left the cottage. The lukewarm liquid combined with the stodginess of the lambs-fry and potato exacerbated rather than abated her queasiness, but she was determined not to be sick.

"Grab the pig."

They headed to the building where the pig had been stowed overnight, unwrapped the muslin cover keeping any bugs at bay and lowered the carcass from the rafters onto Barry's back. It was still attached to the hook and rope, which was all Moira had to carry back to the bath of steaming water. It took a couple of throws until she had the rope dangling from the branch overhanging the bath. The rope cut into her blisters as Barry stepped out from under the carcass and they lowered it into the water.

A few minutes later, Barry lifted the pig from the water and grabbed at the bristles on its back. They came away in his hand.

"It's ready." He handed Moira a tool that resembled a plunger to clear drains except the bell shape was metal and not rubber. "Scrape the pig."

Stumped as to how one scraped a pig with a metal plunger, Moira watched Barry run the bell over the pig's hide and the bristles peel off, before mirroring his actions. The boar didn't look nearly so fierce in its nakedness and the bath, with a layer of black bristles floating like flotsam, was the last place Moira wanted to relax.

They carried the clean carcass back to the shed and suspended it from the rafter.

"Salt the pig?"

Moira assumed Barry's raised eyebrows meant it was a question not an order. She shrugged her shoulders.

"Didn't think so. What'd they teach ya land girls?" Barry grunted his disappointment. "I'll salt the pig. Ya finish the woolshed."

It felt like punishment. Moira wanted to pretend she hadn't understood the instructions, find an easier job to do or just disappear over the back of the farm and rest in the shade of a tree but she knew there was no one else foolish enough to agree to be a land girl in these conditions, the job had to be done and she was the only one here to do it.

She looked down at her blistered hands and chipped nails, almost laughing at the long-lost manicure she'd left Christchurch with earlier in the year. Digging at the buildup under the woolshed floor couldn't ruin them anymore. It was probably better than salt stinging her wounds.

The thump of a yellow and red tin landing on a chopping block brought Moira's thoughts back to the present. The tin had seen better days, but she knew from its distinctive colours and logo that it was Rawleighs' Salve.

"Put this on ya hands," Barry suggested.

Moira gasped and looked wide-eyed at the shaggy man that had become her employer. *He did care.* He'd already busied himself sharpening knives on a steel, so she took her time rubbing the salve into her hands, gently coating the blisters with a protective layer.

⌘

For the next fortnight, Moira's routine involved moving the sheep in the morning, each day to a paddock closer to the yards and cleaning the woolshed in the afternoons, spreading the accumulated muck over the paddocks as fertiliser. She could finally see the end of the task; the relief renewed her energy as she disappeared beneath the slatting of the woolshed floor for the last time.

Melodic singing drew her out some hours later. She wondered if delirium had set in. It was as if a choir of angels had come to rescue her. She couldn't recognise the song, the words formed in a foreign language flowed together with an eloquence she longed to mimic.

Her throat was parched, coated with a veneer of dust she'd inhaled. She struggled to straighten, imagining she'd be permanently bent at ninety degrees. She'd heard people say farming was back breaking work, she'd never believed it would relate to her literally.

A rusty truck came over the brow of the hill, the same track by which Barry and Moira had arrived, the only way into and out of Moira's new dilemma. *Out of the frying pan and into the fire.* That's what she'd done, left the nastiness of Anne to come to the end of the earth, perhaps the end of her, she was expected to work so hard.

Peering into the sunlight, the truck looked driverless, a darkness pierced by hovering white lights. Moira rubbed her eyes. Was she seeing things? Had she already died and gone to heaven? She poked her finger into her ribs. Ouch! No! The vision was real.

When the truck pulled up beside the woolshed and half a dozen Maori jumped down from the back, she laughed at her mistake. Three more Maori filled the cab, cheerful white smiles amidst dark wiry hair, and skin the colour of chocolate, their language native not foreign. They weren't angels but perhaps the shearers would provide an escape route. She'd have to get friendly with them and see where they were heading next.

"*Kia ora*." The driver of the truck appeared to be in charge. "*Kei konei* a Barry?"

Moira heard Barry's name and pointed like a mute to the cob cottage.

"She look like red-headed Waikato *wahine*." An older woman spoke, her thick grizzled hair woven in a plait hung down over her breast. "But she no speak *te reo*."

The women's dark eyes looked straight through Moira as if she was seeing into her very core, judging her essence. A shiver ran down Moira's spine.

The group shrieked with laughter and Moira realised her skin, caked in dirt, was coloured as if she too was Maori. She hurried to the trough to wash her face and arms, removing the source of their amusement.

"*Kia ora*, Tama." Barry and the truck driver clasped hands, leaned in, and touched foreheads and noses.

Moira blinked and shook her head slowly, disbelieving. She'd heard of a *hongi*, the traditional greeting but she'd never witnessed it, never thought Barry would engage in such a reverent moment. How was she going to get the shearers to help her leave when the mutual respect was evident?

"Cup of tea?" Barry and Tama headed off to the cottage chatting away like long-lost friends who had a year of catching up to do.

Envious of their relaxed demeanour, Moira walked off. Her work under the woolshed was finished and with Barry preoccupied she had a moment to catch her breath before she was assigned her next job. She found a shady spot under a walnut tree, sat down amongst its ancient roots. Like the tree she was an import, out of place, but unlike the tree Moira had no intention of staying forever. She contemplated what the arrival of the shearing gang would mean for her.

Moira had never had much to do with Maori before. There were only ever one or two students at her school. This group looked like an entire family: mum and dad and six children. Perhaps the older woman's look was merely a mother assessing a threat to her offspring. They seemed to know the routine. They gathered their equipment from the back of the truck and headed off to a flat area to set up camp. Moira noted with delight that four young strapping men made up the shearing gang with a couple of women, most likely the rousies who would sort the fleeces the men shore, rounding out the team. She looked skyward and smiled, silently thanking whichever power delivered her desire to her doorstep, just when she'd been thinking she was missing out on all the young men.

Black shorts and woollen singlets appeared to be the uniform for shearers and these men filled them out well. Moira admired their flexing biceps and taut thigh muscles as they pitched tents, gathered stones to set up a fire pit and erected a slab of timber as a makeshift table, all to the rhythm of song.

Every so often one of the men glanced her way and smiled. His black hair was cut short, dark eyebrows framed equally dark eyes. He looked serious, as if he kept his mischievous nature under wraps. Moira imagined his dark skin against her, like ebony and ivory on a piano, side by side but never completely joined, creating a delightful harmony. She hoped he spoke English, she wanted to talk to him, to discover what it took to ignite the humour in his eyes.

Barry and Tama emerged from the cottage jovial and affable, shaking hands as if a mutually beneficial deal had been sealed.

"Moira!" Barry's summons was loud and clear, her rest was over. "Fetch a horse, release the dogs, get the sheep into the yards."

Walking off to the horse paddock, Moira sensed she was being watched and glanced back. The young Maori man smiled and winked at her. The fatigue she'd been feeling, fell away. She had a skip to her step, knowing there was fun to be had. She just had to get through the rest of the chores and not do anything to make herself look silly.

"Right, Storm," she murmured to the horse. "Help me out, will you? I promise to reward you some extra hay if we impress that handsome man over there."

Storm neighed and lowered his head to receive the bridle. Moira drew confidence from the horse's movement, as if they were a team working together on a mission. She tried to look casual as she walked the horse back to the yards, like she was an experienced shepherdess, not an inexperienced land girl with blisters on her behind.

The shearers had moved indoors to set up their equipment in the woolshed. Disappointed she had no audience, Moira released the dogs and opted to ride bareback rather than bother with the saddle she didn't know how to correctly harness.

At the paddock, there was little for her to do. Thankfully the dogs knew the routine, once the gate was opened, they circled the flock and funnelled it towards the exit. The resulting cacophony of barks and baas wasn't nearly as harmonious as the Maori song, but it was getting the job done. Moira sat atop Storm, pride straightened her spine, all thoughts of leaving the high-country station suspended.

The dogs ensured the flock kept to the track. Once the lead sheep had been herded into the yards the rest followed. Moira dismounted and chased the stragglers in, waving her arms and yelling until she could push the gate closed. A black and tan heading dog ran across the carpet of wool formed by the backs of the sheep packed into the yards. The dog leapt over the gate to scoot off for a drink from the trough. Moira licked her lips; she wouldn't mind a drink. Perhaps this would be her last job for the day.

The shearers were sitting on the steps to the woolshed sharpening the blades of their clippers. It dawned on Moira that without power, all the sheep had to be shorn by hand. She'd been hoping she'd get to help them, a means of getting closer to the handsome one but it was probably better she stayed far away.

"Here, load these up." Barry interrupted Moira's thoughts and handed her a hessian sack.

Surprised by its weight, she let it drop to the ground. "What is it?" she asked dubiously, expecting some disgusting offal.

"Carrots," Barry replied. "Take 'em to the rabbit paddock. Drop them in the trench. One every couple of feet."

"More food for the rabbits." She peered into the sack, nodded and sighed. More dead rabbits meant more skinning of hides.

"Poison! Don't eat them. They're injected with strychnine. Wear these." Barry chucked a pair of crusty leather gloves at Moira.

"How will I know if I've been poisoned?" she asked.

"Spasms from a little. Death from too much."

Moira gulped. "Is there an antidote?"

"Nope," Barry replied with his usual matter-of-factness. "Don't get poisoned in the first place."

A feeling of dread seized Moira, she hurriedly shoved her hands into the gloves, tied the top of the sack with baling twine and lugged it towards Storm.

"Let me help you with that." The handsome shearer appeared at her side, lifted the sack as if it were a feather and hitched the twine to Storm's saddle.

"It's poison. Be careful," she warned as her limbs melted with a tingling warmth. Had she already been poisoned or was it the man's presence? "Thank you ...." She placed her hand on his forearm, felt his strength but at the same time sensed a gentleness. "I'm Moira," she said, wanting but not daring to lean in for a hongi.

"Matiu," he replied with a smile.

Time seemed to hang in the air between them, an awkwardness neither appeared certain how to overcome.

"The rabbits won't poison themselves," Barry yelled out.

"Doesn't Barry have a rabbiteer?" Matiu asked. "There's an old fella usually does the rounds, takes the skins as payment."

"I'm it, apparently. Barry trades the skins with the hawker." Moira unhitched Storm's reins from the fence rail. "I'd better be off."

"I'll give you a leg up." Matiu bent with his fingers entwined to make a stirrup for her foot.

She felt guilty putting her dirty boot onto his bare hands as he lifted her with ease up onto the horse.

"See you later." Matiu stepped back out of the way.

Moira certainly hoped to see him later.

⌘

Reaching the rabbit paddock, Moira was still unsure how she'd manage the task assigned to her. She couldn't drop the carrots from the great height of Storm's back, and neither could she lug the sack around the paddock herself. When she reached the trench, she opted to dismount, walk alongside Storm, grabbing a handful of carrots at a time, careful not to let them touch her bare skin.

She paused to rest when she reached the corner of the paddock, looking back with a smidgeon of pride at the line of orange running parallel to the fence. A bead of sweat ran down her forehead. She had to stop herself from wiping

191

it away, worried that any poison on the gloves would get on her skin.

Storm bent his head down and sniffed at the overturned earth. There was no grass for him to eat and he nibbled at the closest carrot, the last one Moira had dropped.

"Oh no you don't." Moira gasped and yanked on Storm's reins, pulling the horse's head away from the carrot. "Are you trying to get us both killed?"

Moira imagined Barry's reaction if his precious horse died of strychnine poisoning. It didn't take much of the poison to kill a rabbit, how much would it take to affect a horse? Fear mixed with panic. She pushed her fingers between Storm's lips. Was it safe to prize a horse's jaw open? Would she get bitten? Would she poison the horse by doing so? The horse's teeth, stained with green, had no traces of orange.

"Either you didn't eat one or you've swallowed it whole." Moira resigned herself to a game of wait and see and continued around the paddock. "No more, do you hear me?"

RROR

CHAPTER
16

"Do we not all eat together?" Moira asked.

She and Barry were in the cottage dining, yet again, on rabbit stew. She could hear the banter of the shearers and wanted to join in on their laughter and seemingly carefree conversation.

"They're Maori," was all Barry offered as a reason.

It was always when she wanted to know so much that Barry chose to say very little. What did he mean? His greeting with Tama indicated there was a mutual respect. Was that only because Barry knew he needed the shearers to do work for him? Was he like Frank and American soldiers, seeing them as lesser than himself? If no one was going to give Moira answers, she'd have to get them herself. She hurried through her meal, eager to discover all she could about the people with skin a hundred shades darker than hers.

By the time Moira made it back outside, the shearers had settled around a fire, Tama was strumming a guitar and singing quietly. The young women held *poi*, intricately decorated in traditional designs in red, white and black; their graceful wrist actions had the *poi* dancing to the rhythm of the music. Matiu was sitting on a log, a half-fill bottle of beer in his hand and a smile on his face, while his bare foot moved with the beat. He looked up, his smile widening as he saw Moira and motioned for her to join them, patting the log beside him.

Never one to turn down an invitation from a handsome man, Moira joined the group and sat next to Matiu, grateful for a hollow in the log that meant his long limbs touched hers.

He took a swig of beer then offered the bottle to her. "You want a drink?"

Why not? The glass bottle was cold and the beer equally so. Moira copied Matiu and gulped down the liquid like it was a golden elixir, burping loudly as she handed the bottle back.

"Oops!" She giggled, the beer having an immediate effect. "How do you get it so cold?"

"Trough." Matiu pointed to a nearby water trough where several crates of beer were submerged. "Gotta have a cold beer after a hard day working."

"Matiu, *ko wai tenei*?" The older woman waved her hand towards Moira and studied her face.

Moira flinched as if she'd been touched, an uncomfortable feeling that she was being judged.

"Moira." Matiu's reply confirmed she was the subject of the conversation, but his easy tone bolstered her confidence.

"What's she saying?" She nudged Matiu and murmured.

"She, Anihera, was just asking your name."

Moira relaxed slightly, smiled, and nodded. "Hello, Anihera, nice to meet you."

"*Kua hapu ia.*" Anihera's face remained unreadable with no smile softening the curve of her mouth or the corners of her eyes.

Moira felt Matiu tense beside her. She cocked her head to one side and arched her eyebrows. "What did she say now?"

She wished the log was further away, that she could put a distance between herself and the knowing eyes that kept staring at her. She could just leave them to it, go to bed, it was likely to be another big day tomorrow.

She grabbed the bottle back from Matiu, she needed courage to ready herself for his answer. He leaned in and whispered as if it was a secret not to be shared.

"She thinks you're pregnant."

Moira's spine went rigid, and her eyes went wide. She shook her head in denial. *The old women didn't know what she was talking about.*

"She has a wisdom," Matiu continued. "She can see things, others can't."

Moira thought back over the past few months. An image of Bill and her came to mind but that had been before the shooting, and she was certain she'd had a period since then.

"Well, she's got it wrong this time." Moira continued shaking her head. "There aren't any babies in my life plan. I just want to have some fun."

One of the other young men roared with laughter. "Matiu's your man for fun. Just a big kid at heart."

Matiu wrapped his arm around Moira's shoulder and pulled her into his side. "Ignore Nikau. He's just jealous. Ari here," Matiu waved his hand towards one of the young women. "Ari is Nikau's beautiful wife who would string him up by his earlobe if he was to flirt with another woman."

Ari smiled, her *poi* continuing their dance. "*Kia ora*, Moira, nice to meet you."

"*Kia ora*, means hello," Matiu added.

"*Kia ora*, Ari, Nikau." Moira tried to emulate their pronunciation.

Matiu drank the last of the beer before introducing the others.

"Now that you know everyone," he stood and reached out to take Moira's hand, "how about we go for a walk? Leave them all to it."

Moira weighed up her options, it would be fun staying with the group, learning some more Maori, but a walk with Matiu held an unknown her curiosity and playfulness couldn't resist. The mischief she saw in Matiu's eyes, confirmed taking his hand, trusting him to lead her away was a good choice.

"You're like one big family," Moira observed as they walked off, hand in hand. "Are Tama and Anihera your parents?"

Perhaps Anihera's prediction was more of a warning to stay away from her son. Another woman like Anne trying to save a man from Moira.

Matiu laughed. "No, but you'd think so sometimes. We're just a gang for the shearing season then we go our own ways."

"How long are you here for?" Moira asked.

They passed the sheep in the yards, all quiet except for the odd bleat.

"A few days, by the look of that lot." Matiu's strong fingers, capable of crushing, gently entwined with hers, woven together like the fibres in the *poi*. "What about you? Wasn't expecting to find a beautiful woman like you in this remote spot."

"I wasn't expecting to find myself in the back of beyond." Moira laughed at herself. "There only seems to be one road in and one road out, and not many travelling it. Where will you go when you leave here?"

"Next farm over, I guess. Tama and Anihera organise all of that. I just go where I'm told."

Moira sighed. "Well, you're not going to be any help getting me out of here then, are you?"

"No, sorry." Matiu stopped on the brow of the hill and turned towards Moira, pulling her into his chest. "But I can make sure you have a good time while I'm here."

His finger tipped her chin up and he lowered his mouth to hers. The invitation was enticing, and Moira accepted with pleasure. There was no language barrier to be bridged, no cultural divide to cross, a simple melding of man and woman, a blending of their desires.

In the distance, a morepork hooted and the wind whistled down the valley.

⌘

Moira woke alone. Anihera's prediction still had no chance of being right. Not because there had been no desire to take things further but sitting on the brow of the hill, snuggled into Matiu's side, the after-effects of the beer had eased her to sleep. She'd woken cradled in his arms at the door of her hut, where Matiu, like the perfect gentleman, kissed her forehead, lowered her to stand on the steps while he opened the door and sent her to bed.

She made a mental note to forgo the beer tonight if the opportunity to spend more time with Matiu arose. Meanwhile, the noises of another day of work were urging her to get up and dressed.

"Take a sack. Skin the rabbits. Bury the carcass." Barry gave the order for the day's work while they ate their breakfast.

He was oblivious to the slump of Moira's shoulders. She was hoping to spend time in the woolshed helping the women sort the wool, welcoming the soothing feel of lanolin on her hands. There was no point complaining though so off she went.

Walking down the track, it looked as if the rabbits had outwitted them, the paddock was a myriad of browns, the dirt of the bare ground speckled with the taupe of rabbit pelts. But where Moira had expected the blotches to move, there was stillness, when she expected to hear the collective rabbit squeak there was an eerie silence.

She hesitated in the gate. Gulped down the lump that choked her.

"They're only rabbits," she told herself, attempting to assuage the sick feeling deep in her gut.

One sack wouldn't be enough. Ten sacks probably wouldn't be sufficient. The paddock was littered with dead rabbits, their beady vacant eyes stared accusingly at her. Yes, she was their murderer and now she had to deal with the consequences.

Again, she wondered, where was Barry? Why was she being expected to do this alone? He was off-loading all the horrible jobs to her. It confirmed she had to leave, she had to find a way to get a message out. Someone needed to rescue her.

Moira started at the gate, picked up her first rabbit, turning its head away as she poked the blade of her knife into its chest and sliced from top to bottom. She gagged as she pulled out the innards and chucked it into the trench. Wanting the task over and done with as soon as possible, she concentrated on the method Barry had shown her, cutting off feet, decapitating and stripping the skin free until she held a limp pelt in one hand and a naked carcass in the other. The stench was horrific, she stretched her head skywards straining for fresh clean air.

Disgusted at the sight and disgusted at herself, she chucked the carcass into the trench, kicked at the dirt to bury it, and lay the pelt on the sack. Rabbit by rabbit she worked her way around the paddock. The only one monitoring her progress was a hawk that hovered overhead, gliding on the updrafts, awaiting the opportunity to dive in for a tasty morsel.

"Bugger off," she yelled at the bird. "Go do your own dirty work."

As the morning wore on so did the monotony of the task. Moira tried to keep a tally but lost count around fifty-one, or was it sixty-one? The pile of pelts was like the leaning tower of Pisa Moira remembered from her geography textbook at high school. It buzzed with flies instead of tourists. Not wanting the stack to topple into the dirt and ruin her hard work, she packed them into a sack and trekked back up the hill.

The woolshed doors were wide open, affording Moira a perfect view of Matiu on the shearing stand. His brow was beaded with perspiration, his muscular body bulged and flexed, the tendons in his arms, taut beneath his dark skin, pulsed as he deftly clipped at a sheep's fleece.

"Ya finished those rabbits?" It was Barry bringing her back to reality.

"No!" Moira snapped. "One sack wasn't enough."

"Good kill, eh!" He was oblivious to the sarcasm in her voice. "Better get those pelts on the fence and get back to it then."

Moira gritted her teeth, stifling the abuse she wanted to hurl at Barry. Tears threatened instead but she wouldn't give into them. She unhooked dry pelts from the fence wires and stretched the new ones out in their place.

⌘

Late in the afternoon, Moira was still at the task, her hands covered in dry blood, her fingers aching like an aged arthritic woman's. Over the course of the afternoon she'd thrown a tantrum, kicked a dead rabbit as far away as her blistered foot could manage, and screamed at the clouds scurrying across the sky as if they feared bearing her wrath. At one point, she simply lay on the hard ground and wept. All of it got her nowhere, except delaying her finish.

The actions of gutting and skinning a rabbit became second nature, Moira's robotic hands could do it without concentration nor care. Her thoughts wandered and Anihera's words filled her head with fears and doubts. Did the woman think she was already pregnant or was she predicting the future? Surely, she was wrong on both counts, but what if she wasn't? A baby. They were things other people had. People like Alice, happily married to Fergus, and most likely Betsy, now she could admit her true feelings for William and act on them. But not Moira. She couldn't be a parent. She'd most likely repeat the same mistakes as her mother and father and look what that did to a child. No, Moira wasn't going to be held responsible for that.

She tried to remember the timing of her last monthly. She couldn't. How long had she been here in this high-country hell? Days were rushing by in a blur, but she was certain she wasn't overdue.

'There's something special about you, Moira. I know it.'
Frank's words in his American accent were as clear as if
he was standing directly in front of her. She shook her
head. She'd forgotten about Frank and more importantly,
she'd forgotten all about their brief interlude beside the
river. He'd used protection though, hadn't he? Moira froze,
pinned to the point where her life may have changed
forever and not in the good way she'd thought. What if?
What if Chad's interruption had messed up more than their
romantic picnic?

"Don't be stupid," she admonished herself. "What can an
old grey-haired woman possibly know that you don't know
yourself."

⌘

The line of rabbit pelts spanned both sides of the fence
the length of the paddock. If Moira hadn't been exhausted,
she would have taken some delight in the sense of
achievement the line-up wanted to convey. Instead, she
trudged back to her hut, pushed her suitcase to the side and
lay down next to it on the bottom bunk, fully clothed,
gumboots and all. The stench of rabbit permeated her
clothes, seeped into her pores, and clung to her hair but she
had no energy left to care. She slowed her inhales and
elongated her exhales signalling to her muscles they could
finally unfurl and relax. Inch by inch, one vertebra at a
time, her back gradually straightened. Her heavy eyelids
closed, the weight of the day too much. In the fading light,
the noise of the dogs hurrying the last of the sheep to be
shorn into the shed wasn't enough to keep her awake.

The chill of the evening air woke her several hours later, the door of her hut still wide open. Molly wandered in and licked Moira's face.

"Hello, Molly." She ruffled the dog's ears. "Yes, unfortunately, I'm still here."

She swung her legs off the side of the bed and sat up, careful not to hit her head on the top bunk.

"Sounds like they're having a good time out there." Singing, laughter and animated conversation told Moira shearing had finished for the day. "We should go join them but no beer for you, okay?"

Molly wagged her tail and wandered off. Moira washed her hands and face before heading over to the group. Flames from the fire cast an orange glow over the shearers' faces, their broad smiles giving no indication they'd slogged away shearing all day.

"Hi, Moira. Come join us." Matiu waved her over.

"You look like you've had a good day," she observed.

"What about you! Look at all those pelts."

Matiu's obvious admiration made Moira blush, not something she'd normally do. She'd just blame the heat of the fire if anyone noticed.

"Yeah," Ari added. "You've nearly skinned as many rabbits as Matiu has shorn sheep."

Everyone laughed, Moira included. It was nice to be a part of their conviviality.

"Did you want a beer?" Matiu offered his bottle. "You've definitely earned it."

"No, thanks." Moira smiled suggestively at Matiu. "I'd like to stay awake tonight and not miss out on anything."

"Would you like to learn the *poi*?" Ari offered the cords of her *poi* to Moira.

Matiu nodded his encouragement.

"I hope it's as easy as you make it look." Moira tried to get the *poi* to spin in a circle.

"It's all in the wrist, just turn them like this."

Moira copied Ari's actions and soon had the *poi* spinning.

"That's it," Ari encouraged. "Now move your arms up and down and keep spinning."

The *poi* had a mind of their own. One went clockwise, the other anti-clockwise. Moira lost all co-ordination and gave up in a fit of laughter when one of them hit her square in the forehead. Luckily, they were soft.

"Perhaps you'd be better learning some *te reo*," Tama suggested.

"Yes, yes, please, I'd like that." Moira clapped her hands together with delight.

"Repeat after me," Nikau suggested, grinning broadly. "*Haere ke te Reinga e nga kuri paru.*"

Moira repeated the words out loud as best she could, and then silently in her head to commit them to memory. "What does that mean?" she asked.

"It's what you should say every morning when you get to the woolshed." Nikau slapped his knee and roared with laughter.

"Nikau!" Ari swatted at her husband.

"What does it mean? Matiu, tell me what he made me say."

Matiu shrugged his shoulders and laughed. "Go to hell, you dirty dogs."

"*Haere ke te Reinga e nga kuri paru.*" Moira pretended to be hurt for a couple of seconds then burst into laughter with the rest of the group.

CHAPTER
17

The embers of the fire glowed a vibrant orange by the time Tama put his guitar away in its case, and said goodnight, reminding the shearers there was another big day tomorrow. It had been easy to blend with the group, except for Anihera, but Moira ignored the woman who sat plaiting strands of harakeke into a fibre rope.

Soon the others retreated to their tents and Moira and Matiu were left alone, basking in the warmth of the fire and each other. Matiu wasted no time in making his intentions obvious when he pulled Moira onto his lap, the centre of his desire pressing into her side. He kissed her neck, the tip of his tongue flicking like the flames of the fire, adding to the heat burgeoning inside her. She'd never imagined a man with the strength of a warrior could treat her like she was a delicate flower. It was tantalising but she wanted more, she needed to feel his power, draw from the energy he exuded. She released herself from his hold, stood momentarily, just long enough to turn, face and straddle Matiu. His hardness was now right where she wanted it, albeit with several layers of clothing affording protection so Anihera's prediction remained unfulfilled.

Matiu groaned, a deep rumble of rapture. His mouth claimed hers, silently voicing that the moment couldn't be allowed to end.

"Your hut or my tent?" he murmured.

The tents were closer, their needs would be satisfied sooner but they were too close to each other. Moira didn't want to be heard by anyone other than Matiu. She wanted nothing to ruin the moment.

"How about we shower?" she suggested, remembering the smell of death was still on her skin.

Matiu wrapped his arms around her and stood in one fluid movement, the might of his muscled legs lifting them from the log.

"We normally bathe in the river, but a shower sounds good," Matiu said. "Whatever I have to do to see you naked."

Moira rested her head on his chest, listening to the thrum of his heartbeat, as he carried her to the area under the tree. The wind whistled up the valley, whorled up the hillside and crested the brow of the hill with a velocity that threatened to blow Moira over when Matiu set her on her feet. She imagined Anihera had sent the gods to scare her off. Matui clearly wasn't hearing any message, and they quickly discarded their clothes.

"Brrr," Moira shivered, goosebumps prickling her skin. "Perhaps this isn't such a good idea. There's no fire to heat the water."

"You're so hot." Matiu turned the tap to on. "That's all I need."

The pipes creaked, an eerie screech that pierced the night.

"Ssh!" Moira raised a finger to her lips. "It'll wake everyone up."

She glanced back to the cluster of buildings and tents where the others were hopefully asleep. The only movements were tree branches bending in the wind.

"I think the water's frozen in the pipes." Matiu bent to gather up their clothes. "Quick, we'd better get to your hut before you freeze."

They must have disturbed Molly. She followed them to the hut, tried to sneak inside as Moira closed the door.

"Oh, no you don't, Molly." Moira patted the dog's head. "There's only room for two in here."

While wild winds raged outside, behind the closed door of Moira's hut the couple created their own heat, a desire finally sated.

"You do have protection, don't you?" was the last question Moira asked before she surrendered to the strength of the warrior on his mission to rescue her.

⌘

Moira wondered if it was nothing more than a beautiful dream when, once again, she woke alone. The storm had passed, the morning's chorus was loud and clear, not just birds but men whistling, dogs barking, and sheep bleating, all backed by the harmony of female voices chanting in their native tongue. She glanced at the clock; it was after eight. She'd slept in. *Never mind.* She felt carefree and content.

Matiu's aroma still filled the room. Memories of his touch, his hands on her body, his mouth devouring hers, the feel of skin against skin. Moira purred like a cat who'd had its belly rubbed and stretched and yawned.

"Wake up, sleepyhead." Barry's rap on the door interrupted her dreamy state. "Ya needed at the woolshed."

She felt like a mischievous toddler. Perhaps she could pretend she wasn't in the hut; Barry might think she'd already gone down the farm to work. She froze, lifted the sheet up over her head to muffle the giggle that escaped. Of course, he'd never imagine her capable of that.

The woolshed. It slowly dawned on Moira that Matiu would be at the woolshed. Barry's instructions were finally something she'd follow with pleasure.

"Coming," she called out as she pulled the bedding away from her naked body.

Skipping breakfast, she arrived at the woolshed a few minutes later to find Ari had come down with a stomach bug and was unable to work. Moira was to be a rousie for the day. With four shearers, the two rousies split the workload in two, each clearing, sorting, and folding the fleeces created by two of the shearers. Moira grinned from ear to ear when she saw she'd been assigned to Matiu and Nikau.

Tama operated the wool press, compressing the fleeces to fit as many as possible into the woolsacks which Anihera stitched and stamped with the brand for Barry's station to ensure he received the proceeds when the bales went to auction.

They stopped for morning tea, drinking from a communal billy.

"Would you like some *rewena paora*?" Matiu asked.

It just looked like bread in the flax basket Matiu held out to her.

"Potato bread." Matiu must have seen the confused look on her face. "It's traditional bread that Anihera cooks on the hot rocks."

Moira took a slice and ate greedily. The bread had been lathered with a generous dollop of jam and the sweet taste of blackberries, contrasted with the sourdough, and satisfied her hunger perfectly.

She wanted to talk to Matiu, to have some private time to be sure in the reality of a new day he'd enjoyed their night of pleasure, but everyone stayed close, chatting away about their progress, the number of sheep left to shear, the quality of the fleeces, and life in general.

"I don't know if we'll be able to come back next year, Barry." Tama poured himself a second mug of tea.

"What!" Barry's forehead creased into a deep frown, his eyebrows joining into one.

"The lads are all joining up," Tama continued. "The Maori battalion is accepting them in droves, appealing to their warrior spirit."

Moira searched Matiu's face for any sign he was one of the new recruits. Not that it mattered, she hadn't considered a long-term relationship with him. She gulped, almost choking on a mouthful of tea. What if Anihera's prediction came true, Moira got pregnant and Matiu was the father? She knew they'd used protection but what if it failed? There were so many warnings that condoms weren't full proof but with the alternatives being marriage or abstinence Moira decided it was better to take the risk.

Lost in images the tea leaves formed on the bottom of her cup, Moira wondered whether a baby conceived from their joining would be born fair skinned or dark or a blending of the two. Matiu was handsome, a child with his genes would be attractive. *What? What are you even thinking about babies? They aren't in your plans. Don't be silly. Just have fun. Life with a baby can't be fun or your father would never have left.*

"The war should be over soon," Barry said.

That would solve all Moira's problems. No more land girls. She could leave the high country, move back to the city, find another job working in a shoe shop, an easy job that left her with plenty of energy to dance away her weekends.

"An end to the fighting would be good." Tama's voice indicated he didn't believe it to be true though. "Too many of our *whanau* have been killed, no *tangihanga* to return their spirit to the *marae*."

"We'd better finish shearing the sheep then." Nikau stood, chucked the dregs of his tea onto the ground, and walked off.

Tama should his head. "He wants to go. Thinks it'll be more exciting than this. If only he knew."

⌘

211

By afternoon teatime, enough of the sheep had been shorn, to reveal another problem. In the corner of the yards two sheep, trampled and suffocated by the flock jammed together, were now blown up, their bellies like inflated balloons, an infestation of buzzing flies already feasting on the remains.

"Better skin them." Barry looked directly at Moira, ensuring he had her attention. "Cut out the kidneys and livers for breakfast."

"But ..." Moira gagged before she could voice the rest of her protest. She turned away from the yards, certain that she'd lose the contents of her stomach.

Frustration turned to anger. If only it wasn't so late in the day, she had little energy left to go into battle with Barry. What use would it do anyway? He only seemed to trust her with dead animals. Did he think she was just a useless land girl? If only Bill hadn't been injured. He was the only man who treated her as if she were equal.

Moira found the knife she'd used to skin the rabbits and headed towards the dead sheep.

"Not now," Barry yelled. "After supper. Finish shearing first."

Moira's knuckles went white as she clenched the knife's handle. It took all her effort to restrain herself from pointing the blade at Barry. Instead, she stabbed it into the nearest post, exhaling through gritted teeth as she stomped back to the woolshed.

⌘

The clippers were oiled for the last time and laid to rest for the night. The end of another big day.

"How about we take the truck down to the river and go for a swim?" Matiu suggested. "Want to come with us Moira?"

Moira sighed with exhaustion. Flowing from the high country, the water in the river would be cold. It might be just what she needed to feel human again.

"That'd be great," she replied. "I don't think I could walk there but if a ride in the truck is on offer, count me in."

Back in her hut she changed into her bathers, grateful she'd packed them, and grabbed a towel. She heard the truck's engine roar into life and hurried to join the others as fast as her tired legs would allow. Matiu hoisted her up onto the tray of the truck and she sat between his legs, not caring what anyone thought of their familiarity.

"Isn't Ari coming for a swim?" Moira liked Ari. She'd made her feel welcome, like one of the 'gang'.

"She's still sick," Nikau replied.

"Oh, I hope it's nothing too serious." Perhaps Anihera had been right about a pregnancy, but it was Ari who'd fallen victim not Moira.

"Anihera's not sure," Nikau replied. "She thought it was just a stomach bug, but the Kawakawa tea doesn't seem to be making it any better."

Tama drove back down the track, the one where rocks rose on one side of the vehicle and fell to the valley on the other. The track where Moira had been terrified Barry would crash, plummeting them to their death. Nestled between Matiu's legs, she felt safe. She leaned back on his chest, and he wrapped his arms around her, their hands meshing in her lap. This late in the day, there was no fog sealing the valley roof, it spread out before them, expansive and endless. Rocks looked like freckles, streams looked like veins, carrying the life blood of the earth.

The ever-present hawk hovered overhead. She hoped it didn't discover the dead sheep before she reluctantly dealt with them.

The truck was parked by the riverbank where jagged rocks jutted out above the water creating a natural diving platform above the pristine river. The rock strata rose on a forty-five degree angle as if they'd been squashed out of the earth in a prehistoric time.

Matiu helped Moira off the truck and then dashed off after Nikau in a race to see who could jump into the water first.

"Yahoo!" Matiu cheered as he dive-bombed into the river.

Rocks lurking beneath the surface had Moira's heart racing with worry. She closed her eyes until she heard a splash. Matiu disappeared below the water, and she sucked in a breath, unable to move until he resurfaced.

"Come on, Moira." Matiu shook the water from his head and beckoned her in.

"I'm coming. I'm coming." Moira sounded annoyed but it was with herself not Matiu. She struggled to understand her body's reaction to the possibility of him getting hurt. This was all meant to be fun. She wasn't supposed to fall for anyone. He was just another man who would be gone from her life soon enough.

Nikau and the other men joined Matiu while the women took the more slow and graceful route over the rocks that sat at the river's edge. Moira was right, the water was cold. Slowly submerging herself, inch by inch, she sucked in a breath as goosebumps prickled her skin. Once her shoulders were covered, she kicked off into the middle of the river, gradually adjusting to the freshness of the water. Paddling with her arms and kicking her legs out under the water she managed to stay afloat.

"Watch out!" Nikau yelled as he pointed to the water beside Moira. "There's an eel!"

She squealed and thrashed, bobbing below the surface until Matiu swam up behind her and wrapped his arms around her middle.

"No, there's not," he said. "Nikau's just being a big tease."

"Well, it's not very funny, Nikau," Moira growled but she was glad it meant she was back in Matiu's arms.

"I bet there are eels," Nikau argued. "They'll be living under the bank over there, in the shade."

"Well, you swim over there then," Moira challenged him.

"I'll get the spear." Nikau left the river to grab a three-pronged spear from behind the seat of the truck. "I'll catch one for dinner, then you'll be grateful."

He did just that, soon emerging with his spear stabbed through the head of a long slimy grey eel. It didn't look very appetising, and Moira wasn't sure she would be grateful to eat any of it.

"Right, we'd better get back then." Tama headed towards the truck. "It'll take a while for Anihera to process and cook that."

⌘

Moira was too busy gutting and skinning the dead sheep to notice how the eel was dealt with. She'd had to drag them from the yards, terrified their bloated stomachs would burst. Fortunately, Matiu came to lend a hand.

"What are you going to do with the sheep heads?" he asked as he finished digging a hole for the offal.

Moira looked askew at Matiu. "Why?"

"If you don't want them, we'll set a trap for *koura*."

"You're welcome to them." It was one less thing for her to bury. "What are *koura*?"

"Fresh water crayfish." Matiu mimicked kissing the tips of his fingers as if they were delicious. "Eel today, crayfish tomorrow. There's nothing better."

"The eel does smell good cooking." Moira's stomach rumbled loudly.

Matiu laughed. "It'll be ready soon. I'll go take the heads to the river and set the trap. See you around the fire."

Moira buried the inedible innards, loaded the sheep skin, carcass, and offal into a rickety wheelbarrow to deliver her efforts to Barry in the cottage.

"I'm going to eat eel for supper." She dumped the sheep kidneys and liver on the table where Barry was dishing up another plate of rabbit stew. "If I never see another rabbit, it'll be too soon."

"Um, what?" Barry shook his head.

"Never mind. I'll see you in the morning." Moira didn't wait for Barry's response. "The rest of the sheep is outside in the wheelbarrow. I'll leave you to deal with that."

She walked away with a mixture of pride and trepidation. She'd drawn a line in the sand and spoken to Barry like she never had before, sticking up for herself, and demanding something of him. A niggly speck of doubt hoped her newfound assertiveness didn't backfire.

She washed her face and hands, scrubbing away the incessant smell of dead animals and headed over to the shearers' camp.

The eel had been wrapped in *rarekau* leaves and roasted amongst the hot embers of the fire. Anihera peeled back the leaves to reveal chunks of eel, golden on the outside and smoky white when broken open. It tasted as good as it looked. All of Moira's doubts about the slimy fish dissipated. It tasted so much better than rabbit.

CHAPTER
18

"Ari's no better, Tama. I'm worried. Her stomach pain hasn't eased, it's probably worse."

Anihera and Tama stood away from the tents to afford their conversation some privacy, but they were close to Moira's hut, and she was wide awake after Matiu's early morning visit. She overheard every word.

"We'll be finished up here today," Tama replied. "We could defer the next job for a day and take her home. She'll recover quicker there and if she needs to see a doctor, she can."

"A doctor …" Anihera's voice rose a pitch.

"I know, I know," Tama interrupted his wife. "I know you don't like the pakeha medicine but sometimes it is necessary. For Ari's sake, Anihera."

"Alright," Anihera conceded. "You'd best get on with it then, in case we need to go today."

The shearers were leaving. Maybe today. Moira's mind was all a flurry, not with worry about Matiu leaving or Ari's health but totally selfish concerns. Could she leave with them? Where was their 'home'? What would Barry do if she left? She quickly discounted that question; she didn't care what happened to him. He'd managed before she got here, and he'd survive after she'd gone. Where would she go? One place would be to see the Placement Officer to ensure that no other land girls got assigned to Barry's station. What would she do? She glanced down at her hands, covered in callouses, nails ingrained with dirt. Farming really wasn't for her. No, she'd find something else to do. Perhaps she could go to see Grace, see if there were any jobs at the linen flax mill. That wouldn't do either, no man was going to be attracted to a woman who stunk of rotting flax. Grace really should find another job too. Maybe they could move to the city. Not Christchurch. Further afield to Wellington. That's where the American soldiers were based. As a plan formulated in Moira's head, a lightness filled her. For the first time since leaving Orari, she felt like there was light at the end of the tunnel.

She left her bed unmade. There was no point in tucking in the sheets nicely if she was going to have to pull it all apart in a hurry. She headed to the woolshed where Matiu was already bent over his first sheep.

"You're looking happy." Matiu released the shorn sheep and smiled as if he believed he was the source of her joy.

"Where are you from?" Moira gathered up the fleece and carried it to the sorting table.

219

Matiu frowned. "Why?"

Tama was at the wool press, so Moira waited until she'd finished processing her fleece. She picked out the dags and dirty wool, folded the fleece and delivered it to Tama to squash down into the bale. Back at the shearing platform she leant close to Matiu.

"I overheard Tama and Anihera say you might have to leave and take Ari home," she murmured. "I want to know where home is?"

Matiu continued clipping at the wool running down the sheep's back. "And here I was thinking you wanted to know about me."

Moira saw a hint of hurt in his look.

"Well, aren't you all from the same place?" she asked to keep on Matiu's good side. It wasn't that she never wanted to see him again, but he was a shearer, and she had no plans to be a rousie, sleeping in a tent, for the rest of the war.

"Yes and no. I'm from Waianukarua. My *whanau* still live there."

Moira nodded her head as if she understood, but she couldn't even pronounce where Matiu's family lived, and it wasn't the answer she wanted.

"And Tama and Anihera are from ....?" Moira struggled to sound patient.

"Otipua Creek, just out of Timaru is the base we head back to at the end of each season."

"Timaru!" Moira almost sang the word.

"Moira," Matiu caught her attention. "It's great you want to come back to the base, but I won't be there long, we have other jobs to go to, the shearing season has another six to eight weeks to run yet."

"That's fine," Moira replied casually. "I can catch a train from Timaru to Orari."

"Oh … I suppose so." Matiu focused on the sheep "You'd have to ask Tama, he's the driver."

Aware that she had disappointed Matiu but not wanting to witness a grown man sulking, Moira busied herself picking up bits of wool that had dropped on the floor.

When she took the next fleece to the wool press, she secured her way off the farm.

"Tama, would I please be able to hitch a ride with you when you leave?" she asked politely.

"I guess so. There'll be room on the back," he replied. "You realise we're not coming back though."

"That's fine, neither am I."

With her ride secured that left one more problem to deal with. Barry. The confidence she had last night when she'd left him with the dead sheep seem to have dissipated. Perhaps she could just leave without telling him. No! He hadn't paid her yet. He owed her four weeks wages, and she couldn't afford to leave without it.

⌘

"Well, that's a job well done," Barry said to Tama as the last wool bale was stitched up. "Thanks, Tama. Ya best join me for a celebratory whisky tonight."

"Won't be able to do that, sorry, Barry. We're going to pack up and head off. Ari needs to get to a doctor."

"Surely ya can wait until morning." Barry lit his pipe and puffed a cloud of smoke into the air.

"Best not. Ari's in a lot of pain. Anihera's worried it might be her appendix."

"Ya best get loaded up then. Get on the road before it gets dark. I'll get Moira to clean up here when ya gone."

"Umm ..." Tama hesitated and glanced over Barry's shoulder at Moira who mouthed *'help me out'* with a pleading facial expression. "You might have to sort things out yourself, Barry."

"What'ya mean?"

"Moira's leaving with us."

"She's what!"

It's now or never. Moira joined the two men. "I've decided high country station life isn't for me."

"Ya've only just arrived." Barry looked accusingly at Moira. "Ya haven't given it a chance."

"I've been here long enough." Moira dug her hands into her overall pockets. "Four weeks, in fact. Dealing with a dead animal of one sort or another every day. That's not what I signed up for."

"That's farming." Barry shrugged his shoulders. "If ya want live animals, ya going to have dead animals. I don't know what they teach ya land girls but it clearly ain't enough. Be on ya way then. I managed before ya arrived, I'll manage after ya gone."

"I'll write up an invoice for the shearing," Tama interrupted. "And collect a cheque from you before we go."

"I'd like a cheque for my wages at the same time." Moira was determined not to cower in front of Barry. "Please," she added as a precautionary gesture.

Barry stormed off, huffing, and puffing on his pipe.

"I hope he doesn't withhold payment," Moira spoke quietly to Tama.

"I'll add a bit onto my invoice," Tama suggested. "For your work in the shed. So, you'll get paid one way or the other."

"Thanks, Tama." Moira appreciated his support. "I'll come with you when you go to collect the cheque if you don't mind."

"That'll be fine. Best get packed up now then."

Moira had a quick wash and hurried back to her hut, pulling the sheets from the bed, stuffing them and her clothes back into her suitcase. She had to sit on the lid to get the locks to click into place. Molly wandered in and sat on the floor in the doorway.

"At least you look like you're going to miss me, Molly." She leant over and patted the dog's head.

The tents were all packed down, rolled up and stowed on the back of the truck along with the shearing and cooking equipment and everyone's gear. Ari was wrapped in a woollen blanket and helped into the cab of the truck.

"We'll just collect our pay and be on our way," Tama said to the group. "Coming, Moira?"

She followed Tama to the cottage where Barry was bent over a pot hanging above the open fire, the familiar odour of rabbit filling the room, adding to the unsettled feeling in Moira's stomach. He didn't look up at them.

"On the table," was all he muttered.

"See you next year. Hopefully." Tama picked up the cheques and handed Moira her pay.

Barry nodded but kept his attention on the pot. Moira was glad he was a man of few words. It made leaving easier.

She looked around the collection of buildings that had been her home for the last month, with a sense of relief she looked skyward, grateful to be leaving. Her relief was short-lived when she reached the truck and Matiu was nowhere to be seen. Had she been too heartless, hurt his feelings? Surely, he knew their relationship was just a short-term fling, nothing serious.

"Where's Matiu?" she gasped.

He ran up behind her, panting. "Oh, did you miss me? I didn't think you cared."

He was laughing but Moira heard the double meaning in his teasing.

"I thought you were going to miss your ride," she replied trying to sound casual.

"Tama wouldn't leave me behind." Matiu jumped up onto the back of the truck with a wet sack writhing with *koura*. "Not when I've caught dinner."

⌘

There wasn't a creek to be seen when they reached their destination.

"Why's it called Otipua Creek when there's no creek?" Moira asked Matiu as Tama pulled the truck off the road and drove down a long driveway.

"It's back over there towards Timaru, hidden in the trees. I'd show you but you probably haven't got time if you're catching the train to Orari tomorrow." Matiu sounded despondent.

Moira pretended she hadn't heard the hurt in his voice. "I'll telephone the train station and check on the schedule. There might be a train tonight."

"No phone here," Nikau chirped into the conversation as everyone began unloading their bags. "Never needed one, we're on the road so much."

"Looks like there's a storm coming," Matiu added, his downturned mouth flipping into a wide grin. "You might as well stay the night; I'll keep you warm."

Matiu was right, ominous grey clouds darkened the sky and gusts of wind rustled leaves and bent branches. And his offer to keep her warm was already doing so, a heat stirring within.

"Well, hottie, lead the way, where do we sleep?" She nudged Matiu, hurrying him along.

"I wasn't planning on sleeping," Matiu leaned in and murmured. "But the bunkhouse is this way."

"Bunkhouse?" Moira's eyes went wide as Matiu opened the door and flicked on the light switch.

"More comfortable than a tent and sleeping bag on the hard ground."

"But not as private." A sudden chill made Moira shiver.

"I'll get the fire lit, warm the bunkhouse up and heat some water." Matiu came up behind her and wrapped his arms around her waist, resting his chin on her shoulder. "Perhaps we could enjoy a bath together. You find a bed, and I'll cook the *koura*."

The bath sounded delightful. The *koura* was more of a wait-and-see. Matiu had said they were freshwater crayfish, but Moira was none the wiser having never tasted saltwater crayfish either.

The oblong building was plain and functional with a serviceable kitchen and wood burner at one end and wooden framed bunks jutting out from the side walls at the other end. Moira didn't mind the bunks, if they weren't infected with fleas like her last bed; it was the lack of privacy that had her thinking sleeping was all she would be doing. Hanky panky with an audience wasn't something she wished to participate in.

⌘

The *koura* and some sweet potato and *puha* were cooked by the time Tama, Nikau and Anihera arrived back from the doctor.

"Where's Ari?" Matiu asked.

"They've put her in the hospital," Nikau replied, a worried look on his face. "They'll probably take her appendix out in the morning."

"Just as well we came back then." Matiu carried two large pots to the table which he and Moira had already set with plates and cutlery. "Help yourselves everyone."

Moira happily sat back and watched the others fill their plates, then tuck into their food, fingers cracking open the belly and tails of the *koura*. The combination of odours radiating from the two pots wasn't at all appetising, but it seemed Moira was the only one who felt that way.

"Mmm, delicious, Matiu," Tama sighed with pleasure. "A good catch."

"Aren't you hungry, Moira?" Matiu nudged her gently with his elbow. "Quick, eat up before they're all gone."

Gingerly, she picked up the smallest of the crayfish, avoiding its pincers. Its beady eyes were long dead but still they appeared to look accusingly. She copied the other's movements and snapped the tail off to reveal the cooked white flesh. Biting off a small amount at first, Moira was surprised how good it tasted. The texture and flavour were much better than rabbit. She finished the tail meat and cracked open the body. *Koura* were fiddly to eat but worth the effort.

When the pots had been emptied and everyone's plates cleaned except for shells, pincers, and heads, Anihera stood and began clearing the plates.

"Thank you for cooking, Matiu," she said. "I'll clean up. You young ones have a day off tomorrow.

Go and have some fun before the storm comes."

"We could play cards," Nikau suggested. "Who's ready to lose their wages to me in a game of poker?"

Matiu looked across at Moira with a smile that said he had something else in mind.

"I'll take Moira for a walk and show her the creek," he said with a cheeky grin.

There wasn't room in his statement for her to decline, not that she wanted to, a tingle of anticipation began bubbling away inside her. They left Nikau shuffling the cards, waiting for the others to join him, and wandered outside hand in hand.

The creek was just a creek, clear waters ambling over a muddy bottom, reeds bending with the water, tiny shimmering silver fish swimming against the current.

What happened at the creek filled Moira with a glow that carried her through the night, snuggled in a single bunk with Matiu's strength cradling her protectively.

⌘

Nikau was anxious to head to the hospital first thing in the morning to check on Ari, so farewells were brief which suited Moira fine. She didn't want to feel the guilt that Matiu's hurt look piled on her.

"Take care of your *pepe*," Anihera said, waving her hands in front of Moira's stomach.

Moira was caught off-guard, not only by the reminder that Anihera thought she was pregnant, but also by the heat that radiated from the Maori woman's hands like a protective energy.

"Y-y-yes," was the only response that spilled from her mouth before she climbed into the front of the truck and quickly shut the door, feeling the need to create her own barrier.

Nikau dropped her at the train station where she bought a ticket to Geraldine after deciding arriving at Orari without warning and without the ability to telephone anyone, she would end up stranded. Who would she call anyway? She couldn't imagine Anne welcoming her back with open arms and Betsy would be busy with William and the new land girls at Whipsnade. The other option was Christchurch, but Moira wasn't ready to go from remoteness to city, just yet.

⌘

It was late morning when Moira climbed down from the train at Geraldine. She looked around the others on the platform. Some soldiers made her heart skip a beat until she noticed their uniforms were New Zealand and not American. The soldiers' tired faces and slumped shoulders carried the weariness of battle signalling they were home for a well-deserved rest.

On the train she'd decided to head to the boarding house where Grace had been staying. At least there she could get a room until she decided her next move, and Grace being Grace, would be full of suggestions no doubt.

The double-storey boarding house was only a short walk from the railway station. Moira strode up the path between the rose beds inside the white picket fence. She expected a grim-looking woman would answer the door, one dressed in black who would want her 'lights out by ten o'clock' rule respected. She paused in front of the door's brass doorknocker and silently questioned whether she was doing the right thing. The decision was taken out of her hands when the door opened, and Grace appeared.

"Moira!" Grace squealed excitedly, hugging her tight. "Finally. We wondered if you were going to turn up in time. And I've got a pile of mail for you. You've really got under someone's skin this time."

CHAPTER
19

Moira sucked in a breath when Grace finally released her, from the physical bind and the stench of linen flax that Grace exuded. The fresh air wasn't enough to stifle the bile she felt rising. She clamped her hand over her mouth.

"Where's the toilet?" Her desperate plea was mumbled but fortunately Grace understood, moved aside, and pointed to a passage heading to the back of the house.

It wasn't the nicest start to the visit, but Moira felt better once she'd vomited. She returned to Grace who was still standing in the doorway as if she was too stunned to move.

"Are you alright?" A worried frown creased Grace's forehead.

"Yes, I'm fine." Moira stood back from Grace to avoid any repeat performance. "It's just you don't smell too good."

"Oh, you soon get used to that."

Moira didn't plan on having to. Dead animals were more pleasant.

"Anyway, it's nice to see you too." She changed the subject. "I was hoping I could get a room. Does your landlady have any spare?"

"If she doesn't you can top and tail with me," Grace offered. "We'll worry about that later; we've got to go, or we'll be late."

"Late for what?" Moira asked.

"Alice's baby shower." Grace's face lit up. "She's come to town and Nel is hosting. Lunch and games."

Moira sighed. Lunch sounded good, but games? What sort of games did they play at a baby shower?

"Come on, we'll put your bag upstairs and be on our way." Grace took Moira's suitcase before she had time to protest and was halfway up the staircase by the time she followed.

Grace's bedroom was the middle of three facing the road, lace curtains hung in the sash window opposite a single bed with a wrought iron bed head and a patchwork quilt in pinks and mint green. It was all very feminine and luxurious compared to the hut at Barry's.

"Are all the rooms like this?" Moira hoped there'd be another one that didn't reek of linen flax, she was beginning to feel queasy again.

"Yes, I think so." Grace picked up a bundle of letters from the dresser. "These are yours. From that American soldier by the looks of it."

232

Moira's hands quivered as she turned the bundle of envelopes over to read the sender's address: Paekākāriki. It confirmed the neat writing addressed to her was from Frank. There were at least a dozen, meaning he'd written several times a week. The effort required felt weighty like it might require a response from her that was more than she was prepared to give. She rocked backward and forward, unsure what to do. Her curiosity itched to be satisfied by sitting and devouring every word at once. Why had he written? What did he want from her? She pictured his perfect teeth, his smooth face, his boyish grin, his muscled torso. What did she want from him? She licked her lips.

"Come on then." Grace snatched the letters, put them on Moira's suitcase and grabbed her hand. "No time for that now. You can devour them when we get back."

Their mode of transport was Grace's bicycle, Moira on the carrier and a gift wrapped in white tissue paper carefully stowed in the cane basket hitched to the handlebars.

"Ouch!" The steel bars of the carrier dug into Moira's behind as Grace cycled through rather than around a pothole.

"Sorry, didn't see it," Grace called out, her own bottom bouncing up and down in front of Moira's face as she tried to pick up momentum.

"We aren't biking all the way to Orari are we?" Moira's bottom was still tender from riding Storm. She'd be jumping off the carrier if they had to go all the way by bicycle.

"No, just to Brian's. He's going out to the farm, so we'll catch a ride with him."

Wasn't Brian the soldier who'd returned from the war with shell shock? Was he healed and capable of driving?

"Is he alright to drive?" Moira frowned.

"He's a bit jumpy still but I like to go with him and encourage him."

Nothing had changed in the short time Moira had been away. Grace was still trying to help everyone and solve their problems.

Brian was already in his mother's car, the engine idling quietly, by the time they reached the McPherson's house. Grace leant her bicycle against the side of the garage and retrieved the parcel.

"Hi, Brian." Grace made sure Brian had seen her before she greeted him cheerfully. "You remember Moira, don't you? She's coming out to the farm too."

"Hi, Brian," Moira added as they climbed into the vehicle, Grace in the front seat and Moira in the back.

He gave no acknowledgement other than to put the car into reverse, glance in the rear-view mirror, release the brake and back down the driveway. His face looked as if it had been frozen in time, not a muscle twitch nor an emotion gave away whatever was whirring away inside his head.

The leather backseat may have been more comfortable than the bike carrier, but Moira wasn't convinced it was safer.

⌘

Arriving at *Whipsnade* was like going back in time. Moira reflected on all that had happened since she, Grace, Betsy, and Alice had begun their land girl training.

She breathed a sigh of relief when Brian turned the car off outside Duncan and Nel's house. His driving had been fine, but it was a long quiet journey, with baited breaths, as if a bomb was going to explode any second. Driving past Bill's farm brought a flood of memories both good and bad, and a raft of unanswered questions about Bill. Was he improving? Would he make a full recovery and return to farming? Would there have been a future for them if he did?

"Hello, Brian." Nel came out to greet them. "William's over at the implement shed working on the plough. And look at you two." Nel held her arms out to Grace and Moira as Brian wandered off.

"Hi, Nel." Grace had the first hug. "Thanks so much for inviting us, all."

"You're most welcome. Having a baby is a joy to be celebrated, isn't it, Moira?" Nel wrapped her in a motherly hug.

Moira stiffened and did a double take. Nel's comment could have been mere chatter, but it felt like a dig directed solely at her. She didn't see anything joyful in having a baby and she had no intentions of doing so anytime soon. What was it with older women? First Anihera and now Nel. Once they lost their own ability to reproduce, it seemed they all assumed the younger generation would immediately oblige.

All this talk of babies was annoying. How was Moira going to make it through the afternoon? She'd much rather be back at the boarding house reading Frank's letters.

"Come inside." Nel ushered them towards the house. "Betsy and Alice are getting everything ready."

"I'll just have a smoke first," Moira replied, pulling the packet from her handbag, ignoring the frown that Nel sent her way.

She needed a nicotine hit to calm herself. She'd been rationing them since she'd left Orari, and this was the last of a precious supply. She'd have to find her ration coupons and cash one in tomorrow to stock up again.

The new trainee land girls were at the pig sties. Moira heard their squeals of horror and disgust as they cleaned the sties and shovelled the dirty hay and effluent onto the compost stack. There was one smell worse than rotting flax and that was pig excrement. Moira's memory was so vivid she felt like she was cleaning the pig sty herself. Her stomach churned in protest, and she drew on the cigarette to suffocate the feeling. It was more evidence, as if she needed confirmation, that farming wasn't for her. By the time she'd smoked the cigarette down to its butt and stamped it out on the ground, her mind was made up. Moving to Wellington and finding a job in the city, that's what she'd do next. Meanwhile, she just had to get through Alice's baby shower.

The familiar warmth of the coal range filled Nel's kitchen where the table was laden with baking: scones with dollops of cream and jam, a bacon and egg pie, club sandwiches and a plate filled with lamingtons, both chocolate and strawberry. Not a cooked rabbit in sight.

236

The last time Moira had seen this much delicious food would have been Alice's wedding and there Alice was, standing in the corner, looking like she'd eaten the entire table.

"I know you're eating for two, Alice, but really," Moira teased. "You've gone from being the smallest among us to the biggest."

"Hi, Moira, nice to see you too." Alice waddled forward. "Fortunately, it'll all be gone soon and the bundle of joy I'll be holding will make it all worthwhile."

"So, you're looking forward to being a mother?" Moira's eyes went wide. How could anyone look forward to that? Alice had always been the one to rescue lambs, calves, and piglets. "I guess it's no different to you saving dying animals."

Alice wrapped her arms lovingly around her swollen belly. "Very different, Moira, very different. Fergus and I have created this baby out of love."

"Who would have thought, shy little Alice, the first to find love." Moira felt a tinge of jealousy but quickly reminded herself she was here for a good time not searching for elusive love. It was much safer that way, she couldn't be hurt.

Betsy came into the kitchen carrying a bundle of nappies and cradling a life-sized baby doll.

"Oh, no, Betsy, have you and William beaten Alice and Fergus to parenthood?" Moira joked.

"Ha ha, very funny, Moira," Betsy retorted as she tossed the doll to Moira. "Here, you look like you need some practice."

The doll's big glass blue eyes stared blindly up at Moira as it lay cradled in her arms, head nestled in the crook of her elbow, lips painted rose pink were pursed as if ready to latch onto her breast.

"You look like a natural," Alice teased. "You can come and babysit when I need a rest."

Moira felt giddy imagining that the doll was real, a tiny human she was responsible for.

"What's wrong, Moira?" Grace pulled out a seat at the table. "Here, sit down. You've gone as white as a ghost. Is there something you'd like to tell us?"

"Are you alright, Moira?" Betsy's voice was laced with concern. "You look exhausted."

Moira managed to sit but any audible response was beyond her. She had to blink away the tears that welled up. What was wrong with her? Why had she become so emotional holding a silly doll? She should just pass it over to Alice, but she couldn't let it go. The innocent blue eyes begged to be held, to be nurtured and treasured above all else. She inhaled deeply, squeezed her eyes shut, and masked her inner turmoil, pushing the niggling doubt that Anihera was right, into a tiny ball to be hidden away and ignored.

"Nothing's wrong with me." She forced a laugh and painted her face with a smile. "High-country station farming is tough. I just need some of Nel's delicious food."

"Let's have lunch then," Nel suggested. "Then we can have a good catch up and find out what you've all been up to."

⌘

Moira felt as bloated as Alice looked by the time they'd all finished lunch and moved through to the sitting room for the gifts and games.

"Sorry, I don't have a gift," Moira apologised to Alice. "I didn't know I was coming here until two minutes before we left."

"That's alright. It's nice just to have you here." Alice's face lit up as she unwrapped the tissue paper on Grace's present to reveal a white woollen jacket knitted with a lacy pattern down the front and matching bootees with ribbon ties.

"They're so tiny." Moira gulped, the thought of being responsible for a miniature human terrified her.

"Oh, they bring back memories." Nel's eyes went glassy. "I could never keep booties on William, he managed to hook them off every time."

"I wonder what you're having, Alice?" Betsy asked, passing over her gift.

"Well, her baby bump is all out front," Nel observed. "So, that usually means it's a boy."

"What sex would you like, Alice?" Grace asked.

Moira laughed. "I think she's had enough sex, it's what got her looking like she's about to pop."

239

Alice's cheeks coloured a deep scarlet. She kept her head down as she unwrapped a parcel to reveal a pretty baby brush and comb set, two cards of safety pins and a bottle of baby powder.

"Thank you, Betsy." Just as she used to, Alice ignored Moira's teasing. "Fergus would obviously like a boy, to help him on the farm when he's older. I'll be happy with either, so long as the baby is healthy."

"That's all that matters." A tear trickled from the corner of Nel's eye.

"Sorry, Nel, I didn't mean to upset you," Alice said.

"Just me being an emotional old duff." Nel blew her nose. "Have you had a good pregnancy, dear? Did you suffer from morning sickness, at all?"

Alice sighed and rolled her eyes. "Every morning for nearly three months, any unpleasant smell would send me running for the toilet."

"Really?" Moira's eyes went wide, and her voice rose an octave.

"Yes, I think I spent more time getting rid of my breakfast than I did eating it."

"They say," Nel shared some more wisdom. "That the worse the morning sickness, the stronger the pregnancy. I didn't know that at the time but with the babies I lost I never had morning sickness, only William. It seemed to go for the whole nine months with him."

"Nine months! That'd be exhausting." Alice patted her stomach. "Thank goodness this one hasn't done that to me."

"You soon forget it, once you're holding them in your arms and they reach out their tiny hands."

Moira was oblivious to the conversation that continued, she was lost in her own thoughts. What if Anihera was right? What if what she thought was merely a dislike of stewed rabbit and dead animals was really morning sickness? Being sick at Grace's too; that couldn't be blamed on dead animals. When was her last monthly? She hadn't endured that as well while she was at Barry's. What if, it wasn't hard work and exhaustion that made her cycle irregular when it never had been before? Possibilities barrelled on through like a driverless fully laden freight train.

"What other symptoms did you have?" Moira blurted, desperate for reassurance that her life wasn't about to drastically change.

"Pardon. What?" Alice frowned at her.

Moira realised everyone was looking at her. She shrugged her shoulders and leaned back, trying to look casual and carefree.

"Nothing really. Morning sickness sounds awful. I just wondered what else happened when you got pregnant. Does it get any worse?"

"My breasts got really tender." Alice blushed again. "Fergus couldn't go near them."

Moira involuntarily looked down at her chest. Her nipples tingled as if to say 'yes, we are sensitive, and it wasn't just Matiu's touch that made us so'.

241

"Right, we should play games now." Moira had had enough, she needed distracting.

"Patience, Moira, patience," Nel chastised as she handed over a large parcel, wrapped in brown paper and tied with string. "Alice needs to open the present from Duncan and I first. Sorry about the wrapping, dear. All this rationing. I'm getting tired of it."

Inside was a cot-sized knitted blanket which Alice unfolded and held to her cheek.

"Thank you, Nel. It's beautiful. So warm and soft."

"Fold it in half when you've got baby in the bassinet," Nel suggested.

"Fergus is finishing building a cradle while I'm here." Alice's love and admiration for her husband showed in her smile. "It'll be perfect."

Moira's smile was more of a grimace. Nothing seemed perfect in her life, and she had no idea what to do about it.

She couldn't see any point to the first game they played. The others giggled as they wrote their guesses for Alice's baby gender, birth date, weight, and length on small squares of paper which were then stowed in an envelope until after the birth.

"We'll see how good you are at folding nappies now." Nel handed a nappy to each of them, put the naked baby doll on the floor with some safety pins all the while laughing as if triggered by another happy motherhood memory. "It's your worst nightmare when baby's nappy leaks and you have poo from here to Kingdom come."

No! Moira's worst nightmare would be if she was pregnant. She hoped to never get to dirty nappies. She had no idea how to fold a square piece of cloth so big compared to the doll that it could be wrapped three times around and used to smother the defenceless being.

Figuring Nel would be the most expert among them, she glanced over as Nel's hands deftly folded the cloth, but Nel was too quick for Moira to learn what she'd done. Moira tried to remind herself it was only a game, what did she care if the nappy worked or not. She folded the cloth into a triangle, over and over until she judged it was small enough to fit the doll.

"You go first, Moira." Nel's suggestion had everyone else looking expectantly at Moira.

She grabbed the doll by its ankle and dragged it across to her. Betsy faked a baby's cry.

"What?" Moira scowled.

"You're hurting her."

"It's only a game, not a real baby." It took all of Moira's effort to shove a safety pin through the multiple layers of cloth and she was rewarded, or punished, with a stab to her thumb. "Ouch! Bloody stupid thing."

Blood oozed from the wound. Tears trickled from the corners of her eyes. Moira tried to blink them away, but she couldn't stem the flow. She stuck her thumb in her mouth and cried like a baby.

"It's alright, Moira." Alice patted Moira's hand.

The gesture was probably meant to comfort but it only served to irk Moira.

"I'm fine," she snapped and yanked her hand away. "I just hurt my thumb."

"It's the silly little things that set me off too," Alice continued. "The midwife tells me it's just pregnancy hormones but knowing you, Moira, that's not going to be the case."

CHAPTER
20

"I think we need to have a chat, Moira."

Grace didn't knock on the door to Moira's new room at the boarding house but barged in, all authoritative and perched herself on the end of the bed.

Ignoring her friend, Moira continued unpacking, hanging her dresses in the wardrobe, organising her shirts and cardigans in the drawers, and chucking her farm clothes into a pile in the corner. She planned to never wear them again, but they'd at least need washing first before they were stowed or given away. She was unsure how long she'd be at the boarding house, but it was nice to stop living out of a suitcase.

"You're pregnant, aren't you?" Grace didn't mince her words.

The direct question jolted Moira to a halt. She'd asked herself the same question in the quiet of the night. It was easier to ignore when it was only inside her head but spoken out loud it demanded an answer Moira was a little scared to voice.

The underwear she'd been about to put in the drawer remained scrunched in her hands as she sought support from the edge of the bed. The wirewove mattress creaked under her weight as if it, too, felt the burden. Her movements stalled; she sucked in a deep breath and exhaled long and slow.

"Maybe," she mumbled, chewing on her lip.

"You've got lots of symptoms; being sick all the time, crying at the littlest of things."

"I know, I know." Moira impatiently brushed away tears. "I thought it was all the hard work at Barry's. It was horrible, Grace. I worked from dawn till after dark, backbreaking work, dealing with dead animals, day in and day out. I'm just exhausted. That's all it is."

"When was your last period?"

Moira wished Grace would stop asking questions, prying into her business. It wasn't as if she could help solve this problem.

"When I was back at Bill's," Moira admitted.

"You've only been away four weeks, haven't you?"

A study of the calendar pinned to the wall beside the landlady's telephone had already told Moira at least six weeks had passed since her last bleed. It would be easier to let her friend assume it had only been four.

246

Grace's face screwed up. "You didn't sleep with Barry, did you? Wasn't he old and ugly?"

The idea was preposterous. "And smelly and grumpy and …. no, Grace, I didn't sleep with Barry. It'd be a good six weeks since my last period."

Grace's face twitched. Moira could almost hear her brain calculating the most likely moment of conception.

"Frank!" Grace's eyes went wide. "You've got yourself pregnant to an American soldier. Oh, Moira, how much more of a mess could you have made?"

It may have been a rhetorical question, but it demanded an answer, a defence against the accusation. Moira huffed and threw her underwear at the open drawer. She stood, placed her hands on her hips and looked indignantly at Grace.

"Firstly, I don't know that I am pregnant, for sure."

"Well, a quick visit to the doctor will remove any element of doubt."

Moira skipped the next point, a dilemma that she wasn't sure how to solve and certainly not one she was ready to share. What if Matiu was the father and not Frank? How would she know before the baby was born?

"Secondly," she paused, unsure of Grace's reaction to her next revelation. "I don't think I'll be keeping any baby, *if* there is one."

"Oh, Moira." As Grace reached out to her, Moira pulled back and clasped her hands together.

Any acceptance of a kind gesture would likely bring on more tears and Moira had cried enough to last a lifetime since coming back to Geraldine.

"I know being a single mum wouldn't be easy, but you've got friends and family who would help you. I'd help you," Grace offered.

"Family!" Moira scoffed. "You haven't met my family. We don't make good parents. Divorced. Philanderer skipping out on his duty without a consideration."

"You don't have to be like your parents. You can choose a different way."

"Yes. But look at me, I'm here for a good time. I haven't had a relationship that's lasted more than a few months. How can I make a lifetime commitment to a little baby? That wouldn't be fair."

Grace sighed. "Well, you don't have to decide now. One day at a time. The first job is to see a doctor. There's one down on the corner. You can go along there tomorrow."

A noise outside the door drew their attention and lowered their voices.

"I hope nobody was listening," Grace whispered. "The landlady won't want you here if she knows you're pregnant."

"I'm not going to be here for long anyway." Moira didn't bother to whisper. "I'm thinking of moving to Wellington."

"Wellington?" Grace frowned. "Why not Christchurch? It's a big enough city if you're tired of country life." Her frown dissipated as her mouth broke into a wide smile.

"You want to go to Wellington to be near Frank. Have you read his letters? Does he want to marry you? That would be the best solution to everything except you'd have to move to America when this silly war is finally over."

Moira raised her palms. "Slow down, Grace. You're like a wild horse galloping at full speed."

"Well ... have you read his letters?"

"No, not yet." The bundle of letters sat untouched on the top of the dresser and Moira eyed them with trepidation.

Grace stood and moved to the door. "I'll leave you to read them then. I'm sure you'll think differently once you know how he feels. A man doesn't write that many letters unless he feels something."

"I'm thinking of moving there regardless of what Frank says. You should move to Wellington too," Moira suggested.

"Why would I want to do that?"

"Escape that putrid smell you bring home from the linen flax mill." Moira pinched the bridge of her nose. "It's not good, Grace. You're never going to get a man smelling like that."

"Ben ..."

Moira cut her off. "Is stuck in prison. They're not likely to let any conscientious objector out until the war is over and done with."

"Well, I guess I would be there to support you." Grace rubbed her chin as if contemplating the possibility. "Betsy and Alice are settled and don't need my help, but I'd need

249

to get a job. There won't be any land girl positions in the city."

"You can type. You could get a job with the government," Moira suggested. "Maybe deciphering secret war messages. That would be exciting."

"Mmm."

Moira could see Grace was warming to the idea, so she continued. "There'd be lots of dances for us to go to. The stories I've heard, the Americans are always partying. You might see that soldier you danced with at the Orari hall. He was a charmer, wasn't he?"

"Mmm, their accents are easy to listen to." Grace sighed as if she was lost in memories.

"We can go to the station tomorrow to book tickets." It was Moira who was now rushing forward with her plans. "Catch the train from here to Christchurch and get the ferry to Wellington."

"Now, you're getting carried away, Moira." Grace sat back down. "I've got work tomorrow so won't be able to go anywhere to book anything. Besides, that's the ferry that nearly got torpedoed by the Japanese. I'm not sure I want to go anywhere on that."

"Come on, Grace, where's your sense of adventure? If a disabled man like William can survive a ferry crossing, then so can we."

⌘

The letters were neatly arranged in date order and while Moira itched to skip to the latest one, she resisted the urge and opened the letter dated the day after she'd last seen Frank, the Monday she'd left Orari with Barry.

Dear Moira

Today is my last day of leave. Tomorrow, we head back to Paekākāriki and I couldn't go without letting you know how much I enjoyed our time together and regret that it was cut short. I never would have guessed I'd come halfway around the world to fight a war and have the good fortune to find you.

Chad keeps teasing me that there'll be plenty more fish in the sea, but I think you've caught me, hook, line, and sinker.

I'm will send my letters to your old address and hope that someone passes them on to you.

Whatever happens with this war, I will happily defend New Zealand, knowing that in doing so, I am protecting you.

Yours sincerely, Frank

"No declarations of love in there." Moira wasn't sure if she was disappointed or glad. She folded the letter back into its envelope and opened the next, postmarked two days later.

Dearest Moira

Moira licked her lip with cautious hope when she noted the subtle difference between *dear* and *dearest.*

We're back doing drills, practising for combat. Where and when that will happen, I don't know, and they'd likely censor it out of my letter if I tried to tell you.

I hope you're well and enjoying your new position. I picture you looking very sexy in your overalls and gumboots. You'll be deserving of a holiday when you've finished. It'd be great if you could come to Wellington. I won't be eligible for any leave for a while, but we get weekends off and I'd sure enjoy dancing and having a good time with you again.

She knew the *good time* he was referring to and smiled at the memory of their lovemaking on the picnic blanket under the rustling leaves of the willows.

I hope my letters are being passed on to you and you can write back soon.

Yours Frank

Letter number three, written later the same week, continued a similar vein. Letter number four was after the weekend.

My gorgeous Moira

A weekend in Wellington just isn't the same without your presence. The lads kept sending women my way, but I wasn't interested. It confirmed there is definitely something special about what we had together.

I hope you haven't gone off into the countryside never to return. You're too beautiful to be stuck in the back of beyond, unless it is with me. Please write soon.

Missing you, Frank.

That was four weeks ago. Moira couldn't imagine a handsome man like Frank not taking advantage of all the women throwing themselves at him. He might be able to abstain for one weekend but an entire month. She picked up the bundle of letters, curious as to the date of the most recent, sceptical that Frank would still be so amorous.

A stern-looking Queen Victoria appeared to frown at her from the postage stamp on the letter on top of the pile.

"Yes, I know," Moira spoke to the Queen as if she was sitting beside her. "You'd tell me no good can come from this. He'll have moved on. He won't be looking to become a father. That's alright, though, because I'm not looking to become a mother. I don't have the good fortune of nannies and servants to look after my children, like you."

Where are you, my beautiful Moira? the fifth letter began. *Please write. Please let me know you aren't merely a figment of my imagination. I see you in my dreams. I wake and the need to have you next to me is painfully obvious.*

I thought perhaps you believe my feelings not to be genuine, that we should spend the time when we cannot be together getting to know one another, so here goes. I am the eldest son in a family of four boys. Before the war, we lived on the family cotton farm in Ferriday, Louisiana. After the war, God willing, I will return to home and take over from my father. The farm is 1800 acres, most of the hard work is done by slaves. My mother has always wanted a daughter and I'm sure she would love you.

Moira's head jerked back. "Your mother would love me," she repeated with disbelief. "My own mother thought I was a burden when she had to raise me single-handed. Just because yours has got a husband and slaves, doesn't mean she'd shower me with affection."

253

It was all too much. Moira needed the calming effect of a cigarette. She rummaged amongst her things until she found a cigarette packet, forgetting that she'd smoked the last of her supply yesterday.

"Oh, blast." She scrunched the packet and threw it at the wicker basket in the corner before searching for her ration book, which was safely tucked in the pocket of her handbag.

A walk to the store was just what she needed: fresh air with a nicotine fix at the end. The sudden realisation that she'd be expected to give up smoking if she was pregnant added to the list of reasons why it wasn't a good idea.

⌘

With a ration card swapped for cigarettes, Moira decided to walk around the block back to the boarding house, prolonging the moment when she would read that Frank had tired of waiting for a response from her, received a better offer and moved on. That's what all the previous men in her life had done. Frank wasn't going to be any different despite his terms of endearment.

She found herself in front of the hospital where she'd last seen Bill and a raft of memories flooded in. Both literally and figuratively, she'd gone around in circles, ending up back where she started but worse off.

"Moira! Is that you?" The nurse who'd helped Moira avoid the censoring eyes of the matron to sneak a visit with Bill, was sitting on the same garden seat puffing away on a cigarette. "Whatever brings you back here? How is that man of yours? Is he home yet, or is he still in Christchurch hospital?"

Moira stalled. How could she admit she didn't know anything about Bill? Had he ever really been her 'man'? She'd thought so at first but when he wouldn't acknowledge their relationship in public, that said something else altogether.

"Hello … I … um …" Moira searched for the right words; words that would assuage the guilt that tightened her chest. "I've been away. I was assigned to work on a high-country station. I wasn't needed at Bill's, not with his sister and brother-in-law arriving."

The nurse patted the seat beside her. "Come and sit. You look like you've got the weight of the world on your shoulders."

Moira accepted the invitation. The nurse had helped her before and that sparked a twinkle of hope that maybe she could do so again.

"Did you want a cigarette?" the nurse offered.

Moira withdrew her new packet from her bag. "Thanks, but I've just got another packet."

"Oh, lucky you. I've used up all my coupons. I guess the soldiers need them more than we do but I'll be glad when we're no longer rationed."

Inhaling the nicotine, Moira waited until its calming effect took hold before she spoke.

"I … I was … I was wondering if you might be able to help me. You were so good to me last time."

"Sure." The nurse's cheerful smile buoyed Moira. "What do you need? Matron is in a real grump today, but I have my ways to get around her." She tapped the tip of her forefinger to her nose.

"Um, I'm not really sure how to ask." Moira hesitated, taking another big draw on the cigarette.

"Go on, spit it out, nothing can be so bad that it can't be fixed."

"I need a pregnancy test," Moira blurted.

The nurse turned and stared wide-eyed at Moira. She didn't know the woman well enough to tell whether her reaction was shock or horror, whether she'd be judged for having to make such a request.

"Mmm. Um. Well, I see why you're looking so worried." The nurse glanced back at the hospital building and lowered her voice. "I can certainly help you with the test, but beyond that …"

"Thank you." Moira sighed with relief, her first hurdle overcome, although she realised it would be a marathon with many more obstacles rather than a sprint.

"If you are, you know, if the test is positive." The nurse cast another glance over her shoulder. "You should find a way to get to Christchurch."

"Christchurch?" Moira was confused. Did she know of someone who could terminate the pregnancy?

"Yes!" The nurse's face lit up. "Wonderful news like this would help Bill so much in his recovery. You do know, he and his late wife, what was her name … Miriam, that's right. Anyway, Bill and Miriam were never able to have children. They were devastated. Oh, this is a blessing. Come on, I'll help you get that test straight away."

It was Moira's eyes that widened now, like a possum caught in the headlights, blinded into inaction. Stuck between revealing the truth that any baby wasn't going to be Bill's and having to bear the weight of the judgement that would surely come if she did.

The nurse stood, took a last puff on her cigarette before stubbing out the butt with her shoe.

"You do realise, you should really give up smoking if you're having a baby." She reached down and took Moira's hand. "Come on, no time like the present. You're better off knowing than not. Quiet though, we'll have to sneak past Matron."

The door creaked as they entered.

"Is that you, Nurse Humphrey? You're late." The matron's stern voice bellowed from her office. "There is a bedpan in room five that needs emptying. Please attend to it immediately."

"Certainly, Matron. I'll get right onto it."

They peeked into the matron's office and made sure she was head down in paperwork before scooting past the door. At the end of the corridor, the nurse ushered Moira into a bathroom with several toilet cubicles.

"Here." She took a paper cup from a stack beside the basins. "Get me a urine sample and I'll be back in a minute."

Moira's fingers trembled. She peered into the bottom of the cup as if expecting tea leaves to predict her future.

"Better to know than not." Nurse Humphrey must have sensed her reluctance; she patted Moira on the arm and went to deal with the bed pan.

Unsure whether she'd even be able to go, Moira took the cup into the end cubicle, lifted her skirt, dropped her underwear, and sat down with a thud. Her bladder obliged and the sample was collected.

She was still there, staring blankly at the cup, when Nurse Humphrey returned.

"Have you finished yet?"

The question brought Moira back from the myriad of thoughts that were making her temples throb. She gingerly put the cup on the floor, careful not to spill the fluid that would determine her future. It all seemed so surreal, as if time had stalled. This was the end of her life thus far and the beginning of the next chapter lingered like an ominous storm cloud on the horizon.

When she finally exited the cubicle, Nurse Humphrey waited, one hand ready to take the cup, the other holding a taper that would provide the results. Moira sucked in her breath as the taper was dipped into the urine.

CHAPTER
21

Moira gritted her teeth. The urge to rip the pregnancy test to pieces filled her; the thin taper sat like an exclamation mark, its telltale tip colouring with a positive result, demarcating Moira's life before and after. She scrunched her hands into tight fists and shoved them into her pockets, stifling the need to scream.

She reached for her cigarette packet; a smoke was just what she needed now, but a subconscious maternal instinct told her otherwise.

"You have these." She retrieved the packet and handed it to the nurse. "Thank you for your help, Nurse Humphrey."

"Sally … call me Sally." Sally took the cigarettes and opened her arms to Moira. "You look like you need a hug."

Moira shook her head; her shoulders tense as her entire body trembled with shock.

"No, I'll be fine," she said, as much to convince herself, as Sally. "I'd best be going. There's lots to be done."

"You've got plenty of time," Sally replied. "You don't look like you're very far along. I can make an appointment with the doctor if you want. He can examine you, work out your due date."

"No," Moira repeated. "I'm leaving Geraldine."

"Yes, best you go to Christchurch, see Bill." Sally made assumptions Moira didn't have the heart to refute. "Everything will look so much better when you know he wants this too and will support you. I imagine you could do it alone, you seem like a woman of the world, and there are plenty of single mums out there, especially with this war taking all our men away, but it'll be so much easier with a man at your side."

Moira's eyes glazed over. It was all too much to take in. Bill. Frank. Matiu. Pregnancy. Abortion. Adoption. Motherhood. They all swirled about her head like a tornado, her life caught in the eye of a storm and about to be torn into a million pieces. She needed some fresh air.

"Thanks again, Sally. It'll take a while to digest, but at least now I know."

Dazed, Moira turned, left the bathroom, and walked along the corridor.

"You, again." The matron, hands on hips, blocked Moira's path. "What are you doing here? Causing more trouble."

"She was just borrowing the toilet," Sally called out, helping Moira yet again.

Sally would have made a good friend if Moira had been planning to stay.

She let herself out the front door, yanked it shut, inviting its slam as a response to the grumpy matron.

⌘

Grace welcomed Moira's news with joy and excitement. It was just as well she had enough positivity for the pair of them.

"I've handed in my notice at the mill," she announced. "I think you need me more than they do and like you suggested, with my typing skills I should easily be able to get a job in Wellington. I'll give the landlady notice as well. I'm already paid up until Friday. We'll need to get the train tickets tomorrow and see if the ticket office can get us passage on the ferry as well. I'll telephone my parents. We can stay with them until we catch the ferry. It's nearly Christmas so I imagine Mum will insist we stay for that."

For once, Moira was happy to let Grace organise her. It allowed her to wallow in self-pity for a while longer. She'd pull herself out of her melancholy soon enough; she always picked herself up and got on with it. Life was too short not to.

⌘

The next few days passed in a blur, the requisite tickets were purchased, clothes were repacked in suitcases, a last-minute visit to farewell Betsy was enjoyed, and arrangements were made for Grace's father to collect them from the train station. So it was that they found themselves on the same train that had brought them to Orari as green land girls less than a year ago, albeit going in the reverse direction. It didn't feel like a backwards step, just an unexpected diversion.

Grace's father was a tall finely built man who embraced his daughter with more love than Moira could remember ever receiving from her own father. When he'd finished showering Grace's forehead with kisses and repeating how good it was to see her, he turned his attention to Moira.

"And you must be the effervescent Moira, Grace has written so much about." He enclosed her hand in his big uncalloused palms and gently shook. "Hello, Moira. Any friend of Grace's is most welcome in the Ford household." He turned and wrapped an arm about each of their shoulders. "Come, we'll collect your luggage and get you home to your mother. She wanted to come to the station too, but I insisted there wouldn't be room. Truth is, I wanted you to myself for just a little while."

Moira knew the words that filled her insides with warmth were meant for Grace, but she lapped them up as if she were another daughter. No wonder Grace was always so bright and cheerful and wanted to help everyone; she came from a family— real family in the truest sense of the word.

The Fords' house was a modest weatherboard abode. It occupied a large corner section in a suburb of Christchurch Moira had never visited before. Flowers, vegetables, and fruit trees—all that was needed to nurture a family— surrounded the house like a warm cape.

A Christmas wreath hung on the front door and the view through a window adjacent to the door was blocked by a large Christmas tree whose pine scent escaped when Mrs Ford burst onto the veranda, eager to greet her daughter.

"Oh, my beautiful girl, it's so wonderful to see you again." Mrs Ford wrapped Grace in a motherly hug, the kind Moira only got when she'd hurt herself, not an everyday hug like this appeared to be.

"Hello, Mum. It's lovely to see you, too."

Grace's slender build, blonde hair and blue eyes had come from her mother. The blonde was now greying at her temples, but her blue eyes carried the same cheerfulness that Grace's always held.

"Shall we let these girls get inside, dear?" Mr Ford interrupted the hug. "It's likely they're parched after their journey and might enjoy a cup of tea or a glass of juice."

"Yes, yes, darling." Mrs Ford released Grace and moved aside. "I've been waiting for my children to come home for so long; I needed to make sure they're real and not just my wishful thinking."

She glanced down the path to the front gate with a wistful look as if hoping there would be more arrivals before shaking her head and turning her attention to Moira.

"Hello, my dear. Grace's letters have told us so much about your escapades, it's wonderful to finally meet you."

Moira was embraced for the second time in half an hour. She wondered what escapades Grace had relayed, but there was no judgement in the welcome, so she took it for what it was.

"Thank you, Mrs Ford," she replied. "I can see where Grace gets her beauty."

Mr Ford turned to show off his side profile and chuckled. "Yes, she does look like her father, doesn't she."

"Oh, Dad." Grace playfully swatted at her father. "Good to see you haven't left your sense of humour in the garden."

"I've got to dig the potatoes for Christmas day so I'm sure I'll find it if I have." He wrapped his arm around Grace's shoulder, and they walked into the house together.

⌘

Several cups of tea and freshly-baked scones were shared with stories and laughter in the front room where the Christmas tree towered over them. The war raised its ugly head several times. The absence of Grace's four brothers, all serving overseas, left a void that the Fords tried to fill by keeping busy.

"What plans have you made?" Mrs Ford asked. "Nothing until after Christmas, I hope. I've been saving my sugar ration to make plum pudding."

Moira looked down at her stomach, and then across at Grace. Her hands rested protectively in her lap, and with the slightest shake of her head, she silently conveyed that her secret needed to remain so.

"We can't stay for too long, Mum," Grace answered on their behalf. "We've got to get to Wellington and get jobs and find somewhere to live."

"Everyone is coming here on Christmas day." Mrs Ford counted off the guests on her fingertips. "Your grandmother, Aunt Daisy and Uncle Bob, Aunty Jean and cousin, Meredith. Oh, and Alison with her adorable twins. You won't want to miss them. It'll just be like old times but without the boys."

"You won't have to fight to shell the fresh peas then." Mr Ford made light of his son's absence.

"We haven't booked our ferry tickets yet," Grace shrugged her shoulders as she looked at Moira. "I guess we could stay for a few days."

Moira replied with a smile. The thought of a real Christmas celebrated in a room full of people, with a delicious meal, fun, and laughter filled her with the joy she needed.

"Wonderful news." Mrs Ford clapped her hands with delight. "The best present I could have hoped for."

"We'd better make the most of our time while you're here," Mr Ford suggested. "There are no Christmas lights this year, not with the blackout out but they're still going to run the Christmas parade tomorrow. No doubt, you girls will want to do some shopping on Monday. We could go for a picnic in Hagley Park."

On the journey up, Moira, calmed by the rhythm of the train, had decided to visit Bill. She needed to close that door of her life before she waltzed on to the next.

"I have a friend in hospital, I'd like to visit as well," she said.

"An injured soldier?" Mrs Ford asked. "I can't decide whether that would be a blessing or not. All a mother wants is for her boys to come home safely."

"Not a soldier ..." Moira hesitated, unsure how much to disclose. "But the victim of a shooting incident."

"Is that the Stanley Graham saga? I read about it in the newspaper," Mr Ford said. "Terrible incident to happen so close to you. I'm glad they caught the blighter and kept you all safe."

"You didn't say anything about it to me." Mrs Ford looked perturbed that she'd been left in the dark.

"I didn't want you to worry, sweetheart." Mr Ford patted his wife's hand. "The police had it all under control."

They didn't, or they wouldn't have needed the Home Guard to capture the fugitive, Bill wouldn't have been shot, and Moira wouldn't be in the predicament she was in. The list of unfortunate events that brought her to where she was, made her temples throb.

"Are you feeling alright, Moira? You're looking a little pale," Mrs Ford put her teacup back on the tray and asked in a motherly tone.

"It's been a big day," Grace answered on Moira's behalf. "We're both tired. We might go and get settled in. Are we sharing my room?"

"Yes, if you don't mind." Mrs Ford glanced at the door. "Just in case the boys arrive home and surprise us. It'd be just like them."

⌘

The following morning, Moira dressed and undressed several times. The first time she didn't quite make it to the toilet before a splodge of vomit splashed down her front. Rinsing it off left a wet mark she didn't want to have to explain. Eventually, she settled on the cinnamon-hued dress she'd worn to Bill's on her first day. It was more snug-fitting now. She turned side-on to the mirror to check her waistline hadn't expanded to the point where her pregnancy would be noticeable.

"Thank you." She pressed her hands to her stomach, almost unable to imagine there was a baby growing in there. "Just slow down. Give me time. Please."

She finished her outfit with red toe peepers and the Besame Victory Red lipstick. They were like her armour, affording her strength and courage and letting her be the Moira of old for just a while longer.

Mr Ford dropped her outside the Christchurch Hospital. The solid building was constructed in dark red brick, rose three storeys, and towered over Moira. Rows and rows of white-framed windows looked down on her and, she imagined, judging her. She sucked in a breath, pulled a compact from her handbag and checked her lipstick in the tiny mirror.

"No time like the present," she murmured as she stepped up to the entrance and pulled the heavy door open. "You've got nothing to lose."

"How can I help you?" The friendly question came from a nurse who sat behind a sliding glass window in an office directly opposite the entrance.

The opportunity for Moira to change her mind disappeared.

"Oh … um … can you tell me which room Bill De-Ath is in? Please."

"Are you family?"

Moira flinched. The same obstacle she'd faced in Geraldine. What was it with hospitals and needing to be related to visit someone? She instantly decided a lie was justified. She wasn't going to come this far and be denied a visit.

"Yes, yes, I am." Moira straightened her stance.

"Very well then. You'll find him on the first floor in room twenty-two." The nurse pointed to the stairwell at the end of the corridor. "Take the stairs and turn left at the top, fourth door on your right."

"Thank you." Moira turned and walked quickly to the stairs. The further into the building she went, the less likely she would be asked to leave.

The name board outside room twenty-two listed four patients sharing the ward. The door was ajar, and Moira could hear their cheerful banter. It stopped when she entered, and all eyes looked her way.

"Well, well." A man in the bed beside the window pulled himself up further on his pillows. "I'm feeling better already, and the doctor hasn't even been."

"She's not here to see you, Harry; you, silly old fool," the patient closest to Moira teased.

"Moira!" Bill's voice rose. "Moira," he repeated as if he didn't believe his eyes. "Moira."

"Hello, Bill. Yes, its me." She moved to his bedside.

"Well, well, Bill, you, old dog." The teasing continued. "What did you do to deserve a visit from a beautiful young woman?"

"You're turning green with envy, Harry." The oldest of the patients joined the banter.

"Pull the curtains, Moira," Bill suggested, his eyes still wide with surprise. "Give us some privacy."

"Careful of your stitches, Bill." Harry wasn't to be hushed without a final jest. "You don't want to rip them open. Go gentle on him, Moira."

Moira couldn't help but give the men a suggestive smile as she pulled the curtains closed around Bill's bed, sashaying her hips. Laughter echoed across the ward but not in Bill's cubicle. If he appreciated the effort she'd made, he didn't say. He looked more shocked than pleased to see her.

"What are you doing in Christchurch, Moira?" He rubbed his bristled chin. "Anne wrote that you'd left the farm, but I didn't expect to see you here. Why did you leave? I thought you would have kept the farm going while I recovered." His voice dropped to a whisper. "I thought you'd be there when I came home."

Moira gulped. The lump that sat in her throat held back any response to Bill's questions. Anne's letters had obviously only relayed her side of the story. Moira shouldn't have expected anything more. Should she retaliate, let Bill know how nasty his sister had been or should she just leave it in the past? She opted for the latter, casting aspersions on Anne wouldn't achieve anything.

"John has everything on the farm under control, he didn't need me."

Bill glanced at the curtains as if to ensure their privacy and reached out to take her hand.

"But I need you." His plea was little more than a whisper.

Moira felt the warmth of his hand on hers, but the heat didn't reflect in his tone. Did he whisper because their relationship was to remain evermore a secret? She opted to avoid the topic, knowing that she was pregnant with another man's baby, returning to Orari wasn't possible for the foreseeable future.

"How is your recovery going? When do you expect to go home?" She could tell he'd improved since she'd last seen him, but he still looked far from one hundred percent; his cheeks hollowed, a bony frame detectable beneath his hospital pyjamas.

"They think they've got the infection under control this time." Bill pointed to the line hidden by a bandage on his lower arm. "Intravenous antibiotics, but it's caused a bit of damage. I'll be here for a while yet. There is more surgery planned. The skin graft hasn't taken like it should."

"At least you're in the best place to get the care you need." Moira could hear the other men chatting. "And you seem to have made some friends for company."

"Yes, they're a good bunch." Bill smiled but became serious again when he looked at her. "What have you been up to?"

Getting pregnant. The first answer that came to mind was the last response she would give Bill.

"The placement officer assigned me to Barry Master's high-country farm."

"Really!" Bill stiffened. "How did he pass the vetting process? Oh, my poor Moira, that must have been terrible. I hear he lives in horrid conditions."

"It wasn't at all what I expected." Neither was Bill's reference to her as 'my Moira."

"I'm so sorry all this happened." Bill patted her hand. "If only I hadn't got shot."

"If only …" Moira left the thought hanging.

"So have you come back to Christchurch to stay with your mother?"

"No." For a moment, Moira considered visiting her but quickly discarded the idea. Her mother's opinion about her pregnancy was the last advice she needed to hear. "I'm staying at Grace's parents' house. We're catching the ferry to Wellington this week."

"Oh." Bill released her hand and sighed heavily. "What's in Wellington?"

It felt terrible to disappoint the first gentleman in her life. She wanted to say something to give him hope, but it would be wrong to give false expectations. Telling him the truth felt equally as cruel. He didn't need to know her predicament, not when she didn't yet know how she would deal with it.

"A fresh start."

CHAPTER
22

Moira kissed Bill on the cheek, leaving a red telltale smudge. Knowing he wouldn't openly admit to their relationship, there was a satisfaction to be derived from leaving a hint that would feed the others' curiosity. She pulled the curtains back and smiled at the men who were alert and watching for any sign of what had transpired behind the curtain.

"He's all yours," she said. "Look after him, please."

She left the hospital confident that shifting to Wellington was the right decision. Bill had treated her well in private, but the gentleman in him wouldn't extend to making any relationship public, and that was without the added complication of a baby. Heaven forbid, how he would react to that news.

She caught a bus from the hospital back to the Ford's house, where Grace was sitting on the front veranda reading a book, rocking gently in a swing seat. Her parents were busy in the garden, Mrs Ford picking flowers and Mr Ford tending to the vegetables.

"How did that go?" Grace put the open book face down in her lap. "Did you tell him your news?"

Moira checked that Mrs Ford was out of earshot before she replied.

"I told him I was moving to Wellington. That was all he needed to know. Any relationship we had is long over."

"So, are you going to write to Frank?" Grace always asked the hard questions.

"He's not the reason I'm going to Wellington, you know." Moira paced up and down the veranda, staring at her unpainted toenails. Perhaps she could dip into her savings and spoil herself with a pedicure.

Don't be silly! You'll need every penny. Keeping the baby, raising it herself, would cost more than she'd ever had in her bank account. And if she decided that wasn't an option, an abortion was unlikely to come cheap.

"I just thought he might like to know you're coming," Grace said calmly, patting the seat beside her. "He did write you all those letters."

Grace had a point. Moira accepted the seat and allowed herself to be rocked back and forth in a calming rhythm.

"Yes, he did." She remembered Frank's letters as if he were standing before her, reading them aloud in his smooth American accent. The feelings that absence seemed to intensify, flowed easily off the page and into her heart. Her heart? Hadn't she built an impenetrable wall around that, erected a barrier to protect her from being hurt? Wasn't Frank just another man in a long line of men who would give up on her after a while? Perhaps, but at least she could have fun with him in the meantime. She didn't have to tell him about the baby, not just yet. She planted her feet on the veranda and brought the swing seat to an abrupt halt.

"Yes!" Moira stood, enthusiasm consuming her. "I think I'll go and write him a note right now. Just to see if he knows of any dances on New Year's Eve though."

Grace nodded. Her smile was more of a smirk, as if she saw straight through Moira's response.

"The writing paper is in the top drawer of my bedside cabinet," she said.

"Thank you." Moira inhaled deeply as she entered the house; the pine scent permeated every corner. Thank goodness it wasn't a smell that sent her stomach into a spin.

She closed the door to Grace's bedroom, found the writing paper and sat cross-legged on the bed that had become hers for the duration of their stay. There were matching single beds, with a gap of no more than three feet in between, both covered with rose pink candlewick bedspreads. It was a 'girly' room and thoughts of growing up with a sister close by had Moira dreaming about how her life may have turned out differently had she not been an only child. Could she do that to another generation? Force her child to grow up alone, without the support and comradery of siblings?

You're getting ahead of yourself again! If she had to spend so much time mothering herself, she wouldn't have any energy left to raise a child, let alone more than one. Perhaps Frank …

Dearest Frank she began.

Thank you for all your letters which I received in bulk on my return to Geraldine.

I've decided that farming isn't for me, and Grace and I will be catching the ferry to Wellington after Christmas. We'll be just in time for any New Year's Eve dances so hopefully the war will stop long enough to grant you some more leave or even a weekend pass so we can see the New Year in together.

She paused, chewing on the end of the pen, contemplating what else needed to be said.

We don't have an address yet, but will likely stay at one of the boarding houses in the central city. Grace hopes to get a job typing for the government, and I'll take whatever is available but hopefully avoid the munitions factory.

The top of the pen rested on her bottom lip as she pondered how to finish. Yours sincerely was much too formal but love wasn't an emotion she could bring herself to declare, nor could she say she was his.

She settled on *Missing you too*. It was true. She missed dancing with him, hearing the sweet nothings that rolled off his tongue with ease, the drawl of his accent, their kisses, the fun they'd had beside the river.

Wishing you a lovely Christmas.

One kiss or two? Frank was a good kisser. She'd decided the first time their lips had met that he ranked at the top of her list and there were a few on it. She could easily put a dozen kisses at the bottom of the letter, but she didn't want to appear too keen. She grabbed the bundle of his letters and snatched the most recent from the envelope. Three kisses adorned the bottom of the page. Three kisses it was then.

She copied the address from the back of his last letter to the front of an envelope, wondering just how far Paekākāriki was from Wellington. Moira had never been to the North Island before. Shifting was an adventure in more ways than one.

With the letter finished and safely stowed in her handbag for posting, Moira headed to the front room where the Fords had a collection of books neatly stacked on a bookshelf. She scanned the shelves and eventually found the distinctive red cover of a well-used Collins New Zealand School Atlas. She remembered having to search the pages at school and quickly found a map of the Wellington region showing Paekākāriki sitting on the coast to the northwest with the key showing her a train track ran between the two and beyond. If Frank couldn't get leave then Moira could catch the train up to see him; the thought made her smile.

⌘

Moira woke with a familiar queasy feeling that didn't dissipate until she made her new routine visit to the toilet. Hanging her head over the porcelain bowl, she wondered what Christmas Day would bring her.

276

She washed her face and hands, sprayed some perfume to ensure there were no lingering odours to give her condition away and made her way to the dining room hoping everyone was none the wiser.

Mrs Ford placed a piece of dry toast and a cup of tea on the table.

"Here you are, dear," she said. "The perfect remedy for an upset stomach."

Moira gulped and looked wide-eyed at Grace.

"Moira was just making room for all the Christmas treats she's going to enjoy today." Grace's attempt to lighten the moment was appreciated.

"After a month of eating rabbit, morning, noon and night, my stomach isn't used to all the delicious food you cook," she added.

Mrs Ford nodded as if she agreed, but Moira guessed from the look on her face that that wasn't the case. She quietly sipped the tea and nibbled the toast, avoiding further eye contact until she'd finished.

"Here you are, girls." Mrs Ford handed Grace a bowl. "Please pick some peas for our meal."

Grace giggled and nudged Moira. "Come on, Moira. This'll be fun."

Half of the back section of the yard was occupied by the vegetable garden. Mr Ford was already amongst the rows of potatoes, loosening the earth with his fork and shaking the potatoes from the dirt.

"Pea picking time." He pointed to the row where criss-crossed bamboo stakes supported a healthy crop of peas. "Remember the rule, one for you, one for the bowl."

"Yes, Dad." Grace laughed and pretended to salute her father.

There was obviously a ritual to pea picking that Moira had no knowledge of. Something else she had missed out on as a child.

Grace squatted down beside the row of peas and picked her first pod. "One for me," she chimed as she split the pod, loosened the fresh peas with her thumb and scooped them into her mouth. "Mmm mmm, my favourite."

Seeing Grace's delight, Moira followed suit and soon enjoyed the sweet and earthy taste.

"Remember one for the bowl," Mr Ford called out as they both reached for another pod.

It took a good hour to shell enough peas to fill the bowl.

"I'm not sure I'll have any room left for lunch." Moira patted her full stomach.

"You'll find room," Grace replied. "You are eating for two, you know."

"Sshh!" Moira growled, glancing around to ensure no one else heard the comment. "I think your mum might have guessed already."

"Maybe, but she won't say anything, she's too polite for that."

⌘

The guests began arriving mid-morning, bringing with them a buzz of anticipation. There were hugs all around. Each time Moira was introduced to someone new, arms, fat, skinny, short, or long, were wrapped around her as if she were a long lost relative.

The oak dining room table was extended, additional chairs were retrieved from the back room, and fine china, silver cutlery, and linen napkins were perfectly laid out. A candelabra with holly twined around its arms was placed in the centre of the table, its flickering flames bringing an ethereal glow to the room's magic.

Moira was spellbound. She'd never experienced the laughter and joy of so many people at Christmas. After her father had disappeared from their family, Christmas Day was always just her and her mother. Her mother had tried her best to make the day special, but Moira always sensed something was missing. She watched the delight and heard the giggles of Grace's nieces and nephews and knew that any child of hers deserved that too.

Apart from the absence of the young men, there was no evidence that New Zealand was in the middle of the war. The table was laden with delicious food; bowls of peas, potatoes, pumpkin and carrots, a steaming gravy boat waiting for Mr Ford to carve the mutton roast that sat on a platter in front of him.

He paused before doing so. "Let us say grace, show our thanks for all that we have been blessed with."

Mothers hushed their children, the room went quiet, and the group bowed their heads while grace was recited and a collective 'amen' given. Moira wasn't religious, but her gratitude was heartfelt.

The reverent moment was quickly swamped by lively chatter. Christmas crackers were pulled, the snap igniting giggles of delight as paper hats and novelty items fell to be claimed by the winner. When everyone had a make-believe crown atop their heads, the food was served. Plates were passed to the head of the table for slices of meat, and bowls of vegetables were passed around. In a time of rationing and making do, the meal was fit for royalty.

There was a lull in the chatter while everyone ate. While Moira chewed quietly, she contemplated the baby growing inside her, imagining a tiny human to be loved and shown the joys of life. She was no longer certain she could end that before it had the chance to begin. She still doubted she'd make a better mother than her own but if she could find a family like this one, a family that would love her child, provide brothers and sisters, cousins and Aunts and Uncles, and most importantly a life that allowed the child to blossom, then she would happily bring her baby into the world.

"I hope you've left room for dessert." Mrs Ford stacked Moira's empty plate on top of the pile she was collecting.

"Let me take those for you," Moira offered. "Grace and I can do the dishes."

Moira thought it would give them an opportunity to chat, but the kitchen soon filled with people. Mrs Ford carefully lifted the plum pudding from the pot where it had been boiling away for most of the morning. She sighed with relief when a perfectly shaped and cooked pudding was released from the flour bag used to hold the mixture suspended in the water.

"Perfect again."

"You always did make the best plum pudding."

"Mum's never-fail special recipe complete with lucky threepence and sixpence."

A cousin peeled and diced a couple of apples into the fruit salad, Grace's aunt whipped the cream and spread it over the pavlova, and a niece was responsible for arranging sliced strawberries in a pretty pattern on the top. Her cheeks bulged as she adopted the rule, 'one for me, one for the pav.'

Back in the dining room, dessert plates now made the journey around the table, receiving a slice of plum pudding, a wedge of pavlova and a spoonful of fruit salad.

"Why do they call it plum pudding when there are no plums in it?" an inquisitive child asked.

"Good question, Joe. Perhaps they used to put plums in it."

"I hope I find the lucky coin." Another of Grace's nephews eagerly scooped up a spoonful of pudding.

"Slow down," warned his mother. "It won't be lucky if you swallow it."

The child's eyes widened, and he slowed his munching to a careful chew. Moira heeded the warning, too, content to savour the sweet and spicy flavours, the child within her wanting to find a sixpence. She bit down on something hard, thought it was likely just a nut until she couldn't crunch through. Her smile grew as she carefully swallowed the pudding to leave the coin sitting on her tongue. King George, stamped into silver, looked down on her as she pulled the coin from her mouth and held it up

"I've got one, I've got one," she squawked like the coin's *huia*.

"Make a wish," came the instructions from around the table.

"Aww, I wanted to get it, that's not fair," groaned a child.

Moira closed her eyes, inhaled deeply, and caught up in the moment, casting a silent wish that one day she and her family would enjoy a Christmas just like this one.

"What did you wish for?"

"She can't tell you; it'd be bad luck."

Moira didn't want anything to ruin the dream. In that moment, she felt anything was possible. She held the sixpence tightly in one hand while she finished her meal.

"Can we go outside now?" Another child asked after their plate had been scraped clean.

"Yeah, we can play hide and seek."

"Put your plates on the bench first," a mother requested. "And be careful in the garden, don't go squashing any flowers."

Moira licked the last remnants of pavlova from her spoon and leaned back in her chair, replete both physically and emotionally.

CHAPTER
23

On the morning of their departure, Moira was packing the last of her things into her suitcase when Mrs Ford entered the bedroom.

"Here's a little gift for you, dear, for the future." Mrs Ford handed her a small parcel wrapped in crinkled Christmas paper. "I hope you don't mind the second-hand wrapping."

"Thank you." Moira clutched the surprise gift to her chest, blinking back tears, silently cursing her out-of-control emotions. "I've had a wonderful time. I should be getting you a gift, not the other way around."

Moira froze when she unwrapped the parcel to reveal a tiny pair of knitted white bootees. Mrs Ford knew; the bootees were confirmation. A kind gesture, not a judgement. But they were so tiny. They sat in the palm of her hand, soft and delicate. How would she ever take care of a human so small and dependent upon her? All her fears and self-doubt came flooding back, bringing tears.

Mrs Ford wrapped her arms around Moira and patted her back like she was the baby.

"Now, now, don't worry, dear. Everything will work out in the end. It always does."

⌘

Despite the sea being calm, Moira still had to rush to the toilets once the ferry left the shelter of the harbour. Looking at her washed face in the mirror, she silently prayed her days of morning sickness would end soon. She rinsed her face and hands and returned to the seat Grace had found for them.

"You can keep an eye on the land if we sit here." Grace patted the seat beside her. "It'll help settle your stomach."

"I'm not sure it's seasickness," Moira murmured, not wanting the other passengers to hear. Watching the coastline might help if her queasiness was merely from the motion, but Mrs Ford's plain toast and a cup of tea seemed to be the only remedy for morning sickness.

The other passengers appeared oblivious to her condition. A family of four sat at a nearby table, enjoying a game of cards, with claps and squeals of delight from the children when a hand was won. In adjacent chairs, two women, with grey hair styled in matching buns sitting at the nape of their necks, were engrossed in reading books.

Moira followed Grace's suggestion and watched the coastline as the ferry sailed up the eastern coast of the

South Island. A pod of dolphins joined them on the journey, jumping out of the water as if enjoying a fun game of hide-and-seek. Vast areas of native bush covered the hillsides, at times meeting gentle bays of black iron sand, otherwise growing down to brush the waves breaking over rocks where seals fished amongst the seaweed or basked in the sunshine.

Moira was busy daydreaming about the tranquillity of the environment when the distinctive voices of American men filled the room and she turned on her seat, eager to get a better look.

"Well, well," she said to Grace. "I think the view is better this way now. I don't feel queasy at all."

"Oh, Moira, you're incorrigible." Grace rolled her eyes. "Is Frank one of them?"

"Just let me have a closer look and then I'll tell you." Moira chuckled. With all traces of morning sickness temporarily banished it felt good to have her flirty, fun-loving self back again. She was beginning to fear she'd either left that behind in the high country, or that a sense of humour was something you lost with pregnancy while you grew a baby instead and prepared yourself for the seriousness of parenthood.

The four soldiers all wore the distinctive brown American army uniform: neatly pressed shirts and trousers and shiny boots. Their matching haircuts were short on top and shaved at the sides, framing clean-shaven faces. They were handsome, but none of them were Frank.

"No," she replied. "Don't you remember? Frank's much better looking than them."

285

The men stood and scanned the room, like hunters scouring the terrain for their bounty. Their eyes eventually settled on Grace and Moira, and their mouths curved into wide smiles as they strode confidently over.

"Howdy, ladies, do you mind if we join y'all? The view looks lovely here."

"I'm not sure there is enough room." Grace looked at the limited space on either side of her and Moira.

"Of course there is." Moira gathered her coat and handbag onto her lap, clearing the seat beside her.

The boldest of the Americans immediately accepted the invitation.

"Thank you, Miss ....?" He held out his hand, not to shake but beckoning Moira to place her hand on his.

Moira ignored Grace's tsk of disapproval and lifted her hand, wishing they weren't chapped and calloused from farming.

"You can call me Moira," she purred as he brushed his lips across her knuckles.

"Lovely to meet y'all, Moira. I'm Henry." He sat beside Moira, not leaving a polite space but snuggling close like they were long-lost lovers reconnecting.

"Henry likes to make himself feel at home wherever he goes," teased one of the other soldiers. "I'm Drake, this here is Hudson, and the shy one at the back is Theodore, but everyone calls him Teddy."

Drake squeezed in next to Grace and Hudson sat beside him, leaving Teddy half a seat beside Henry.

"Have you been on leave?" Grace asked.

"Yes, in Christchurch." Henry replied. "We're heading back to base at Par-cack-car-rye-kie. Is that how y'all say it? I can't get my tongue around these native words."

"Paekākāriki," Grace corrected him. "You might know a *friend* of Moira's, he's based there."

Was *friend* an apt description for Frank? Moira had expected him to be a brief interlude, some fun before she went away but now, the implications of their friendship had gone far beyond.

"What's his name, Moira?" Grace's question came with an elbow nudging into her side.

She had no option but to reply. "Frank Davis."

"Haven't heard of him," Henry said. "But there are more than twenty thousand of us in camps all over the place. We're all based in Camp Russell, Camp Par-cack-car-rye-kie is up the road and Camp McKay is across the road. Then there are some other smaller camps closer to the city."

"We could ask around if you like," Teddy offered.

"Teddy! Why would they need to find an old friend when they've got us four to entertain them?"

"Thanks, Teddy." Grace ignored Henry's question. "Moira has written to him, let him know we were coming."

"Are there any other lucky men awaiting your arrival? Husbands? Boyfriends?" Drake directed his question at Grace.

Ben, the escaped soldier Grace had tried to help at *Whipsnade Farm* was still detained as a conscientious objector. He was hardly waiting for her arrival.

"Definitely no husbands," Grace replied.

"Nobody who's going to meet us when the ferry docks," Moira added.

Frank wasn't officially her boyfriend. His letters hinted he'd like to be but if or when he found out Moira's condition, she'd probably never see him again.

"Do you know of any New Year's Eve parties?" Moira wasn't going to let Grace ruin the chance for some fun with the soldiers.

"There's bound to be something, it depends on what y'all like to do." Henry turned and winked at Moira.

"I was hoping to dance the New Year in," she replied.

"The Majestic Cabaret will be yo'all best bet for a Chatanooga Choo Choo." Henry waved his arms and swayed as if he was already on the dance floor, causing everyone else to rock from side to side and pushing Teddy off the end of the seat.

"Oh, Teddy, are you alright?" Grace looked concerned.

"Grace will take care of you if you're not," Moira teased.

"I'm fine." Teddy's cheeks coloured bright red as he eased himself back onto the seat. He smiled timidly at Grace. "Thanks for inquiring."

"Where do y'all live?" Henry asked. "We could pick y'all up around seven."

"We might have to stay in camp this weekend, Henry?" Hudson appeared to be the serious, quiet one of the four. "Can't see us getting a pass when we've just been away."

"It's New Year's Eve. They can't stop us from celebrating, not when we'll likely be deployed into the South Pacific any time now. Leave the passes to me." Confidence oozed from every word Henry spoke. "I'll sort it. So where shall we pick y'all up from? What part of Wellington do y'all live in?"

"Nowhere yet. We're just moving there now. We'll find a boarding house in the city to start with, until we can get jobs."

"We'll have to catch the train down and walk to the Majestic. We might have to meet y'all there. It's on Willis Street. Ask any local, and they'll point the way." Henry took Moira's hand in his. "It's not very gentlemanly of us, but I'm sure I can find a way to make it up to y'all, Moira."

"Are all Americans smooth talkers like you?" Moira teased as she enjoyed the tingle his gentle touch ignited.

"Why, Moira!" Henry feigned offence. "I'm merely taking pleasure in the beauty that surrounds me. It'd be a foolish man who let the opportunity pass."

It felt good to be appreciated. Bill had treated her well but never where others could see, never as brazenly as the Americans did. Having some fun with Henry would be a wonderful way to farewell the year, but she'd have to let Frank know too.

"We'll see you there." Moira smiled as she freed her hand from Henry's. She didn't want to encourage him too much.

289

"What sort of work are y'all going to do?" Hudson asked.

"I'm a typist so I'd like to get a job with the government," Grace replied.

"Decoding top-secret messages," Moira added with a chuckle.

"And what about y'all, Moira? What hidden talents do y'all have?" Henry winked again at his innuendo.

"I used to work in retail," she replied. "Before we volunteered as land girls, that is."

Henry nodded and grinned. "Mmm, multi-talented and good at dealing with people."

"Y'all could volunteer at the Red Cross Club," Teddy suggested. "There's one right by the train station, in the Hotel Cecil. They have a canteen where we can get hamburgers, doughnuts, and ice cream sodas, just like at home. There's table tennis and pool."

"It sounds great, Teddy, but I can't afford to volunteer, I need a job that pays."

⌘

When the ferry left the shelter of the mainland and sailed into the open waters of the Cook Strait, the wind buffeted the side of the vessel, the bow rose and fell as the ship crested each wave, sea spray splashed over the railings and splattered against the windows.

Moira clutched her stomach and rushed to the toilets again, grateful that the American soldiers were no longer sitting with them to bear witness. The toilets were full of passengers in the same predicament. A queue formed out the door until the paper bags handed along the line were hurriedly used. Moira was grateful the toilets were strategically placed in the middle of the ship where the rolling motion seemed less, but the stench of vomit set her going again until she felt she had nothing left. She leaned against the wall while she waited to dispose of the bag. Her turn finally came; she glanced in the mirror as she washed, the face that looked back at her bereft of colour. She took another paper bag as a precaution and headed back to the seat.

"You look terrible."

"Thanks, Grace," Moira replied sarcastically. "I feel terrible."

"Lie down," Grace suggested. "Use my lap as a pillow."

"It's just seasickness." It had to be. Moira disliked pregnancy even more if it wasn't.

She lay down, curled her legs up under her coat and rested her head on Grace's thigh. Grace gently smoothed Moira's hair, brushing the wisps away from her face. Exhausted Moira soon dropped off to sleep.

⌘

The vibration of the ship's engine breaking woke Moira several hours later. She sat up with a start, dazed, trying to regain her bearings.

"Where are we?" she asked, her voice croaky.

"Good evening, sleepyhead. We're about to dock in Wellington." Grace rubbed her thigh. "You're looking much better. I can't say the same for my leg, you've put it to sleep."

"Sorry, Grace." Moira stood, shook her arms, and jigged from leg to leg, gazing out the window at the city. "Look, Grace. Isn't it exciting!"

The cityscape spread out in front of them, rising like a grandstand into the scrub-covered hills behind. The cargo sheds of the shipping yards had a prime position beside the water, for convenience obviously and not as an attractive sight to greet the visitors. A train, a trail of black smoke billowing behind, chugged along a railway track that wound its way around the bay. Multi-storey office buildings with ornate facades lined up parallel to the shoreline as if reporting for duty. They sat in a grid-like fashion with streets, busy with cars and pedestrians, dividing the sectors. The corrugated iron roofs of houses sat amongst pockets of greenery in the foothills.

The ship buzzed with excitement as passengers gathered their belongings and lined up to disembark.

"Welcome to Wellington." The purser in his crisp white uniform stood beside the exit door. "And where would you young ladies be heading this evening? Will there be someone to collect you and your belongings?"

"Hello, Sidney." Moira read his name tag. "There's no one to meet us. We need to find somewhere to stay. Can you suggest anywhere?"

"Well, I'd be remiss if I didn't recommend the YWCA hostel. It's perfect for young ladies like yourselves." Sidney replied. "It's in Boulcott Street. Do you know Wellington at all?"

"No, it's our first time."

292

"I'll give you this map." Sidney took a brochure from a shelf behind him and opened it out to reveal a street map of the city. He pointed to Boulcott Street and glanced down at their feet. "It's a bit of a walk but you've got sensible shoes on so you should be able to manage it. Otherwise, you'll find a taxi behind the train station."

"Thank you, Sidney."

A loud blast on the foghorn signalled that Sidney could open the doors to allow the passengers to disembark.

"Enjoy your stay in Wellington," he farewelled them.

"I intend to." Moira smiled, all remnants of morning sickness, seasickness and fatigue banished.

The American soldiers had already disembarked and were making their way to the train station. Henry turned, caught Moira's eye, and waved. She couldn't hear what he said above all the excited chatter, but she was certain he'd confirmed their New Year's Eve date. His broad smile of perfect white teeth reassured her there was fun to be had in Wellington.

The hustle and bustle of the city created a cacophony of sound: vehicle engines revving, horns tooting, and trams' squealing brakes. Moira and Grace crossed the busy road that divided the city from the shipping yards and railway tracks.

No sunshine reached them as they stood in the shadows of the buildings to gather themselves. Around them, office workers were heading home for the day, their heels scuffing the pavement. Pedestrian chatter blurred into a low hum, punctuated by raised commands and calls for taxis. The windows of the buildings gradually disappeared as shades were lowered, curtains drawn, or black cloth hitched into place. Everyone was abiding by the blackout rule designed to make it more difficult for the enemy to find their target.

"We'd better look at the map, Moira." Grace put her suitcase on the footpath and took the map from her handbag. "It'll be blackout soon; we'll have to get to Boulcott Street."

They orientated the map, turning it until the sea was behind them, in reality, and on paper.

"Look, Boulcott Street joins onto Willis Street." Grace pointed. "If we cross here, we'll get to Willis and then we can just walk until it meets Boulcott."

"But look, Grace. Boulcott Street goes for miles. What if we start at the wrong end?" Moira looked down at her red toe-peepers. "I don't think my feet will like that."

A passerby must have seen their lost looks and stopped to help. They soon learned the YWCA hostel was in the middle of Boulcott Street and there was no shortcut to get there.

"Thank you." Grace folded the map and stowed it back into her handbag. "We'll walk as far as we can and get a taxi if we need to."

⌘

They were both shivering by the time they finally reached the YWCA building. A southerly wind had whirled its way between the buildings, whisking the hems of their dresses and ruining their hairstyles, making Moira feel like she'd been through the wringer of a washing machine.

"Oh, thank God for that." She dumped her suitcase on the front steps of the hostel and sighed with relief.

"Moira!" Grace growled.

"What? What have I done now? I just need to catch my breath."

"This is the YWCA. Young. Women's. Christian. Association." Grace spoke slowly to emphasise each word. "I don't think any blaspheming will be appreciated."

"I wasn't blaspheming," Moira groaned. "I was thanking him for finally getting me here. I'm frozen."

"Well, pick up your suitcase then, and we'll get inside where it'll be warm."

Moira gritted her teeth. Grace's mothering wasn't appreciated. Her annoyance was soon forgotten when they entered the reception area, even with its high ceiling it was noticeably warmer. The happy sound of women's singing to the upbeat tempo of a piano drifted in from a nearby room, and the aroma of a hot meal wafted from the opposite direction. This would do fine.

CHAPTER
24

After both securing jobs—Moira's in one of the many milk bars dotted around Wellington and Grace's for the government—they read the advertisements in the *Evening Post* in search of accommodation. By Friday, they'd secured more permanent accommodation at *The Moorings*, a boarding house in the suburb of Thorndon, but could not move in until the first week in January. Meanwhile, Moira had to watch her language. 'God' had slipped into the conversation several times and was met by stern looks and frowns from some of the other female guests at the YWCA.

The night curfew was another rule that Moira was having trouble with. She quickly learned to arrange for Grace to sneakily open the door at the back of the building, the entrance staff used for deliveries, at an agreed time. Grace wanted to make the right impression in her dream job working for the government, so she was happy to stay in on weeknights. She wasn't so happy when Moira was late, and she had to stand around in the cold kitchen in her nightgown.

"Moira!" Grace's muffled growl echoed around the kitchen. "It's nearly midnight. What have you been doing at this hour?"

"We went to the movies tonight, *Arsenic and Old Lace*. I haven't laughed so much in ages." Moira broke into giggles again. "You should have come, Grace. You need a good laugh."

Grace put a finger to her lips to hush Moira, grabbed her by the hand as if she was a naughty child, dragged her through the kitchen and headed back upstairs to the room they shared.

"Whose we? Did Frank come to town?" Grace asked when the door was closed behind them.

"No, but before you get all grumpy, I have written to him and let him know we'll be at the Majestic Cabaret on New Year's Eve."

"Whose 'we' then?" Grace stood, hands on hips, demanding an answer.

"Just some Yanks I met at the milk bar." Moira spoke casually as she undressed for bed. "They asked if I'd like to go to the movies after work and I said yes, simple as that, Grace. Just young people enjoying life while they're still here."

"No, need to be sarcastic, Moira." Grace climbed into her bed. "I'm just trying to look out for you, that's all."

"I know." Moira turned the light out and slipped between the cool sheets of her bed. "And I am grateful."

⌘

Grace had already gone to work by the time Moira conceded she had to leave the cosiness of her warm bed and begin the day. She'd discovered that staying in bed as long as possible kept her morning sickness at bay. Her work day at the milk bar didn't start until ten o'clock, so it was perfect.

The job meant she was on her feet all day and it didn't pay that well, but milk bars were the favoured spot for the American soldiers, or Yanks as everyone referred to them. The milkshakes, burgers and doughnuts on the menu reminded the men of home and Moira was always happy to chat and make them feel welcome.

Dressed in her uniform, a short-sleeved dress with a white apron, Moira washed her delicates in the handbasin and pegged them to the string line a previous tenant had strung across the room before heading out for the day.

"Is there any mail for me?" Moira stopped by the reception desk. "Moira Harvey," she said in response to the receptionist's vague look.

The young women flicked through the letters filed in the 'H' slot. Moira's heart skipped a beat when she recognised Frank's handwriting on the envelope passed to her.

"Thank you." Her voice quivered.

She'd been eager to get to the department store and buy a new dress for the cabaret but now, with the letter tightly held, she headed to the reading room in the opposite direction. Moira chose an armchair in the furthest corner, avoiding the other women who were reading the latest news in the paper or engrossed in a novel. She returned their nods and polite smiles but was grateful nobody spoke to her.

Her fingers trembled as she edged her thumb under the envelope's flap and eased the letter out, her heart thumping in her chest.

Dearest Moira

Receiving your letter has made me the happiest man on earth. I was beginning to despair that you had been a figment of my imagination when I wrote so many times and got no reply.

It's wonderful to know you are just down the road in Wellington. I will get leave as soon as possible and take you on a proper date.

Until then, Frank x

He still wanted her. Moira sighed so loud that everyone in the reading room paused to look at her. It was as if time was suspended, anticipating the worst until Moira smiled.

"It's alright. It's good news." She reread the letter just to be sure before folding it carefully back into the envelope.

There was a lightness to her step as she headed to work; anticipation for the weekend filled her with joy.

⌘

"I didn't realise how much I missed getting glammed up." Moira dabbed her lipstick with a tissue and made sure there were enough bobby pins in her hair to ensure the French roll she'd styled would stay in place for a night of dancing. "Imagine what we'd be doing if we were still stuck in Orari and having to get up and milk the cows in the morning."

"I am enjoying my new eight-to-five job," Grace replied. "Wearing skirts and dresses instead of overalls."

"And you've finally stopped smelling like rotting flax." *Thank goodness,* Moira thought but didn't add.

The mirror hanging above the basin was too small for the head-to-toe view Moira needed to ensure that she was ready to dazzle. She was unsure if the butterflies in her stomach were from excited anticipation or nervousness at seeing Frank again. Would he still have the same feelings for her? It was all very well for him to put them in a letter when he was alone and homesick, but would they still be real when they met? Their time together had been so brief. When he really got to know her, would the spark still be there? Her history with men and relationships resounded with a very convincing 'no'.

"How do I look?" She sought reassurance from Grace.

Grace turned and smiled. "You look beautiful, Moira. You'll have Frank eating out of your hand."

Until I tell him about the baby!

"And you'll have a line-up of Yanks wanting to dance with you, Grace." Moira picked up her coat. "It's a pity we're not being collected from here. That Wellington wind is brisk again tonight. I hope my hair doesn't get all messed up on the walk."

"It's not far." Grace put on her coat and hurried Moira out the door. "We'd better go, or we'll be late."

Fortunately, the wind was at their backs, at times strong enough to feel like it was pushing them along. A small crowd gathered outside the cabaret, a mixture of uniforms, naval and army, some with women on their arms, others, clearly single, and looking for fun.

"Moira!"

Moira sucked in a breath. A man's American accent called out her name. Someone was waiting for her. Frank? She turned towards the source and tried to look casual, looking amongst the faces for Frank's smile, his chocolate-brown eyes and his smooth, tanned skin.

"Hi, so glad y'all could make it." Henry bustled through the crowd, a corsage in his hand. "I bought this for y'all. May I?"

He lifted his hand to pin the corsage to Moira's dress.

"Excuse me." Frank arrived from the opposite direction and tucked his arm possessively under Moira's.

"Frank!" she squealed.

"Frank?" Henry's look said he didn't share Moira's delight at the reunion.

"Sorry, Henry, this is Frank. Frank meet Henry." Moira glanced from one man to the other, hoping to diffuse any antagonism. "We met on the ferry sailing. I was telling him about you," she explained to Frank.

Henry was gracious in defeat. "You're a lucky man, Frank. Have a great night. Hopefully, you'll allow me a dance later, Moira."

"That would be nice, Henry."

Henry turned his attention to Grace. "Evening, Grace. Teddy was hoping you'd be here."

He called out to Teddy and waved him over. Teddy arrived, shy and red-faced but his eyes lit up when he spied Grace. He timidly offered her a corsage, his trembling fingers held none of Henry's boldness as the corsage was pinned to Grace's dress.

"I'm glad we got that settled. I thought I might find y'all here, and it looks like I arrived in the nick of time." Frank wrapped his arm around Moira's shoulders and kissed her cheek. "Shall we go inside and get out of this wind?"

With its blacked-out windows, the building looked like any other on Willis Street, but once inside, the Majestic Cabaret lived up to its name in every sense. The spacious room had a grandness that rose all the way to the lofty, ornate ceilings. The Laurie Paddi Dance Band filled the stage framed by velvet curtains, the musicians priming their instruments. Drums, a grand piano and a double bass sat behind a row of brass players—saxophones and trumpets. Behind the band, a large banner displayed the flags of both countries, and an eagle with wings unfurled flew between the two, uniting the allies.

The room was a smorgasbord, a dance full of soldiers, that in other times, Moira would have enjoyed a selection of morsels from, a taste of all that was on offer until she found the sweetest dessert. Tonight though, on Frank's arm, she had no need to partake.

Moira and Frank, Grace and Teddy found a table close to the stage. Frank and Teddy introduced themselves and shook hands before pulling out the chairs for Moira and Grace.

"I think we should have champagne tonight," Frank suggested. "It is New Year's Eve, and there is much to celebrate."

"That would be lovely." Moira saw the sanctioning glance Grace sent her way, but one glass of champagne wouldn't hurt. She could just sip at it, make it last the entire night. She had no intention of ruining their fun by revealing her condition.

The music had started by the time Frank wove his way back through the crowd, carrying a tray laden with four glasses and an open champagne bottle chilling in a silver ice bucket.

"Let's dance." The music's tempo had Moira's toes tapping under the table. "It feels like forever since I last got to dance."

"One toast first." Frank poured the champagne, handed a glass to each of them and raised a toast. "To friends and lovers, together at last."

Moira took the tiniest of sips, the bubbles tickled her nose, the adoring look Frank gave her melted her insides. If only the moment could last. She shook her head to flick away any negative thoughts, reminding herself to stay in the moment and enjoy all the fun and excitement on offer.

Frank held Moira's hand as they joined couples already on the dance floor jiving to the drummer's boogie beat. A saxophonist joined in, then a trumpeter, until the entire band were playing a happy tune, and the dance floor came alive.

With Frank's hand gently wrapped around her, Moira felt like she'd been transported back to their first meeting at the dance in Orari. She knew so little about this man, but he turned her insides on end, made her feel like anything was possible as he spun her out at arm's length as if to show her to the world, then pulled her close to his chest to claim possession.

Conversation was nigh impossible, but neither was it necessary, their eyes met and silently conveyed a mutual desire. Where their skin touched or bodies brushed against each other, an energy charge ignited like an electrical spark. Moira was buzzing.

The music went from jive to swing to foxtrot. Moira's hips never stopped swaying until finally, the band opted to slow the pace to a waltz, and Frank pulled her close.

"Finally," he sighed. "I've got y'all where y'all belong, in my arms."

Was that where she belonged, or was he just sweet-talking her? A niggling doubt kept her from fully embracing the moment. There was a conversation that needed to be had, but not now; she wasn't going to risk ruining their reunion. She wanted to finish the year celebrating all that was, not fretting about all that might be.

She rested her cheek against his chest, listening to the reassuring beat of his heart, a constant and regular rhythm that said it could be relied upon.

Up on stage, Jean McPherson was introduced, her silver sequined bolero sparkled in the lights as she sung her version of the Andrews Sisters' *Rum and Coca Cola.* Frank and Moira returned to the table as Jean continued with the drink theme and sang *Cocktails for Two.*

Frank gulped down his champagne as if it were beer. "Would y'all like another drink?"

"No, no, I'm fine." Moira's throat was parched, but she resisted the urge to copy Frank and finish her glass of champagne. "Thank you."

"I'll leave y'all ladies to drink the champagne and I'll get a beer." Frank stood to go to the bar as Teddy and Grace arrived back at the table. "Teddy, did y'all want to get a beer?"

Teddy's boyish grin said beer was much more to his liking as well and the two men disappeared, skirting around the edge of the dance floor towards the bar.

"Have you told him?" Grace barely waited until they were out of earshot.

"No!" Moira glared at her. "And I'm not going to tonight."

"Don't waste too much time." Grace continued, ignoring Moira's pinched expression. "He deserves to know. What if he gets deployed? It could happen, you know; he could end up battling the Japanese in the South Pacific. That is what they've come for."

"You and Teddy seem to be getting along well." Moira deliberately changed the subject.

Grace huffed but conceded defeat. "He is rather cute, isn't he? He wants me to go and watch a baseball game with him tomorrow. Perhaps we could double date?"

"Baseball? Is that the American version of softball?"

"I haven't a clue, but we could take a picnic, make a day of it," Grace suggested. "I don't want to be late, though;

305

I've got work the next day, and we have to move our things to the *Moorings*."

"That's right." Moira smiled, a secret smile like a cat that discovered a stash of cream. She'd been quietly wondering where and how she would get some quality time alone with Frank, not time to talk but time to explore what they'd started at their picnic by the river in Orari, this time without being rudely interrupted. She couldn't very well bring him back to the YWCA room she shared with Grace, and she imagined it would be the same, or worse if she turned up at the camp where he most likely bunked in with a dozen other soldiers. The *Moorings* provided the answer, separate rooms, and no curfew; there were rules banning parties but nothing to forbid visitors.

Frank and Teddy arrived back with Henry in tow.

"Moira." Henry reached his hand out to her. "Can I claim that dance y'all promised me now?"

Her immediate reaction was to look to Frank for some indication of approval, but she stopped herself, she didn't belong to him, she could dance with a friend if she wanted to.

"That'd be nice, Henry." She stood, placed her hand on his and followed him to the dance floor.

It felt as if Frank's eyes were boring into the back of her head, so she sashayed her hips just a little more before Henry turned to face her, and the band headed into *Boogie Woogie Bugle Boy.*

⌘

Midnight came around all too fast. Moira and Frank danced right up until the band played its last note on a sweet and soothing rendition of *Auld Lang Syne*. Everyone formed a circle around the edge of the dance floor, swinging their linked hands up and down as they stepped forward and back, chanting the words. It was a tradition that united America and New Zealand, joining men and women in a common hope for good times. The song was sung as the clock ticked past midnight before war had engulfed nations, and it would be sung long after the war had finally finished.

Slowly, the dance hall emptied, and couples filed out into the darkened streets, a full moon replacing the light normally cast by the streetlamps.

"We'll walk y'all home." Frank wrapped his arm around the small of Moira's back.

The cold breeze was now on their faces as they headed back the way they'd come. Moira snuggled into Frank's side, absorbing the heat that radiated from him.

"We're staying at the YWCA," Grace said. She and Teddy walked ahead, holding hands. "We won't be able to invite you in."

She was always straight to the point. Bless her, thought Moira. At least everyone knew where they stood. If Frank and Teddy were expecting more, they didn't show it.

"How are we going to get in?" Moira asked. "Won't they have locked the doors by now?"

"The manager said they'd make an exception for tonight. We can ring the bell, and someone will come and open the door but only until one hour past midnight."

They turned into Boulcott Street, grateful to be sheltered in the lee of the building. The footpath plunged into darkness, and the moon was unable to permeate between the buildings on either side of the street. Frank took advantage of the moment, stopped, and pulled Moira into his arms. His lips found hers and devoured hers with pent-up passion. There was no need for light, lamp, or lunar. If this was the only chance they had to express their feelings tonight, it would be sustained until the next opportunity came.

"I think I've fallen for Moira Harvey," Frank murmured when they finally broke apart. "Hook, line and sinker."

Moira couldn't express her feelings; they were a jumbled mess that threatened to spill out in all the wrong ways. So, she poured all her desire into a kiss, winding her hands around his head and pulling his mouth to hers.

"Come on, you two," Grace growled. "We'll be late. You can see each other again tomorrow."

CHAPTER
25

The new year dawned with a sense of hope. Moira lay in her single bed dreaming of happy beginnings: a new home at the *Moorings*, her new job at the milk bar, new friendships with the Yanks, new and fun parties, and outings to be enjoyed. Her light and cheerful thoughts turned to more serious beginnings, the life that was growing inside her. Already, she'd noticed the subtle changes in her body, the tenderness of her breasts, the widening of her waistline. She rested her palms on her belly, a maternal desire to protect the tiny life within.

What would a baby mean for her renewed relationship with Frank? How and when was she even going to tell him? She imagined Grace chastising her, saying it should be sooner rather than later. The tiny niggling doubt that the baby was even Frank's, held her back. What if it was Matiu's instead? What if she told Frank the baby was his, and the baby was born with skin that spoke clearly of Matiu's Maori genes? Waiting until the day all was revealed wasn't an option, though. She glanced at the calendar pinned to the wall, still showing December. Perhaps she could work back, establish some dates, estimate when she would have been ovulating, see if the dates coincided with the dance at Orari, her picnic with Frank, the moment that sex became unprotected.

If— no, not if—but when she told Frank, would he relish the opportunity to have a baby? With her? Or would he just disappear off fighting in the war or go back to America, leaving her to raise a child on her own? Could she do that? Could she be a better parent than her own had been? Or should she terminate this life before it had a chance to breathe? She'd got the job at the milk bar because one of the other waitresses had failed to turn up to work. Apparently, she'd been in the same condition as Moira and had visited a back street clinic to terminate the pregnancy. It hadn't gone well; she lost so much blood she collapsed and had to be taken to the hospital, where she was in a bad way with septicaemia. She could die. Moira wasn't willing to risk that.

The questions couldn't be answered from the safety of her single bed, so she flung back the bedding and swung her legs out over the side, gasping as her toes touched the vinyl floor.

"You look like you're a million miles away." Grace's voice shook Moira from her contemplation. "Are you dreaming about your American lover boy?"

310

"Are you dreaming about yours?" Moira retorted with a cheeky grin, avoiding revealing her thoughts. "A living teddy to cuddle into."

Grace blushed. "He is gentle and kind. I don't think he's cut out to be a soldier. He seems to have joined up because a holiday with his mates in the South Pacific sounded like a good idea."

"And Frank said they might be shipped out any day now, so we'd better make the most of our time together."

"What are we going to take for the picnic?" Grace was ever the practical one.

"It's probably just as easy to go via the milk bar," Moira suggested, pulling on her dressing gown. "Get some Coca-Cola to drink, ask the girls to make us some hamburgers to take away."

"That sounds like a good idea."

The women quickly made their beds. There was no need to be fussy; they weren't going to sleep in them again.

Moira pulled the calendar from the wall and turned the month backwards instead of forward.

"My feet are sore from all the dancing." She faked a groan, not wanting to reveal her reason for studying the calendar. "It seems like forever since we last danced. Do you remember when it was? In Orari?"

"Umm." Grace looked skyward for a second then her eyes went wide. "You should remember that; it was the week after the A & P show."

"I didn't go to the A & P show." Bill had been shot the week before and she'd been too busy trying to prove to John and Anne she could run the farm without them.

"Sorry, that's right," Grace apologised. "I'm pretty sure the A & P Show was the first weekend in November."

"Six or seven weeks then. No wonder my feet hurt. They're more used to wearing gumboots than heels." Moira hoped her musings would disguise her real reason for asking. If only she could remember when her last period had been. She wracked her brain, searching for some reminder that would confirm the father of her baby.

Bill's injuries came at the end of spring. She was already exhausted, and his injuries became her prime concern, whether she'd had a period was of no consequence. She may have been too stressed. Her body may have hit pause, and her hormones were sending out a warning that now was not a good time to create a new life.

Her temples started to throb. There was no memory to stifle her niggling doubt. She shook her head, pushing the dilemma aside, turned the calendar to January and hung it back on the wall.

"Here's to new beginnings," she said to herself as much as to Grace.

⌘

It was a beautiful day to laze around in the sunshine watching a group of men yell and yahoo like schoolboys. It was easy to pretend there wasn't a war going on.

"This game looks just like softball to me." Coca-Cola tingled Moira's mouth. "A diamond with bases, bat and ball, pitcher, and fielders. Why do you call it baseball?"

"Softball is for sissies," Frank teased. "Our diamonds are bigger, our bats and balls smaller. We play like men, no underarm pitches in this game."

"They do throw the ball rather fast," Grace added. "I'd be worried about getting hit in the head."

"We wouldn't want that." Teddy gently touched his palm to Grace's cheek. "You'all too beautiful."

Moira ignored the sentimentality between the couple. "Kiwi men aren't sissies. They play rugby, no helmets, no protective padding, just full-on tackling, scrums with the weight of the whole team behind them. The Yanks might beat us at baseball, but they'd never win in a game of rugby."

"Well, there's a challenge," Frank replied. "I'll suggest it to the lads. New Zealanders against Americans. Allies on the battlefield, opponents on the rugby field." He sidled closer to Moira and took her hand in his. "Enough about them, I want to know all about y'all."

"There's not much to tell." Moira absorbed the warmth radiating from his hand but was wary of relaxing too much, giving away details that would turn him away from her.

"There must be. Parents, siblings, big family, little family, goals, and dreams. I want to know everythin', Moira. What plans do you have now you've moved to Wellington?"

"We're shifting today." Moira focused on the present and smiled suggestively at Frank, it was easier than delving into the past or worrying about the future. "A private boarding house, none of the restrictions of the YWCA."

"I have to head back to base before nightfall, but perhaps I could help y'all move." Frank twirled the tip of his finger around Moira's palm.

"I'd like that," was all she needed to say.

"Once, you'll moved, what are your plans?"

Moira wanted to say that it depended on him, but she didn't. "While the war continues, I'll keep helping in the small way I can. Working in the milk bar, cheering up the soldiers with some good food and a chat."

"Don't cheer them up too much, I'll get jealous." Frank continued twirling his finger around Moira's palm. "And after the war?"

His touch distracted her as if his finger was drilling all the way to her core.

"Who knows when that will even be," she replied, sucking in a deep breath.

"Would y'all ever consider coming to America?"

Moira searched Frank's face for a clue. What was he really asking her? Should she take the question literally or was it an offering?

"I … might …" She didn't want to close any door before it had the chance to open wide.

"I'd like y'all to meet my family. I know my mum would adore y'all. She's always saying I need to find a good woman."

Moira giggled nervously. "You'd better keep looking then."

"No need." Frank kissed the top of Moira's hand. "I've already found her."

The flutter in Moira's stomach wasn't from morning sickness; her pulse raced, and she was grateful she was already seated as her legs turned to jelly. This floating bubble she found herself in would surely burst when she told him about the baby. She should break the news now and accept her fate before she got too deeply entwined. But Grace and Teddy were sitting close, they would hear, even over the noise of the game. Such a talk should be held privately. Moira latched onto the excuse that let her off, for now.

"Oh, Frank, you're one smooth-talking Yank." She attempted to lighten the moment. "I bet you say that to all the girls."

Frank sat up straight as if he'd been offended. "Let me prove it to y'all, Moira." He stood and reached for her hand. "Come on, let's go."

"But the game hasn't finished."

"Bugger the game, this is much more important. Teddy, Grace, we're leavin', you'll be okay to pack up here and take everything home, won't y'all."

Grace's look silently asked Moira if she needed to be rescued. Moira shook her head.

"I'll help Grace." Teddy grinned from ear to ear, seizing the opportunity.

Frank wrapped his arm possessively around Moira as they left the field and headed back towards town.

"Where are we going?" Moira asked.

"I said I'd help y'all move." Frank winked and leaned closer to whisper into Moira's ear. "We'll move your belongings and then I'll move you."

His warm breath tickled her earlobe. It was nothing compared to the heat simmering inside. Memories of their riverside interlude filled her with anticipation. This time, they wouldn't be interrupted. This time, she couldn't get pregnant. She quickened her pace; the sooner they reached the *Moorings*, the sooner she could anchor in a safe harbour.

⌘

The *Moorings* sat amongst the native greenery of the hillside, the steep pitch of its roof rising like the prow of a ship, gifting a view out over the parliament buildings to the harbour beyond. Frank carried Moira's suitcase on their walk from the YWCA to these much grander lodgings and they now stood at the front door.

Moira hesitated before ringing the doorbell. "I've never lived anywhere so grand before."

"Y'all deserve to. A lady should live like a queen." Frank's smooth voice flowed like the fairytale words he spoke.

It was a nice sentiment, but the reality was much different.

The door opened and the landlady, dressed as grand as the house, ushered them in.

"Good afternoon, welcome to the *Moorings*." Her tone was more motherly than matronly. "I'm Mrs Stevens."

The ornate ceiling of the entrance hall floated overhead taking Moira's breath away.

"I … I'm Moira Harvey." She stopped gazing about in wonder and addressed the woman who was now her landlady. "I've booked a room."

"Yes, and your friend, Grace, is she arriving today too?"

"She will be, she's just watching a game of baseball."

"And are you Mr Harvey?" The woman turned her attention to Frank.

"Frank Davis III, ma'am." Frank removed his hat and bowed like a true gentleman.

"I don't usually allow unmarried couples in my rooms unchaperoned." The landlady looked from Frank to Moira and then glanced at the grandfather clock as if it was a sentry guarding the proceedings.

"It is only mid-afternoon." Frank's smooth voice could charm anyone. "I do have to be back at base before nightfall."

"If you were engaged?" She looked like she was wavering.

Moira had to temper her impatience and stop her eyes from rolling. She thought she was moving into an establishment with fewer rules.

"Not yet, ma'am" Frank winked at Moira.

Did his wink mean he was teasing Moira or joking with the landlady?

"I'll show you to your room then." The landlady spoke directly to Moira and emphasised 'your' before she turned and followed a soft carpet runner that led the way to an elaborately carved staircase at the end of the hall.

Moira felt like she was walking the red carpet at the Academy Awards. She had no knowledge of art but the paintings on the walls flanking the hall, looked like they'd been created by the masters.

"This is a beautiful building." Frank followed them up the staircase as if he too was moving in. "Reminds me of my home."

Moira gulped. *Frank lived in a house like this!*

"It was owned and designed by John Sydney Swan, a prominent Wellington architect." The landlady rattled off the details as Moira ran her palm along the highly-polished timber balustrade. "He was a keen sailor, hence the exterior design. He favoured the Edwardian style for the interior, and we haven't had to change anything." The landlady stopped at the first door on the upstairs landing. "I've put you in this room. Grace will be next door."

"Thank y'all, ma'am." Frank's manners were impeccable. "I'll just help Moira settle in and I'll be on my way."

"Be sure you are, Mr Davis." The landlady turned to leave. "Supper is at six in the dining room. Moira, I'll give you and Grace the grand tour before then."

They waited until Mrs Stevens descended the staircase out of view. Frank closed the door, dropped Moira's suitcase on the floor and pulled her into his arms.

"I've waited so long to get y'all to myself." There was no timid testing of the waters, Frank's kiss dived in, exploring, delving, releasing.

Breathless, Moira gave herself willingly, allowing Frank to edge her back to the side of the bed while his lips continued to shower kisses. Thoughts of inspecting her room, unpacking her bag, and admiring the view from the French doors were abandoned. Lust took over and she wouldn't stand in its way.

⌘

They lay naked, bodies still entwined between the now rumpled sheets of the bed. Frank glanced at his watch.

"I might have to love y'all and leave y'all, my darling," he whispered. "Grace should be here soon, Mrs Stevens will growl, and I might miss the train back to base."

They were three good reasons for leaving but Moira was stuck on the 'love you'. He hadn't actually said 'I love you'. It was merely an expression. A polite way of referring to the sex. Wasn't it? In the afterglow of their interlude, she felt loved, but she'd felt like that before, she knew that was only the hormones, it would soon dissipate.

Afraid to say the wrong words and ruin the moment, she leaned in and kissed Frank. Delight, gratitude and a chance for a future conveyed silently.

"We can't have Mrs Stevens growling at you. She might never let you back in," Moira teased.

"I don't know when I'll be able to come back." Frank discarded the used condom in the bin, gathered his clothes from the floor and began dressing.

Moira's heart thudded. She gulped. He hadn't left the room, and it was already over. She stood, frozen in time, admiring his tanned and muscular body as he dressed, capturing an image to preserve for the future, to be able to describe to her child the father it would never meet.

She was brought back to the present when Frank rushed to her side and wrapped his arms around her.

"What's wrong?" The concern in his voice eased her self-doubt. "What did I do? Did I hurt y'all?"

She smiled and made light of the moment. "I was missing you already."

"I wish I could come again next weekend but I mightn't be able to get a pass." Frank pulled his trousers on. "Y'all could always come up to Par-cack-car-rye-kie. There's bound to be a party at Aunty Jean's or a show at the ANA Club, movies at the Saint Peters Hall."

"That sounds exciting." Moira caught a glimpse of her side profile in the full-length mirror on the wardrobe door and quickly grabbed her dress to cover herself.

"Don't cover you'll beautiful body." Frank, who was now fully clothed, pulled the dress away and turned Moira so that her nakedness was reflected in the mirror. "I could look at it forever." He trailed his hands down over her breasts and rested them on her belly.

Moira didn't dare to breathe, to exhale and relax, to allow her stomach to balloon like a pregnant woman.

"I don't think Mrs Stevens will appreciate me turning up for the grand tour in my birthday suit." Humour always served Moira well. "You'd best be on your way so I can unpack and make this room look like that's all we've been doing."

"I'll ask her for the telephone number on my way out." Frank's farewell kiss was full of promise. "I'll phone you durin' the week, let you know what arrangements I can make."

"Sounds like an army manoeuvre."

Frank pulled her into his arms, his eyes locked on hers with undeniable sincerity.

"I want to make sure our next date is as special as y'all are." His smooth words were like a warm coat that Moira never wanted to take off.

CHAPTER
26

The effervescence Moira started the week with dissipated a little each day. She gave herself a pep talk each morning and reinforced her mantra that life was too short not to have fun. Every time she heard the telephone's ring echoing up the stairwell, her heart skipped a beat and was filled with anticipation. It quickly turned to disappointment when another boarder was summoned to take the call or Mrs Stevens herself chatted away. What if Frank had been trying to call and all he got was an engaged signal? He might think Moira had lost interest.

Work was busy. She'd heard there were more than 25,000 American troops in New Zealand. Some days, it seemed they were all in her milk bar. She and the other waitresses were run off their feet, and she came home exhausted, too tired to do more than wash, eat a light supper, and climb into bed.

"I hope you're looking after yourself." Grace stopped by Moira's room one night. "You don't seem to be eating much. You are eating for two, remember."

Moira looked down at her tummy and then wide-eyed at Grace.

"You are still two, aren't you?" Grace's forehead furrowed with concern. "You haven't … have you?"

"It's called an abortion, Grace. You can say the word." Moira had been saying it to herself often enough as she battled with the pros and cons of bringing a baby into a world still battling away at war.

"Have you had an abortion, Moira?" Grace wouldn't let up.

"No. I haven't. And I'm not going to." Moira felt instant relief at giving voice to the conclusion she'd subconsciously reached. "And I am looking after myself."

"Oh, I am so happy for you." Grace hugged Moira, patting her back like she was a baby that needed soothing. "Has Frank asked you to marry him?"

"No!" Moira snapped. "I don't want to marry someone just because of a baby. If I have to I'll do this by myself. Plenty of other women are."

"But haven't you noticed, Moira, most people scorn those women as harlots and slags? Aren't you afraid of what people might think?"

Moira shrugged as if she didn't care. It wasn't true. She'd borne the brunt of judgemental looks many a time, and it wasn't nice.

"You are still seeing Frank though, aren't you?"

"Well, I did last weekend. I haven't heard from him since." Moira's eyes glassed over. Annoyed at the emotions she seemed to have no control over, she blinked the burgeoning tears away. "He's likely moved on to someone else."

"I'm sure he hasn't. He's probably busy. They are supposed to be protecting us from the Japanese."

⌘

When Moira was finally summoned to the telephone, she was tired and grumpy after a restless night.

"Hello," she said gruffly, still in her dressing gown, rubbing the sleep from her eyes.

"Hello, my darling, it's Frank."

He didn't need to announce himself. His American accent was the tonic Moira needed to perk up.

"Hi Frank, it's so good to finally hear from you."

"And y'all too, my love. Can y'all get away early on Friday night? Catch the train up. We can go to the movies on Friday and there's a dance on Saturday."

Moira heard the excitement in Frank's voice and the thought of a weekend together had her slippered feet bouncing on the polished floor.

"That's sounds wonderful." She could have asked where she'd sleep, but if she never slept a wink the entire weekend, it wouldn't matter. "If they won't give me the night off, I'll call in sick."

"I don't want to get y'all in trouble."

"It's alright, if they fire me there are plenty more milk bars, I can get a job at."

"There's one here in Par-cack-car-rye-kie. Maybe y'all could get a job there, and then I could see y'all every day."

Moira hesitated. "Maybe." She tried to keep the brightness in her voice and give no hint that sooner or later she was either going to have to tell Frank about the baby or the pregnancy would reveal itself. She touched her hand to her belly. Perhaps a little distance was better until she knew for sure how Frank would react.

"I'll see y'all on Friday then," Frank said. "I can't talk now, sorry, we're about to go on manoeuvres. Bye, my love."

"Bye." Moira managed to say before the phone clicked off.

It was just as well he had to hurry away. She was left pondering the word 'love' and the ease with which Frank seemed to use it, almost casual as if it didn't carry the burden of the word as she knew it.

⌘

The only way Moira could get off work early on Friday was to swap her afternoon shift for a morning one. That meant an early rise, one her insides let her know they didn't appreciate. She rushed to the shared bathroom and lost the remnants of last night's supper.

"Are you still suffering from morning sickness?" Grace, already smartly dressed for work, whispered to Moira in the hallway.

"No, I just like vomiting for fun," Moira retorted, moving the conversation back to her room, away from flapping ears.

"You should be through the worst of it soon."

"Good, because I'm sick of this." Moira laughed at her own joke.

"It usually only lasts the first trimester." Grace was full of knowledge for someone who'd never had a baby. "How many weeks are you?"

"I don't know." Moira slumped down on her bed. "Nine or ten maybe."

"You'd better tell Frank soon, or it will be too late."

"Too late for what?" Moira rubbed her throbbing temples.

Grace lowered her voice until it was barely audible. "An abortion."

"I've told you." Moira's reply was peppered with impatience. "I'm not having one, even if Frank's not interested in being a father."

"Okay, okay, I won't bring it up again." Grace headed toward the bedroom door but paused, her hand on the door handle. "You could always consider adoption. Plenty of couples can't have children of their own and could provide your baby with a good home.

Moira's face flushed with anger. "I thought you'd come to Wellington to support me. You seem to want me to get rid of this baby one way or another."

"Sorry," Grace apologised. "I just don't think you realise how difficult it will be to raise a child on your own."

Moira stood, legs apart, hands on hips, ready to do battle.

"I know exactly what it's like. My mother raised me by herself. Remember!"

Grace looked guilty. "Sorry. I've got to get to work. I've got an important meeting with my boss."

She was gone long before Moira calmed herself with deep, long breaths.

⌘

The morning sickness lived up to its name and persisted right up until the lunchtime rush. The last time Moira exited the toilet, the head waitress met her at the hand basin.

"You're pregnant, aren't you?" The waitress' righteous tone was mirrored by her hands-on-hips stance.

Moira should have stopped to think about her reply, but she was exhausted and snapped.

"What business is it of yours?"

"It's very much my business. If you cannot do your job properly, then perhaps you should reconsider your position here?"

"What?" Moira's red-headed temper took over. She untied her apron, screwed it up and threw it onto the floor. "Keep your stupid job. There are plenty more milk bars I can work at. I'll find one where the women stick together and support one another."

She stormed from the room and stomped through the kitchen to the back door, where her coat and handbag hung.

"We'll need your uniform back," the head waitress called out as Moira disappeared through the door, letting it slam behind her.

Walking down the street, she let the noises of life continuing as normal wash over her as her heartbeat gradually slowed. Vehicle engines revving, horns tooting, brakes screeching, an accompaniment to the chatter of pedestrians all going about their day as if nothing had changed. Yet it had in Moira's world. She conceded to herself that her reaction had been a little rash. She needed the money from her job if she was going to stay at the *Moorings*. Could she, as she'd claimed, get a replacement job at another milk bar? She hoped so, or she'd be back living at the YWCA before she knew it.

⌘

The train to Paekākāriki was full of women chattering excitedly, glammed up, hair styled in the latest fashion, makeup impeccable. The majority were around Moira's age but not all. The first spare seat she found was next to a couple of women who, despite their best efforts or because of them, fell into the category of 'mutton dressed up as lamb.'

"Do you have someone special you're going to meet?" the woman seated beside her asked.

Frank was someone special, but Moira thought that about most of the men she'd been in relationships with. The common denominator in all the failings was her. She wasn't special enough for them to want to stay.

"Yes," she replied, smiling about the fun adventures they would enjoy together this weekend.

"Oh, you're so lucky. I'm hoping to find a handsome man, with good manners who'll treat me like a lady, spoil me with lavish presents. The Yanks are all so dishy, aren't they? And their accents are so smooth. I could listen to them talk all day."

Moira noticed the indentation on the woman's ring finger, like a wedding band had been removed especially for the trip to Paekākāriki.

"Did you lose your husband in the war?" she asked.

The woman clasped her hands together, hiding the telltale white mark.

"Oh, no, can you tell? Do you think the Yanks will notice? I just want to have a little bit of fun. My husband has been away for so long. My friends encouraged us to come." The woman glanced nervously around the packed carriage. "They've been showered with gifts and had the best of times. No harm will come of it."

Moira looked down at her stomach. "As long as you are careful," she warned.

⌘

Frank was one of many soldiers waiting on the platform to greet the train. He edged his way through the throng to take Moira's hand as she stepped from the carriage.

"Hello, my love." His kiss declared to all around that she was his, as did the large bouquet of flowers he handed her.

"Thank you, Frank, they're beautiful."

"Just like y'all." Frank's smile revealed teeth as perfect as the rest of him. "Let me take your bag. It's a bit of a walk."

"Where are we headed?"

"I thought we'd do a movie first," Frank suggested. "Peanuts and popcorn, all the works to set us up for a night of partying. There's a shindig at Auntie Jean's. It's sure to be a lot of fun."

"Auntie Jean's?" Moira was confused. "Has your Auntie come out from America?"

Franked laughed. "No. That's what we call one of the locals. A Maori woman who does laundry for the officers and opened her home up to us PFCs. I think it's more because the Maori aren't allowed to have beer in their homes, some stupid rule that is easily got around if we take some hogsheads."

"PFCs?" Moira frowned. "Hogsheads? I thought they spoke English in America."

"Private First Class. That's us army boys that haven't made officer status." Frank laughed. "Hogsheads are eighteen-gallon kegs of beer. The lads get two or three of them to keep everyone goin' for the night."

Moira nodded. Normally, she would have looked forward to drinking beer and partying all night. Perhaps she'd better have a serious conversation with Frank before they went much further. Her other option was to forget all about the pregnancy for the weekend and live life like today was her last day. The latter seemed much more attractive.

z

Ingrid Bergman and Cary Grant dominated the screen at Saint Peter's Hall, but Moira couldn't recall what the movie was about. She was content to rest her head on Frank's shoulder, her hand cocooned in his, warming her thigh. The flowers lay on the adjacent seat, in hindsight a beautiful but impracticable gift with no vase nor water to sustain them.

Around them, couples were more interested in each other than in the movie, lips locked and hands wandering in the darkened theatre. Moira wanted the moment to last, not to be caught up in a sense of urgency, that everything had to happen now, or it wouldn't happen at all. Their closeness was like a simmering pot that would eventually boil, and the heat would be even more pleasurable for having taken the time to enjoy each other first.

Moira dreamed of possibilities. Movies every weekend, flowers, holding hands, chocolates and everything that would lead to. She imagined her dreams weren't dissimilar to the other women around her. One such woman's aspirations were shattered when the lights came on at half-time. An older woman, embracing the authority her Maori Welfare Officer's uniform bestowed, marched down the aisle scanning the audience. She found her target, a younger woman with the same dark skin. There was no polite 'can I speak to you?' but the third degree delivered as she was dragged from her seat and the pair left the building. She never even had time to say goodbye to the Yank she had been seated beside.

"Aren't Maori allowed to go to the movies, either?" Moira whispered to Frank. She should have known the answer, not sought it from him, a newcomer to New Zealand.

"Don't know the rules here," Frank replied. "But we still have all sorts of segregation back home."

What if Matiu was the father of her child and he too would be subjected to prejudiced rules and regulations just because of the colour of his skin. Another reason that it needed to be Frank's seed planted inside her.

The sun was sinking towards the horizon by the time Frank and Moira exited the theatre.

"Come with me." Carrying Moira's suitcase, Frank reached out his free hand out to hold Moira's. "We'll head to the beach and get away from the crowds."

Time alone. Moira's insides tingled with anticipation. She looked down at her faithful red toe-peepers. They weren't made for walking on sand, but it wasn't walking she had in mind.

They covered the short distance to the beach at a quick pace. At the end of the track, where the Kikuyu grass had been kept in check by vehicles and feet, they stopped and removed their shoes. The sand shifted beneath Moira's feet, her toes sinking into the minuscule grains.

Once through the sand dunes, black sand stretched for miles in both directions. The constant rhythm of the waves gave a certainty that life could continue like this forever. There was no possibility of being alone though, couples dotted the beach, walking, paddling in the water, picnicking. Others showed no restraint, entwined in each other's arms, kissing, canoodling, living as if life would end with the sunset.

Moira paused and drew in a breath. Who was she, a woman that believed in happy ever afters or one who lived in the moment without a second thought for the consequences? She'd always been the party girl, the one wanting to have fun. With all the uncertainty of the war, Frank could be sent to the South Pacific tomorrow, he could be killed by the Japanese, she should throw caution to the wind, let the waves wash it away and be like the couple heading to the privacy of the surf club shed.

"Sorry." Frank's apology disturbed her thoughts. "I didn't bring y'all to the beach just so we could make out."

Moira giggled. "So, we can make out, but you had something else in mind as well?"

Frank shifted nervously; his olive skin coloured and his mouth curved into a mischievous grin.

"You're blushing. What else do you have in mind, Frank?" Curiosity had Moira mirroring his smile.

He didn't answer her but turned them towards the high tide mark where a large log, warn smooth by the waves, had washed up.

"Sit down, please, Moira." Frank's voice took on a serious tone which made her worry he was about to deliver bad news.

When he didn't sit next to her, she felt the all too familiar churn of her stomach, but it wasn't morning sickness. Time seemed to stop. The waves' soft murmur became a loud thrum in her ears. She sought reassurance in the depths of

Frank's eyes but just as she watched him sink to one knee before her, the log shook, the rumbling wasn't just in her head, it was audible to everyone on the beach and loud screams pierced the air.

"What is it? What's happening?" Panicked, Moira leapt to her feet.

"Another earthquake." Frank held her hands to reassure her, but his attention had turned towards the surf club shed which was no longer standing on its wooden stilts. "They've been happenin' all this week."

The only earthquakes Moira had ever felt were sharp jolts. This one continued, the sand no longer feeling solid under her feet. She wanted to run back to the safety of hard ground.

"Wait here." The instruction and the calm tone of Frank's voice didn't convince Moira she was safe. "The lifeguard's hut has collapsed. Looks like they might need some help."

"But …" *What about me?* Moira stifled the helpless female who threatened to escape.

"You'll be safe here. Out in the open. There's nothing to fall and hurt y'all." Frank kissed her cheek and ran off. "I'll be back as quick as I can."

The trembling tapered away, and Moira sat back down on the log to wait. She watched as several soldiers clambered over the wreckage of the hut. They pulled aside the broken timbers and helped the injured, in various states of dress, out onto the sand. One woman looked dazed, blood oozing from a wound on her forehead. Another was clasping her arm and crying as if she'd broken it in the fall.

A man struggling to hitch his trousers back up limped away from the wreckage.

Moira was glad. For once, she hadn't gone straight for a home run. The Moira of old would have been the first to drag a man to the privacy of the hut. What had been about to happen at first base intrigued her more. Did Frank down on one knee mean he was about to propose? To ask for her hand in marriage? Surely not. They barely knew each other. The few times they'd been together had been wonderful but were they enough to base a lifetime commitment on? Perhaps she'd just imagined it and he was merely kneeling to kiss her. Yes, that would be it. Just a kiss, not a proposal.

But what if he was going to propose? Would she accept? Live in the moment and seize the opportunity to be Mrs Frank Davis Junior. It had a nice ring to it. At least then her baby wouldn't be born out of wedlock, risk being labelled a bastard by nasty and judgemental busy bodies.

Moira swallowed. The baby. She still hadn't told Frank of her predicament. She'd have to tell him about the baby before she accepted any proposal, let him know that she wasn't just saying yes to trap him, allow him to retract his offer if he wanted. If only she knew for certain that it was his. What if she became his fiancée and she gave birth to a Maori baby? Frank's skin was olive, perhaps he would never be able to tell.

She'd have to let him propose first though. She didn't want him marrying her because of the baby. It needed to be her that he desired as a wife.

Her thoughts were still seesawing when Frank arrived back.

335

"They're going to be alright," he said. "A broken arm, a sprained ankle and maybe a bit of concussion. Someone's gone to get the medics to bring a jeep down."

"That's good." Moira patted the log beside her, hoping Frank would continue where they had left off.

"It's going to be dark soon." He remained standing and put his hand out to pull her up. "How about we head to the milk bar for a shake and some fries?"

As the sun dipped below the horizon, Moira's insides sunk, as if the light that went out of the day, also went out of her. Perhaps she'd imagined the proposal. There was no hint in Frank's demeanour to indicate he had something important to say.

CHAPTER
27

The milk bar was busy. The only space was with three other couples in a corner booth, leaving no chance for a private conversation. Frank let Moira slide into the seat before him. Once the waitresses had taken their orders, the group were all abuzz about the earthquake.

"There'll likely be aftershocks all night," one of the marines said as he wrapped his arm around the shoulder of the woman next to him. "But don't worry, Joan, I'll keep you safe."

"Will they get worse than that one, Thomas?" Joan still looked worried and rested her cheek against Thomas's chest as if she was a damsel in distress and Thomas was her hero to the rescue.

Moira cringed inwardly. She'd never had much time for females who feigned weakness.

"They usually taper off," Thomas replied. "Scared the living daylights out of me when we first arrived. We don't have them at home. But there's been no major damage so far, well, apart from the lifeguard's hut."

"There was an earthquake at Napier about ten years ago nearly flattened the entire town."

"Thanks, Mary." Joan rolled her eyes at her friend. "That really makes me feel better."

The waitress returned with a full tray: bowls of fries, bottles of Coca Cola and several milkshakes, one of which was Moira's. She sucked on her straw, enjoying the frothy milk drink, and keeping herself from joining the conversation as it seesawed from optimistic to pessimistic.

"We're headin' up to Auntie Jean's," Frank said. "Their old house has survived many an earthquake. I reckon it'll just shake on its piles, and we'll be none the wiser."

"We might join you." The marine nodded and smiled.

"Is she really your Auntie?" Mary asked. "Won't we have to be invited?"

"No, we just call her Auntie. She's become an unofficial mother to some of the troops. She's opened her doors to one and all. She loves it when the guitars come out, and we have a sing-song session." Frank laughed. "We've taught them some songs from home, and they're tryin' to teach us some Maori. We're getting' better."

"You might be getting better," Thomas said. "But I can't get my tongue around their pronunciation."

Moira allowed the last slurp of her milkshake to gurgle loudly. She'd had enough of sitting in the crowded milk bar. Getting some alone time with Frank was much more important.

"We'd better get going then." She nudged him to indicate he should stand. "Sounds like you'll need as much practice as you can get, Thomas."

Everyone laughed as the last of the fries were eaten and Coca-Cola bottles emptied.

⌘

The way to Auntie Jean's house was lit by the full moon's light, full directly overhead. A rambling old weatherboard house sitting in the middle of a large section, surrounded by a lawn strewn with vehicles, was their destination. Tentacles of Kikuyu grass wove through the wire netting boundary fence and entwined the house's wooden piles, which appeared to anchor the building to the land. It was easy to see why it survived the earthquakes.

No light spilled from the windows as the blackout rule was rigidly adhered to in this coastal part of New Zealand. The front door was ajar, allowing a slither of light to show the way. The strum of a guitar and the harmony of voices welcomed the group inside.

"Smells like Auntie's got another pot of *puha* and pippies on the boil." Frank rubbed his stomach as if he was looking forward to a feed.

Moira was grateful for the milkshake and fries as the odour emanating from the rear of the house wasn't at all appetising. The long, narrow passage took them from the front door to the kitchen, passing the sitting room where the music was being played.

The first of the hogsheads had already been cracked and sat on the kitchen table with an assortment of glasses and cups beside it. Frank stowed Moira's suitcase under the table, poured her a cup and passed it to her before getting one for himself. One drink wouldn't hurt, she told herself as she sipped the chilled ale, avoiding the chip in the cup's rim.

"Ah, Frank, lovely to see you, my boy."

"Auntie!" Frank hugged the woman who was not at all what Moira had expected.

The title of 'auntie' had conjured a wizened old woman with silvered frizzy hair. This woman was possibly only a decade older than Moira. Her neatly-styled hair had a healthy sheen and not a speck of grey.

"I've just put the kids to bed," Auntie said as she turned to look at Moira. "I see you've brought a friend. Hello, I'm Jean, but as you've probably guessed, all the lads call me Auntie."

"Hello, Jean. Nice to meet you. I hope you don't mind me coming along uninvited."

"Frank's got good taste." Jean winked at Frank as she headed to the pot on the stove.

"Moira's extra special, Auntie." Frank looked adoringly at Moira. "I could spend the rest of my life with her."

Jean cuffed Frank's arm and chuckled. "Oh, you Yanks! Yous are always falling in love. Anyway, welcome Moira. The more, the merrier. Yous go on through. I'll just check on the *puha*. I've been busy *tahu-ing pauas* and mussels to send to our Battalion boys."

Frank ushered Moira back along the passage, his hand on the small of her back. She was grateful he couldn't see her face while she digested his revelation. He hadn't said he loved her, but he wouldn't want to spend the rest of his life with her if he didn't. Maybe it was all just talk. The Yanks all seemed to be charmers, much more worldly than their Kiwi counterparts.

A sea of faces glanced their way as they entered the sitting room, a blending of cultures and a mixture of skin tones, all smiling and enjoying the moment. Frank claimed a chair beside the window. Moira could have sat on one of its wide, faded brocade arms, but Frank settled her into his lap, wrapping his arms protectively around her.

An older Maori man strummed the last chord of a song he'd been singing in his native tongue, and the group applauded.

"Didn't understand a word, Joe, but that was great."

"What d'ya want me to play now?" Joe asked.

"How about *Don't Sit Under the Apple Tree*? Do you know that one?"

"Yeah, but you'll have to sing it." Joe chuckled and cleared his throat. "Ain't no way I can sing as high as the Andrews sisters."

"We can." A trio of women Moira recognised from the train chorused enthusiastically as Joe began.

"Do you know it, Sam?" Joe directed his question at the marine with a piano accordion resting on his thigh.

"Sure do, Joe."

The lively tune filled the room. Thomas and Joan jumped up to dance, adding to the wear of the thread-bare carpet.

"Moira, let's dance too." Frank's enthusiasm was as bubbly as the music and irresistible.

They had to stay close in the crowded room, but that was fine with Moira. Being in Frank's arms felt right, his breath warm on her neck as he sang.

"Don't y'all go walking down lovers' lane with anyone but me until I come marching home."

She wondered if he was merely singing along or, was he asking her to wait for him.

"You'd better come marching home." She chose her words carefully. They could easily be brushed off as a joke.

Frank pulled her closer. "I never want to leave y'all, Moira."

It was now or never. Moira inhaled deeply, seeking the courage to reveal her pregnancy. "Or our baby?" she blurted before she could change her mind.

"What?" Frank froze.

She felt his body stiffen as if immediately on guard for a threat to his wellbeing. She was the danger that could derail his life plans.

He stepped back.

She assumed the worst; the foot between them felt like a chasm. She was going to be raising the baby on her own. It was better to know now rather than later, she silently tried to console herself. Another relationship was over. What was it with her and men?

After flitting towards her stomach, his eyes locked on hers. "Are y'all sure?"

Moira slowly nodded, squeezing her eyes shut as she anticipated the worst.

"Yippee!" Frank hugged her, so tightly she couldn't breathe. He showered her face with kisses. "I'm goin' to be a dad. Yippee!"

Then she was standing on her own again, not abandoned, but witness to Frank's joy as he bounced around the room announcing to everyone.

"I'm goin' to be a dad! I'm goin' to be a dad!"

The singing stopped; the strumming ceased. Everyone was caught up in Frank's excitement.

"Congratulations!" They yelled and clapped and shook Frank's hand.

Then, all eyes turned towards Moira. She felt as if the spotlight had landed on her, centre stage, the star of the show. Fortunately, Frank joined her and wrapped his arm around her waist. Whatever judgement would come her way, she knew it would be easier with him by her side.

But then he was gone, just as quickly as he'd arrived. He stood opposite her; his face became serious. She gulped, swallowing the dread that reality had dawned on him, and he'd changed his mind. The hubbub of the partygoers began again.

"Quiet, please." Frank knelt on one knee and withdrew a small black velvet pouch from his pocket.

Moira gasped. Was that what she thought it was? Frank tugged at the cord holding the pouch closed and pulled a ring out. He had been going to propose to her on the beach. She didn't imagine it. He'd wanted her as a wife before he knew about the baby. She sighed with relief.

"Moira, my darling." Frank had everyone's attention, but his solemn look was solely for Moira. "Will y'all marry me?"

"Yes!" Her reply came out as a high-pitched squeak echoed by the squeals of the women around her as the earth trembled.

The house shook on its piles, the timbers creaked, the overhead light flickered, and a deep rumbling came from afar. Life appeared to pause, holding everyone captive, wondering whether to run for cover or stay put. After several more shudders, it stopped as suddenly as it began.

"Just Mother Nature sounding her approval." Auntie Jean stood in the doorway, leaning on the doorframe, taking it all in.

Moira was reassured by Jean's nonchalance and by Frank still kneeling in front of her.

"Yes," she repeated, just to be certain. "Yes, Frank, I will marry you."

He eased the narrow gold band onto her finger, a row of tiny diamonds glistened under the light. He stood, pulled Moira into his arms and sealed the commitment with a kiss. The room erupted into cheers and congratulations.

"Just as well you are doing good by this lass, Frank Davis III." Auntie Jean came up beside them. "Congratulations to you both. I hope you have many happy years together."

⌘

They didn't even get that night together. Later, the women, Moira, Jean and Joan included went outside to the toilet. There was only one, a long drop, so you either had to wait in the queue or find a spot in the lupin bushes. Moira couldn't hold on any longer, so she found herself a spot behind a lupin. She was stooped down when a haunting call rang out. Eerie tones filled the night sky like a thousand spirits were chanting to the moon.

Unlike the others, Moira stifled her scream but terrified, she lost the urge, hitched her underwear up and hurriedly left the lupins.

"What's that?" she asked Jean.

"Sounds like the ancestors are angry," Jean replied.

As women ran back towards the house, the men rushed outside.

"What the bloody hell is that?" Joe carried his guitar like a weapon. "Sounds like someone's being murdered."

The noise continued. The Yanks, Frank included, looked at the wide-eyed group and cracked up laughing.

"What yous laughing for?" Jean demanded. "What's so funny?"

The Yanks turned towards the Paekākāriki Hill and became serious.

"We've got to go," they replied in unison.

Moira looked at Frank for reassurance.

"That's the Navajo Indian company based on top of the hill," he explained. "They're signallin' the base camp. There's somethin' wrong."

The camp's siren joined the cacophony. Frank gave Moira a peck on the cheek and took off with the rest of the Yanks.

⌘

It was twenty-four hours later before Moira saw Frank again, and the threat of a Japanese submarine was resolved. How the problem was dealt with, nobody was permitted to reveal. At Jean's insistence, Moira had spent the night on the couch. It wasn't at all comfortable, but with a grey woollen blanket tucked around her, she managed to catch a few hours' sleep.

She'd spent the day visiting the milk bars in Paekākāriki, asking if there were any positions available, proudly displaying her engagement ring when she explained she wanted to be closer to her fiancé. By mid-afternoon, she'd secured a job starting the following week and found accommodation with one of the other waitresses, Mavis, a mother who was struggling to make ends meet with three children to feed and a husband away fighting. She offered Moira a room in her home. It had been her youngest child's bedroom, but the five-year-old could sleep with her mother. Moving in with a readymade family wasn't exactly what Moira had hoped for, but the room was half the cost of the *Moorings*, and she told herself it would do for now until she found something more suitable.

In making the arrangements, she felt like she was abandoning Grace. She hoped her friend would understand. Grace's new job with the government seemed to have become very important, so she would likely barely notice Moira's absence.

Moira returned to Jean's house trusting that Frank would find her there. She helped Jean bring in the washing. A wire line, propped up by wooden stays, spanned the backyard and was full of men's clothing: shirts, trousers, socks and underwear belonging to the officers from the camp.

"I hope you get paid well for all of this," Moira said, as they bundled the dry washing into a wicker basket.

"The officers look after me." Jean tapped the side of her nose and winked. "Come on, we'll get this inside and have a cuppa. You look like you need to rest up before tonight's dance."

Moira must have looked as tired as she felt, the medley of her emotions taking a toll. Without Frank's presence she was beginning to think she'd imagined she was now his fiancée. Thank goodness for the ring on her finger, the proof she wasn't about to wake up from a dream.

⌘

The American soldiers' base was a collection of small oblong cabins constructed in rows as straight as the soldiers' morning line up.

"It looks like a small village has sprung up," Moira remarked to Jean as they walked through the gates into camp.

"Mmm." Jean frowned and pointed to a bare area of land to their left. "My family homestead used to be right there."

"What happened to it? Did you sell it to them?"

"Huh!" Jean scoffed. "Not likely. They just took over. Public Works Department. Demolished it. We couldn't do nothing about it."

At the back of the cabins was a large hall that usually served as the mess, but tonight, with some of the trestle tables stacked at the sides of the hall, it was where everyone gathered, ready to dance the night away.

Moira wondered how she would ever find Frank amongst the myriad of men all dressed in uniform, but she didn't have to. The moment she stepped into the hall, she felt his hand slip into hers. He ushered her to the side, drew her into his arms and kissed her. The melding of their mouths was all she needed to dispel her worries.

"How are y'all Mrs Frank Davis III and baby Frank Davis IV?"

She might have entered a dance full of soldiers but only one was for her. The American that had stolen her heart, planted a seed that would bind them forever and loved her like she'd never been loved before. She blushed at his question. He was getting ahead of himself, but she didn't complain.

They danced the night away, embracing the moment and each other, living life like it was too short.

EPILOGUE

"You're doing well. I can see baby's head." The midwife's calming voice was intended to soothe, but her words made Moira tense.

What colour? What skin colour? She wanted to demand. Her short, sharp, panting breaths left no room for questions that would be answered soon enough.

"When the next contraction comes, push."

That's easy for you to say. You don't know my life will be turned upside down if this baby is Maori.

Moira couldn't hold back, the contraction came regardless of her reluctance, despite her fear of disappointing Frank, and with no concern for the painful spasms it caused. She pushed, sensing her child's imminent passage into the world.

The baby took its first breath, found its lungs and announced its arrival by crying.

"What's wrong? Is my baby alright?" Moira strained to look.

"Everything's fine." The midwife busied herself, cutting the umbilical cord and swaddling the baby in a towel. "He's just letting us know he's here."

"He?" *Frank Davis IV?*

"Yes, Mrs Davis, you've given birth to a healthy boy." The midwife placed the baby in Moira's arms. "Congratulations."

He was tiny, precious, vulnerable and he was hers to love unconditionally. How could she have vowed and declared never to want her own child? To deny herself the joy and pride of bringing a child into the world, the total elation and wonder now filled her heart.

Cradled in her arms, his crying softened. Moira inhaled the sweet smell of her newborn; his head was bereft of all but the smallest hint of dark hair. His eyes were yet to open and amniotic fluids still clung to his skin, but in Moira's eyes he was perfect. His tiny pink fingers slowly unfurled, and his perfectly shaped mouth moved as if he already had something to say.

Pink. Moira had been so enraptured with her newborn, captivated by his arrival that she'd forgotten all about the colour of his skin. Pink, not a hint of Maori.

"Welcome, Frank Davis IV." Tears trickled from the corners of her eyes. Tears of joy, tears of relief.

"Right, that's the placenta delivered, and you cleaned up." The midwife appeared at Moira's side and reached to take her baby. "Now let's get him ready to go."

"Go where?" Moira clutched her son tight to her chest. There had been so many hints, suggestions and demands for her to adopt she feared she'd been duped and he was about to be stolen.

"Just over here, Mrs Davis." The midwife, experienced to panicked new mothers, maintained her calmness. "Just over here to wipe him down, check all his bits are in the right place and get him dressed so you can both go back to the ward."

"Oh. Sorry." Moira apologised but stayed vigilant, never taking her eyes off her son.

His eyes had opened by the time he was dressed and returned to her arms. Blue eyes stared blankly at her.

"His eyes are blue." Moira was unable to conceal her alarm. Her eyes were hazel, Frank's brown; however, did her baby end up with blue eyes?

"Lots of babies are born with blue eyes." The midwife inspected the colour of Moira's eyes and then looked back at the baby. "They'll change colour within the first six months if they are going to change. What colour eyes does the father have?"

"Brown. Dark brown." Moira imagined Frank's loving gaze. All of him, the way he looked, the way he spoke were as smooth and velvety as chocolate.

"Hazel and brown. Unlikely that his eyes will stay blue then. Are you alright to walk back to the ward?"

Despite having just given birth, Moira felt energised and ready to take on the world. She bounced off the bed as if she'd just been having a lie-down.

"Careful! Take it easy." The midwife braced Moira.

Her bare feet touched the cold floor and it felt as if all her blood drained away. Lightheaded, she welcomed the midwife's help, and they slowly toddled out of the delivery suite, down the corridor and into a ward.

"I'll get one of the nurses to come and get baby soon." The midwife must have felt Moira tense and clutch baby Frank closer to her chest. "You need to rest up. He'll be safe in the nursery with all the other babies."

⌘

A week later, Moira and baby were back at Mavis's house settling into a routine. The bassinet Mavis had used for her own children had been retrieved from the attic, dusted off, sheets and blankets washed and made up.

"Oh, Mavis." Moira sniffed back tears she was still blaming on pregnancy hormones. "You're too good to me."

"No point leaving it in the attic gathering dust. I'm not going to need it again, not with my Michael away overseas for God knows how much longer."

Moira was lost for something to say that would ease Mavis's burden. She deserved better. She'd taken Moira and baby Frank back into her home. Single mothers sticking together. At least they both had wedding rings on their fingers, so they weren't looked upon with quite as much scorn as those who were labelled harlots. A quick visit to the Registry Office in Wellington, before Frank shipped out to the Solomon Islands, had changed Miss Moira Harvey into Mrs Frank Davis.

"I'd better write to Frank, let him know he's a dad," she said. "The war better end soon so that all families can be together again."

She wanted to send him a photograph of their son, but there was no money for that. Moira and Mavis had planned that once Moira had a couple of weeks to recover, they would ask for their shifts at the milk bar to be alternated. When Moira was working, Mavis would take care of baby Frank, and when Mavis was working, Moira would babysit Mavis's three. It wasn't desirable but a necessary arrangement to make ends meet.

At some point, she also had to make time to catch the train back to Wellington to visit the American embassy office. The United States had passed legislation to make it easier for the wives of American soldiers to emigrate but there was still a pile of paperwork to be completed. That was what her and Frank had planned, that she would move to Louisiana. It all sounded magical when he described the plantation, the grand home they would live in, the nursery where their baby would sleep in the very same cradle that Frank had slept, and his father before him. Moira struggled to comprehend a family home where the roots were so firmly planted. She remembered her small glimpse into that life with the Christmas she'd enjoyed with Grace's family. She'd be the happiest mother if she could give that gift to her children. *Children?* Surely, it must still be her hormones making her contemplate more. She chuckled.

⌘

Life passed by in a blur and it was at least two months before a letter from Frank finally arrived. It was propped against the salt and pepper shakers on the dining room table, waiting for Moira to finish working at the milk bar. She came in exhausted after a busy shift. Baby Frank's nappy needed changing and Mavis's youngest two were squabbling. The letter had to wait until everyone was in bed asleep, everyone except Moira. She sat at the table with a cup of tea, staring at the envelope, anxious that it would contain bad news, that Frank wouldn't want his baby after all, and she'd be a single mother. She wasn't sure she had the energy to continue forever struggling like her own mother had. Her child would have an upbringing just like hers, one without the support of extended family, alone and missing the joy of siblings. Being a mum had given her more empathy for her own mother. Perhaps she could write to her and let her know about her grandson.

She inhaled deeply. It's now or never. Better to know than not. What's the worst thing that can happen? The envelope shook in her trembling fingers.

My darling wife,

He still thinks I'm his darling. The tension in Moira's shoulders eased with each word she read.

I can't wait to see you again and to meet Frank Davis IV. You have brought me so much joy already and I want our family to be all together.

Tears prickled at the corners of Moira's eyes.

You'll have noticed from the postmark on this letter ....

Moira grabbed the discarded envelope and inspected the previously ignored postmark – Louisiana. Frank was back in America, not in the middle of the fighting in the Solomon Islands. Moira gasped, what had happened? Had he been killed? No, stupid. He wouldn't be writing if he was dead, and as his wife, you would have been notified by telegram. Injured? She went back to the letter, her heartbeat racing.

… I'm back home. Don't worry, nothing serious has happened. I contracted malaria so I've been shipped home. I'll come right, eventually, but it'll be a long, slow recovery. But I'm sure with you by my side, I'll recover so much faster.

I've made inquiries. You and baby Frank can come by ship, but that'll take several months. So, I thought you could fly.

Fly! Moira had never been on an aeroplane, even a small plane over a short distance, let alone one big enough to fly from New Zealand to America. She felt breathless. Going on an aeroplane. When? Should she start packing now? It sounded so exciting she wanted to leave immediately.

Then it dawned on her. With a thud, the sound of her hopes hitting the pit of her stomach, she realised she didn't have any money to buy an aeroplane ticket. Probably not even enough to get a berth on a ship.

"Oh, Frank." The letter crumpled in her hands. "I can't afford to come."

"What's wrong?" Mavis rubbed her sleepy eyes to adjust to the light. "I thought I heard one of the kid's crying but they're all sound asleep."

"Frank wants me to fly to America, but I don't have the money for a ticket." Moira sobbed quietly.

"He must realise that. Didn't you say he comes from a wealthy family? Surely, he'd offer to pay. What does the letter say?"

Moira shook her head and laughed at her own stupidity. "Sometimes I wonder at myself."

She unfolded the letter and picked up where she'd left off. She was grinning from ear to ear by the time she reached a line of kisses that convinced her all would be well.

"Well, I can see you've found the solution. Congratulations!" Mavis yawned. "I'm going back to bed."

"Yes! Yes! Thank you, Mavis. I'd better get some shut-eye, too, before Frank wakes for a feed."

Baby Frank must have heard his name. No sooner had Moira folded the letter back into the envelope, she heard his hungry cry. She hurried to their shared bedroom, hoping nobody else would be woken. She ignored the Plunket nurse's advice. She was too excited to not tell her feeding son that they were going on an aeroplane.

"Your Daddy has got us tickets. We're going on a plane. We're going to America. We're going to be a family. It'll be so wonderful."

She caressed the top of his head, inhaled his baby scent and sighed joyfully.

⌘

The novelty of the aeroplane flight was short-lived. There were a number of mothers and babies on board, taking the same leap of faith as Moira and her child. And like the other babies, Frank's tiny ears hurt with the pressure of the take-off. They communicated their pain in the only way possible, howling at the top of their lungs until the noise in the cabin was unbearable. Moira tried to soothe Frank, offered her breast, her knuckle to suck on but nothing would pacify the child. The air hostess's kind words couldn't appease her frazzled state.

The passenger seated beside Moira, who'd introduced herself as Faye, smiled politely as if to indicate she didn't mind the noise, but the cigarette she drew heavily on said otherwise. Moira breathed in the second-hand smoke, felt a hint of the familiar calm nicotine brought that only made her crave more. She'd given up smoking during her pregnancy for the good of the baby, she said, but there was no money to buy them anyway, and the smell continued to make her feel ill, right up until Frank's birth.

"Would I be able to borrow a smoke from you, Faye?" She disliked the pleading tone of her voice. "It'll calm me down and if I'm relaxed, Frank might be too."

"Borrow? You'll hardly be able to give it back when you've finished." Faye laughed as she fished into her handbag for the packet. She lit a cigarette and passed it to Moira.

Moira rested her head on the headrest, closed her eyes and inhaled. The effect on Moira was instant. Her shoulders relaxed. Her spine moulded into the curvature of the seat, but Frank continued to cry, his chubby cheeks red with the effort.

She'd stubbed the cigarette butt out in the armrest's ashtray before Frank finally stopped crying. Whether it was Moira's now calm state, the altitude the aeroplane climbed to, or the baby's exhaustion that finally sent him to sleep, didn't matter. Moira sighed with relief and closed her own eyes to rest.

⌘

Finally landing in America, after several fuel stops where they could walk around the aeroplane but not disembark, made Moira forget all else. Her heart thumped in her chest as she peered out the small window, affording her a view of the airport terminal. She scanned the gathered crowd, searching for her husband, her future.

"Look Frank, your daddy is out there. Isn't it exciting?" She held baby Frank on her knee, imagining he, too, could see across the tarmac.

The plane was abuzz with excitement. Women all eager to be re-united with the men they'd fallen in love with, anxious to be starting new lives in an unfamiliar country, and hopeful that the romance that had whisked them off their feet would still be present without the urgency of war and unimpacted by its remnants.

Moira, with bags hitched on both shoulders and baby Frank hugged to her chest waited in line. She wanted another cigarette to calm her racing heartbeat but Faye, without the worry of a child, was at the front of the queue.

Slowly the passengers exited the aeroplane and Moira inhaled her first smell of American air.

"Moira! Moira, my love!"

She heard Frank's call, his public declaration of feelings, his velvety drawl told her everything would be alright. As soon as her feet hit the tarmac, she stepped out from the line of passengers, searched for the source of the voice and made a beeline straight for her man. His broad smile was like a beacon she was drawn to.

"I've missed you so much."

Moira wanted their embrace to last forever but after showering with her face with kisses, Frank turned his attention to his son. Her frustration turned to joy as baby Frank's face lit up, his toothless grin reflecting his father's.

"Hello, my dear. Welcome to Louisiana. Welcome to the Davis family." The hug that accompanied the kind words was as graceful and sincere as the woman who wrapped her arms around Moira.

Moira hesitated, unsure how to address the feminine version of Frank.

"Hello, Mrs Davis. It's lovely to be here."

"Oh, we can't call each other Mrs Davis, it'll be much too confusing." Frank's mother placed her hand on Moira's as if they were making a pact. "Y'all must call be Deidre, dear. Or Mum, if you'd like. I always wanted a daughter. A shame it took a silly war to bring one to me."

"Thank you, ... Deidre." She silently repeated Deidre's words, the invite to call her 'Mum', the implication that she was a long-awaited daughter. It wasn't the right time and place to utter that precious word, but Moira knew it would come. Her heartbeat slowed. Her body filled with a sense of calmness, an inner peace.

"Now, Frank can introduce y'all to the rest of the family." Deidre reached for baby Frank. "While I meet my precious grandson."

Moira hadn't noticed the circle of people surrounding them. She almost wished baby Frank would cry, demand her attention so she could retreat from the overwhelming welcome, but her son lapped up the attention and gurgled happily.

One by one Frank introduced his family, starting with his father.

"You're more beautiful than my son described. He's a fortunate man indeed." Frank Davis II pecked her cheek. "Let me take your bags."

"Hello, Moira. I'm Frank's Grandmama. You're just the tonic he needs to get better."

"I'm his Aunt Jessica, available for babysitting duties whenever y'all need a rest."

"I love your dress. You'll have to tell me your secret. Getting your gorgeous figure back so soon. Oh, I'm Anna, Frank's cousin."

"Right, enough of the introductions. There'll be plenty of time to get to know your new family." Frank wrapped his arm around Moira's waist. "We'd better get y'all home."

Moira could have danced with delight. Finally, she'd found a man who'd given everything she didn't know she wanted and more.

⌘

Later that night, after a family meal filled with fun and laughter and generous servings of delicious food without a hint of wartime shortages and rations, Moira and Frank settled their son into his cradle.

360

"I can hardly believe my son is sleeping in the very same cradle as I did and my father before me." Frank wrapped his arms around Moira and rested his chin on her shoulder. "Imagine, in another twenty years it might be our grandchild we're watching over."

Moira leaned back into Frank's embrace, unable to find words, absorbing his heat, daring to believe that their future together would extend that far.

"Come, my love." Frank turned Moira so he could lift and carry her to the bed. "I didn't carry you over the threshold, but I can carry you to our bed. I've dreamed of this night, making love to you, waking up next to you. I love you, Moira. Forever."

"I…," Moira had never spoken the words before, never committed to a *forever*. Her heart, overflowing with joy, desire and love for the man beside her allowed her to voice her feelings. "I love you too, Frank. Forever."

AUTHOR'S NOTE

Having reached the end of the Kiwi Land Girls' journey I want to extend my heartfelt thanks to everyone who has travelled this road with me. Especially to you, the readers who have enjoyed the stories of Grace, Alice, Betsy and Moira. Without you, the adventures, struggles, loves and growth of the young women who volunteered as Land Girls would be lost. I hope I have been able to transport you back in time; to take you out into the country to experience life on the farm as women took on roles traditionally reserved for men and made their contribution to the war effort. As Moira discovered, this life wasn't for everyone. Not all the 'bosses' were kind, not all the wives were accepting of young women coming onto their farms and the conditions the land girls found themselves in didn't always offer the comforts of home.

I once again extend my appreciation to *Diane Bardsley* for presenting her interviews with land girls in *The Land Girls, In a Man's World, 1939-1946,* a wonderful source of inspiration and information. In bringing Moira's story to life, I have also relied on the real-life accounts captured in *War Stories our Mothers Never Told Us* edited by *Judith Fyfe* from a film by *Gaylene Preston* and *Rouseabout Jane* by *Jane Dare*.

Once the story is written there are all the other wonderful people who provide support, expertise and encouragement to bring the story to life. Thank you to my writing tribe: Ami, Frances, Joan, Shona and Stella for feedback, wine and laughter along the way. Thank you to the talented Kura Carpenter for the cover designs. Thank you to Annie Seaton for her expert editing skills. Thank you to the wonders of Facebook that brought my high school friend Dixie Carlton back into my life, a vivacious woman whose talent and marketing skills and knowledge I have been fortunate to benefit from, along with more wine and laughter. There are many others whose support and encouragement I treasure. You know who you are, if I haven't mentioned you personally, know that I am grateful for your contribution.

Last, but not least, my heartfelt thanks go to Mike, for going off to play your drums and giving me space to write.

To get updates, excerpts, and bonus epilogues subscribe to my free monthly newsletter, through my website or follow me on Facebook.

Website: taniarobertsauthor.co.nz

Facebook: Tania Roberts Author

Milton Keynes UK
Ingram Content Group UK Ltd.
UKHW042006060824
446613UK00004B/38